LONG-AWAITED KISS

"Perhaps, as your daughters suspected, I intended to trap you into marriage all the time," she said.

"You mock me."

"I do not. Do stop looming over me in that threatening fashion. I am going to get an ache in my neck from looking up at you. You are not intimidating me in the least."

"A mere baronet hardly has the power to do that, has he, *Lady* Catriona?"

She gave a short laugh.

"You would be surprised how much power you have over me," she said. "All right. If you will not sit, I will stand." She rose and before he could step back, she put her gloved hands on his shoulders.

"See here," he said in consternation. "What are you about?"

He could smell the faint floral scent of her perfume. It made him slightly dizzy. Then she put her hand on the back of his head to pull his face to hers and kissed him.

He should have drawn away, but he could not. She was all sweetness and fire as he plundered her soft, lush mouth.

"Lady Catriona, forgive me," he said. "That should not have happened."

Incredibly, she leaned back against her chair and smiled at him.

"You have been wanting to kiss me like that for two years," she said.

He opened his mouth to deny it, but he could not . . .

Books by Kate Huntington

The Captain's Courtship

The Lieutenant's Lady

Lady Diana's Darlings

Mistletoe Mayhem

A Rogue for Christmas

The Merchant Prince

Town Bronze

His Lordship's Holiday Surprise

The General's Daughter

A Hero's Homecoming

To Tempt a Gentleman

Published by Zebra Books

TO TEMPT A GENTLEMAN

Kate Huntington

ZEBRA BOOKS
Kensington Publishing Corp.
www.kensingtonbooks.com

ZEBRA BOOKS are published by

Kensington Publishing Corp.
850 Third Avenue
New York, NY 10022

All Kensington titles, imprints, and distributed lines are available
at special quantity discounts for bulk purchases for sales pro-
motion, premiums, fund-raising, educational, or institutional use.

Special book excerpts or customized printings can also be created to fit specific needs. For details, write or phone the office
of the Kensington Special Sales Manager: Attn. Special Sales
Department. Kensington Publishing Corp., 850 Third Avenue,
New York, NY 10022. Phone: 1-800-221-2647.

Zebra and the Z logo Reg. U.S. Pat. & TM Off.

ISBN 0-8217-7820-X

First Printing: July 2005
10 9 8 7 6 5 4 3 2 1

Printed in the United States of America

*To Bob Chwedyk,
my rock star,
with all my love.*

CHAPTER 1

Dumfries, Scotland, 1817

"Catriona, I am going to die today."

Catriona Grant bit her lip and forced a cheerful tone to her voice as she patted her elderly cousin Sophie's forehead with a cloth dampened in rosewater.

"Nonsense," Catriona said. "You say that all the time. I think you just enjoy the attention. You are not going to die."

"Well, dear. We are all going to die," Cousin Sophie said with the touch of astringency that marked her speech, even on bad days when her voice was a weak, wispy little thread of sound. "I mean it this time."

No, Catriona thought grimly. *I will not let you go.*

Her cousin was ninety years old, and her continued existence was a testament to Catriona's careful nursing. She had been at death's door when Catriona came to live with her two years ago.

"Will you have some chicken broth? You must keep up your strength."

Sophie Tilden's gnarled, old hand clasped Catriona's smooth, young one.

"Chicken broth," the old lady said in distaste. "The problem with officious young people is they have no respect for the dying. Do you think I want to pass from this world with the taste of chicken broth on my lips? Fetch me a glass of port, girl. The good stuff that Sir Michael brought us for Christmas last year."

"Spirits are not good for you in your condition."

"Catriona, my dearest. You cannot keep me alive forever."

"I can try." She would not cry in front of her kind benefactress. She would *not*. There would be time enough to cry for her when she was gone.

"I am tired. Everyone I love except you and Michael has preceded me in death."

"But what would I do without you?"

"What would you do if you were not burdened with an old lady like me? You would get married to a good man and have children. And Sir Michael would do well to have you."

"No more of that talk, madam," Catriona said. "The last thing Sir Michael wants is a wife of questionable reputation whose own family has disowned her."

"What fustian rubbish you talk. That was years ago. Everyone will have forgotten it by now."

"*I* have not forgotten. I do not want to talk about it."

Cousin Sophie gave her a coy look. It quite transformed her thin, pale, wrinkled face.

"What will you give me if I stop?"

Catriona had to smile.

"That glass of port?"

"Excellent. And not your usual pathetic thimbleful, if you please."

"Very well. If you will excuse me . . ."

"I will. And hurry. I have not much time." But she was smiling. When Catriona returned, Cousin Sophie accepted the glass with both shaking hands, and Catriona still had to support it as she took a sip.

"Just a little," Catriona cautioned her as the old lady took a large gulp.

"Do not be so stingy, girl," the old lady said with a sigh of pleasure. She closed her eyes. "More." Catriona tilted the glass carefully to her lips again. Even so, a bit dripped from her lips and Cousin Sophie's tongue snaked out and savored it. "I feel better already. You sent word to Sir Michael?"

"I did," Catriona said as the smile faded from her face. At least once a month at her benefactress's request she sent word to Sir Michael Stewart that he was wanted at Cousin Sophie's deathbed, and, miraculously, the old lady rallied as soon as she had them both dancing attendance on her.

This will be no different, Catriona said firmly to herself. A bit of attention from Sir Michael, and Cousin Sophie would be her old outrageous self.

Sir Michael Stewart was a worthy gentleman who owned the house Cousin Sophie occupied as well as a large estate crowning a hill outside Dumfries and several farms surrounding it. He bred horses and grew oats. He had been widowed tragically young when his beautiful wife, Cousin Sophie's London-bred niece, died in childbirth. His daughters had been married off in ceremonies worthy of princesses, not that Catriona would have been invited to attend them, and lived in London.

Neither of Sir Michael's daughters had been to Scotland to visit their father or Cousin Sophie, who had quite doted on them when they were children, for at least a year. Cousin Sophie wrote dutifully to both of them each week when she was able and had Catriona write to them under her direction when she was too frail to hold pen to paper. They rarely wrote back.

"Why does he not come?" Cousin Sophie said. "You have the letter, do you not, Catriona? Just in case he does not come in time?"

"It will not be needed," Catriona said firmly.

"But you have it?" her cousin asked anxiously.

"Of course. It is right there, on top of the desk, where it always is."

"Good. You will not forget to give it to him when I am dead?"

"No. Although that will not be for many years yet."

Sophie signaled Catriona for another sip of wine. Catriona pursed her disapproving lips at her and then relented. She held the glass as Sophie took a delicate sip.

"Now, that is the flavor I want to have in my mouth when I enter eternity," she said.

"I think that is enough," Catriona said.

Cousin Sophie made a face at her.

"Do you know that Pastor Wilkins says in heaven time goes so fast that centuries can pass in the blink of an eye?" she asked. "When you die, it seems the people you left behind join you almost instantly."

"Cousin Sophie," Catriona said with a long sigh.

"Pastor Wilkins is a silly, sentimental young fool, but I hope he is right," Cousin Sophie said. "I would like to believe that a moment after I close my eyes in death, I will open them in heaven to find you and Sir Michael right beside me."

"No more wine for you," Catriona said dryly as she held Cousin Sophie's hand. "It is making you maudlin."

Cousin Sophie chuckled as Catriona kissed her on the forehead as if she were a beloved child.

Then she closed her eyes and died.

Catriona could hear the maid weeping. She had not stopped for the past quarter hour. In that time, Catriona had closed Cousin Sophie's eyes and tied her slackened jaw to make sure it would not harden in an undignified position. Then she sat quietly next to the corpse and felt strangely comforted.

The world, except for the maid, did not know yet that Cousin Sophie was dead. For the moment, she could almost pretend her cousin was merely sleeping as she did every afternoon at this time, and she would wake a bit confused and querulous, wanting her dinner.

She looked up when Sir Michael Stewart rushed into the small bedchamber with his coattails flying and an expression of concern on his austere, yet handsome, face. His brown eyes were sad, and his ascetic cheekbones were reddened from the wind.

"Is she gone, then?" he asked in a hushed voice. "You are certain?"

"I am certain," Miss Grant said softly. "Her last words were of you and me in heaven. I wrote them down."

He took the paper from her hand, read it, and closed his eyes.

"I should have come sooner. I was out in one of the oat fields when the message came, and it took my farmer some time to find me." He walked to the bed and touched the dead lady's gray curls with an affectionate hand. "The world has lost one of its purest souls, although she would have scoffed to hear me say so."

He glanced at Catriona's face.

"I am sorry for your loss," he said.

Catriona had no words for the moment, so she merely nodded.

The young maid came into the room with her coat in her hands. She was weeping still.

"I am going to my mother's," the girl said. "I won't stay the night with a corpse in the house."

"Very well, Maisie. I shall manage without you," Catriona said calmly as the girl whirled and practically ran from the room. Catriona took the letter from the table and handed it to the gentleman. "Here is a letter from Cousin Sophie, Sir Michael. I promised her I would give it to you."

He glanced at the letter and the wax seal.

"I shall open it later in private," he said.

"As you wish," Catriona said. "I must prepare . . . her."

He hesitated.

"Shall I call on Mrs. Wilkins and ask her to come help you?"

"I can manage, I thank you," she said. "I have bathed and tended poor Cousin Sophie many times. I would not relinquish this office to another now."

"Nevertheless, I do not like to leave you alone at a time like this. I shall go fetch Mrs. Wilkins and bid her take you home with her tonight."

"And leave poor Cousin Sophie alone in the house as if she were unloved and unmourned? How could I do such a thing after her very great kindness to me?" Catriona said. "I will keep watch over her tonight."

"You are not afraid to be alone with the . . . deceased?"

"I could *never* be afraid of Cousin Sophie."

"Very well, then. I shall arrange for a coffin to be brought here."

"One with a sky blue lining," Catriona said, smiling sadly. "It was her wish. She always thought the color became her like no other."

"It shall be done," said Sir Michael. He went to stand by the bed and look upon Cousin Sophie's poor dead face for a long moment. Then he pressed Catriona's hand and left.

CHAPTER 2

As the solicitor's voice droned on with the usual pompous statements that, as a rule, preceded a deceased citizen's last wishes, Sir Michael took a sip of wine, which was unfortunate because he choked and nearly spewed it across the room when the solicitor got to the point.

"She left me *what*?" Sir Michael sputtered.

"Miss Catriona Grant. Her distant cousin who acted as her companion and housekeeper. Mrs. Tilden *would* insist upon phrasing the, er, bequest in this manner, Sir Michael, despite my strong advice to the contrary. The deceased, if you will permit me to say so, was possessed of a highly unusual sense of humor." He cleared his throat. "Mrs. Tilden said you would need a good woman to take charge of you before your house tumbled down around your ears. What she wished, I venture to say, was for you to accept Miss Grant into your household as housekeeper."

Housekeeper, indeed. Sir Michael knew very well the precious old meddler wanted him to accept Miss Grant into his household as his second wife despite the number of times he had told her that he had no intention of marrying again, especially to a woman so much younger than himself. The private letter Mrs. Tilden had caused Miss Grant to give to him on the day of her death made her wishes in the matter of Miss Grant's future abundantly clear.

Sir Michael agreed with Mrs. Tilden completely on the

point that Miss Grant should be married. But surely she should be married to a man of an age more suitable to her own. Until she found this paragon, she must have friends or relatives somewhere who would take charge of her.

Fortunately, as custom dictated, Miss Grant had not been present at the reading of the will to hear how her cousin had intended to dispose of her future, and thus she was spared this awkwardness. He could only assume that she would be as embarrassed by it as he was himself. Sir Michael showed the solicitor from the house and returned to the parlor, where Miss Grant was sitting alone near the large table upon which the coffin had been placed for the funeral. Now her cousin was buried in the churchyard, and Miss Grant was all alone.

She stood when he entered the room.

"It is done, then," she said. Much to his relief, her face was composed, although its lines were solemn.

"Yes. Mrs. Wilkins bade me bring you to her house tonight, Miss Grant."

"Please thank Mrs. Wilkins for me, but there is much work to be done. There is the house to be set in order, for I understand you mean to sell it. And I must sort through Cousin Sophie's belongings. There are some things she wishes me to give to others." She picked up a small box from the table. "Here are some objects she wished to give to your daughters."

She opened the box to show him the small, heart-shaped pendant with the small pearl at its center and the seed-pearl ring, which would be suitable for a girl not quite out of the schoolroom. Possibly Mrs. Tilden still thought of Sir Michael's grown daughters as children, for she certainly had not seen them once they made their debuts and embraced town life. Or perhaps she merely intended for them to give them to the girl children they would have in the future.

"Mrs. Tilden hoped they would pay a visit to her so she could give these things to them in person. She mentioned it several times," he said, feeling ashamed of his daughters, whom he had reared to show respect for their elders. Mrs. Tilden had been an affectionate surrogate grandmother to the motherless little girls. But Dorothea and Marguerite were all grown up now and puffed up in their own esteem as wives of important men. Both hated being quite out of the world in the wilds of Scotland at their father's dull estate and made excuse after excuse to stay in London.

"I will see they get them," he said as he accepted the box. "I do not expect you to prepare the house for sale. You have exceeded your obligation to me and mine by taking such good care of Mrs. Tilden these two years. I will hire some of the village girls for the purpose when you have taken your departure."

"You wish me to leave immediately, then."

"Absolutely not," he said. "I would not turn you out of your home so abruptly, poor girl. You must stay as long as you wish. If I may be of service in contacting any of your relations with whom you would wish to live, I would be happy to do so."

"I have no relatives who will own me, Sir Michael," she said, chin lifted in defiance. "I have no intention of contacting any of them."

"Then where will you go?"

"My future has been taken care of."

He gave a sigh of relief.

"I am heartily glad to hear it. As I said, Mrs. Wilkins would be pleased to have you stay with her tonight. I understand that your cousin's silly maid refuses to return to the house."

"Maisie? Believe me, Sir Michael, I am better off without her. She's a good girl, is Maisie, but she would keep me up half the night babbling of ghosts. Do not worry about me."

"Very well, then," he said. He started to ask again where she would go, but he realized that although he had seen her often in the two years she had lived with her cousin, she was a virtual stranger to him. She might interpret further interest in her destination as being overly familiar. Perhaps she was going to some man. She was certainly pretty enough to attract the interest of one. If so, it was certainly none of *his* business. "Do not hesitate to send me word if I may be of service to you."

"I will not," she said. She extended her hand, and he took it. "I thank you for your kindness, Sir Michael."

Her hand was cold in his, but her grip was steady enough. She would do, he told himself. And he could leave her to her own devices with a clear conscience.

Catriona looked about her at the house that had been her home for the past two years. The mellow wood of Mrs. Tilden's outmoded furniture had been polished to a high gloss. The floors were gleaming with paste wax. Mrs. Tilden's prized Turkey carpet had been beaten, swept clean, and rolled up for transport. Her back wa aching from all her hard work over the past several days. Sir Michael had sent several girls to assist her, but Catriona had dismissed them. She wanted to be alone with her cousin's memory, for she could feel her benevolent soul all about her in this house and draw comfort from it. She would miss Cousin Sophie so much, and the company of outsiders would only make her feel more bereft.

That afternoon, Catriona had folded all the old lady's clothes and placed them in two portmanteaux to be removed by the pastor's sturdy sons. Mr. and Mrs. Wilkins had promised to distribute them to their parishioners who had the most need of them. It had been hard to part with these clothes, for they still smelled of Cousin Sophie's favorite violet scent and the faint, not unpleasant musky odor of aging flesh.

Her favorite hat. Her almost-new gloves. The comfortable shoes that were worn a bit on one side of the heel. Catriona gave them all away.

Catriona kept only the jewelry that Cousin Sophie insisted she must have: the ruby brooch, the amethyst earrings, the cameo pendant, and the stunning emerald ring she had been given by her long-dead bridegroom on her wedding day. Cousin Sophie's Turkey carpet would go to Sir Michael.

Darling Cousin Sophie. How kind she had been to Catriona when she most needed kindness.

None of that, my girl, Catriona told herself. She had cried and cried for Cousin Sophie, but now she was done.

She set her jaw, put on her coat, and went out to the street, where the hired carriage was waiting. She watched solemnly as the driver heaved the rolled-up carpet into the coach.

Her fortnight of self-indulgence was over. It was time to fulfill her last promise to Cousin Sophie.

"A lady? In this weather? And at this time of night?" Sir Michael said in astonishment when his elderly butler came to inform him that he had a visitor.

"A female, Sir Michael," that disapproving man said, looking down his nose at the vicarious affront. "Mrs. Tilden's cousin."

"Miss Grant? It must be a serious matter if it brings her out on a night like this. Where have you put her?"

"In the hall, sir."

"In the hall? You should have brought her in immediately."

"She was dripping, sir. Quite a lot, if you will permit me to say so."

Michael rose at once and went out into the hall.

"My dear young woman, are you all right?" he asked when he saw his visitor. Her fair hair was wet and curling in the damp. Her cheeks were pale. "What has happened?"

She started to answer, but he stopped her.

"Never mind. We will make you comfortable first, and then you may tell me."

He could hear the poor girl's teeth chattering. It was a bitter night for early autumn. Michael helped her remove her wet coat and handed it to the butler, who looked as if he would like to curl his lip in disapproval but did not quite dare. Instead he walked away with it, holding it far from his body as if it might be infested with fleas. In general, Timms, the butler, did not approve of females, but Michael knew he could trust the man to dry the coat by the fire.

Michael put his hand at the small of Miss Grant's back to guide her out of the hall and into his parlor. He seated her in a chair by the fire and poured a glass of brandy for her.

"Better now?" he asked after she had taken a sip.

"Much. I thank you," she said with a faint smile.

"Good. Now tell me how I may be of assistance to you."

"Actually, Sir Michael, I have come to be of assistance to you."

"I beg your pardon?"

"It was my Cousin Sophie's wish that I come to you after her death and take charge of this place. Surely you knew that she intended this. It was in the letter she left for you."

"Well, yes," he said, deeply shocked. "But I assumed she would not tell *you*—"

"She had to. I wrote the letter for her."

"But surely you did not take it seriously."

"Of course I did. She was devoted to you, Sir Michael. It grieved her that since your wife's death you have lived all alone here except for a few servants. She made me promise I would take care of you, and I shall."

"She made me promise I would take care of you as well. To that end, I have arranged with my banker to give you a sum of money. Did he not inform you?"

Incredibly, she looked annoyed.

"I did not ask for your charity. I have come here to work. Surely your banker informed you that I refused your gift."

"I assumed you refused the money in the freshness of your grief, for it would have been natural for you to be confused, at first, by this abrupt change in your circumstances. This sum will enable you to make a new life for yourself."

"Do not patronize me, Sir Michael. I do not need a new life," Catriona said. "I have a life and a purpose, and that is to put your house into order so that on the day you marry again you will not have to be ashamed of the home to which you will bring your bride."

"I will never marry again," he said, "as I have told Mrs. Tilden often enough. I have had one wife, and lost her."

"All the more reason, then, to have someone take charge of this house," Catriona said, wrinkling her nose. "If *I* had the care of it, your chimney would not smoke so badly."

"My dear Miss Grant, you cannot stay here."

"Why not? It is a big place. Surely you have room for one female. I do not take up much room. I have only this one portmanteau of clothes."

"Do not pretend to misunderstand me. Mine is a bachelor household, and you are a young female."

"Not *that* young," she said wryly.

"Surely you have not reached thirty years of age."

"Not quite," she said. "But it is a close-run thing."

"Even so, it would ruin your reputation to stay here."

"My reputation is already ruined. Surely Cousin Sophie told you so."

"She did mention this briefly when you came to live with her," he said, embarrassed. "But she did not give me the details."

"How uncharacteristically discreet of her," Miss Grant said. She almost looked amused. "In any event, you may rest assured that I have no reputation to lose and employ me with a clear conscience."

"But I have no need for a housekeeper. We rub along tolerably well here without one, I promise you. I do not entertain, and a cook, a butler, and a man of all work serve my needs."

"Do these paragons clean your house as well?" she asked with a disparaging look at the furnishings.

"Of course not. A few village girls come in every week or so to turn the place out. The arrangement is perfectly adequate."

Miss Grant shook her head.

"Cousin Sophie was right. You do need someone to take charge of this place." She stood up and removed her bonnet. "Very well. If you will have your butler show me to a room, I will begin first thing in the morning."

"Absolutely not. You will get back in your carriage at once and—"

"Dismissed him."

"I beg your pardon?"

"The driver who brought me here. I dismissed him. And unless you want to turn one of your servants out on a night like this to take me back to Cousin Sophie's house, you are forced to let me stay. You surprise me, Sir Michael. If Cousin Sophie knew you intended to send me out on such a night, she would come back from the grave to haunt you."

"She might at that. My felicitations," he said dryly. "The wily Mrs. Tilden herself could not have check-mated me so effectively. Very well. I shall have Timms show you to a room."

"Thank you, Sir Michael," she said with a brisk nod.

"You may stay only until tomorrow," he told her. "Then we must make some other arrangement for you."

"We shall see," she said.

He summoned Timms, who seemed quite nonplussed

at the thought of housing a female on the spur of the moment.

"We have no rooms made up, Sir Michael," the old man said in consternation.

"Anywhere will do," Miss Grant said, "as long as it is dry."

"The blue room, perhaps," Sir Michael said.

"Very good, sir," the butler said, but his expression was doubtful.

After his disapproving retainer led Miss Grant away, Sir Michael let out all his breath at once.

CHAPTER 3

Once upon a time, a careful mistress—or perhaps a competent housekeeper—had lived here. The sheets that the redoubtable Mr. Timms had managed to unearth from some long-forgotten chest still retained the ghostly fragrance of long-dead lavender sprigs.

The furnishings were of good quality and had been in impeccable taste, Catriona imagined, some twenty years before.

This house had once been beautiful and would be again, Catriona vowed.

With that thought, she hastily washed her face and hands in the bowl of water that Mr. Timms grudgingly brought her, pinned up her hair, donned an old dress fit for nothing but heavy work, and hastened to the kitchen. There she found . . . no one.

Lord, what a household! There was not even a fire, although it looked as if someone had hacked some pieces of bread off an uncovered loaf on the table, leaving a trail of untidy crumbs in the process, and eaten it with cheese. A knob of the hardened yellow cheese was beside the bread.

Well, she was not a guest, so she had not expected any pampering. She rolled up her sleeves and set to work starting a fire. She set a pot of porridge to cook on the stove. In a well-run household, it would have been placed on the fire at dawn. She certainly could not wait for it, for she was extremely hungry. She sliced some of the bread for herself and toasted it and made tea. She frowned at the first sip. It was of a type much inferior to that used in Mrs. Tilden's house and was so old that it retained little flavor. She would tell the cook that she must not order more of it.

She had settled down with her tea and toast and was occupied in adding to an already lengthy list of improvements to be made to the kitchen when the cook bustled in and stood before her with arms akimbo.

"Who are you, lass, and how dare you make free of my kitchen?"

"Well, *someone* should make free of it, if you will not," Catriona retorted. "You are the cook, I presume. I am Miss Catriona Grant, Sir Michael's new housekeeper, and I am making preparations for breakfast since you were not here to do it," Catriona said with raised brows. "You cannot send your master off without so much as a bowl of oats to warm his stomach."

"The master has been up for hours," the cook said. "He rises early and goes straight out to see to his horses and his fields. He has made himself a meal of bread and cheese, as always, and I will put it away, as I always do."

"And in the meantime, it serves as a lovely feast to attract vermin," Catriona said.

"I suppose the master may do as he pleases in his own house," the cook said. "He willna abide females fussing all over him of a morning, he always says, and he willna thank you for your interference. I heard nothing about any new housekeeper."

"I arrived last night, probably after you were gone to bed."

"I willna be taking orders from you, Miss Grant, until the master himself tells me to."

"Very well," Catriona said. "I will speak to him myself."

* * *

Sir Michael narrowed his eyes when he saw a brown-clad female striding with purposeful steps across the yard toward the stables, where he and some of the men were about to take some of the young horses into the pasture. The sunlight turned her hair to pure gold, which left him in no doubt of her identity.

It was Miss Grant, of course, heaven help him. He could tell by the way she was walking that she was irritated. He wondered which of his servants had put that scowl on her otherwise pretty face—Mr. Timms or the cook. Both were extremely territorial about their respective domains.

He could not be more delighted. Perhaps now she would accept his very generous offer of a money gift, shake the dirt of his estate from her sensible shoes, and leave him in peace.

"Were you looking for me, Miss Grant?" he asked as he looked down from the horse he was riding. She squinted into the sun and held her hand up to shield her eyes.

"I am come to tell you that your breakfast is ready," she said.

"My . . . breakfast? I had that hours ago."

"Bread and cheese hardly constitutes a nourishing breakfast for a grown man," she said. "Come quickly, now, or it will be cold and your cook will be peevish. I will say this for her, though. When she is put on her mettle, she does very well."

"When she is put on her mettle—Miss Grant, am I to understand that you have bullied Mrs. Muir into cooking my breakfast? Do you have *any* idea how old she is?"

"She is a vigorous sixty, I should suppose."

"More like seventy. The poor woman has grown old in my service. I will not have her imposed upon."

"Imposed upon! She is a *cook*. In deference to her age, *I* offered to prepare your breakfast myself, but you would not credit how quickly she disabused me of *that* notion.

I believe she thinks I mean to steal her position from her."

The little baggage had the gall to allow a fleeting smile to touch her lips.

"Poor Mrs. Muir," Sir Michael said, shaking his head. He glanced at his men, who quickly wiped the grins from their faces at his expression. Drat all women! He was sorely tempted to ride away and leave Miss Grant and Mrs. Muir to their own devices, but he supposed he had better get into the house and make peace or he might find himself without a cook at all. "I hope all this is not too much for her."

"Not she," Miss Grant scoffed. "She sent me about my business soon enough when I offered to help."

He got down from the horse and handed the reins to one of the men, who gave him a look of commiseration. Then he followed Miss Grant into the house to find a feast fit for a king on the dining-room table.

"Miss Grant, we do not use the dining room for breakfast."

"Today we do," she said.

Mrs. Muir bustled forth from the kitchen with a steaming bowl of porridge in her hands.

"Seems lumpy to me," she said with a sniff as she set it down on the table.

"I like it with some substance to it," Miss Grant said defensively.

"Sticky and lumpy," Mrs. Muir muttered as she signaled for Mr. Timms to set down a platter of ham and bacon. "Put the potatoes by Sir Michael's left hand," she added. She put a plate in front of Miss Grant. "Here you are, miss. Don't dawdle. Put some meat on your skinny frame."

"Thank you," Miss Grant said in surprise.

"I will show you that I still know my way around a kitchen," the cook said with a huff.

Sir Michael watched her leave, and then his eyes snapped back to Miss Grant.

"What have you done to her? I have not seen her move so fast in years."

"I? Merely pointed out that her master has gone out to his chores with nothing but bread and cheese to sustain him, and that no doubt there are many good women in the village who would give their teeth for such a good position in an important household."

Sir Michael shook his head.

"Miss Grant, you are a menace."

He took a bite of bacon, and one of ham. Then he scooped a spoonful of crisp potato onto his plate as well.

"Will you not try my porridge?" Miss Grant said.

"I do not like oats, Miss Grant. I would not eat them if I were starving."

"Nonsense," she said in disbelief. "You live in Scotland. Everyone eats oats here."

"Not I. Give me a nice, warm loaf of bread and a slice of cheese, and I am ready for the day."

Mrs. Muir sailed back into the room with a big dish and set it before Sir Michael.

"Buttered eggs," she announced. The look in her eye told him she did not expect to see a crumb left on his plate. She left the room with Mr. Timms in tow.

"I cannot eat all of this." He passed the bowl of eggs to Miss Grant. "Here," he said sardonically. "Put some meat on your skinny frame."

"Thank you, I will," she said, lifting her eyebrows at the familiarity. "Heaven knows I will need my strength if I am to bring this house into order."

He stood.

"That was very good. Now I must get back to the field *if* I can walk after being stuffed like a Christmas goose."

"Mrs. Muir did well," Miss Grant said, sounding pleased. "I knew that all she needed was a bit of encouragement."

"Miss Grant," he said sternly as he advanced on her.

She leaned back warily in her chair and stared up into his face. "Do *not* give orders to my servants. Leave them alone. Do you understand?"

"Yes," she said. Her blue eyes were full of resentment.

"Very well. Just have Timms order the carriage when you are ready to leave. You may return to Mrs. Tilden's house, if you wish. Or you may stay with Mrs. Wilkins. Or you may order the coachman to take you all the way to London for all I care. Do I make myself clear?"

"Abundantly," she snapped.

"Very well. Good day, Miss Grant."

With that he turned on his heel and strode out of the house.

"Men," Catriona said with a huff of annoyance. "I suppose he *wants* to live in this squalor."

Well, that was too bad. Mrs. Tilden had charged her with the duty of putting this house in order, and so she would.

"What the devil do you think you are doing?" shouted Sir Michael when he came into the house some time later to find Miss Grant on her hands and knees, scrubbing his floor. He reached down and grabbed her by the elbows to hoist her to her feet.

"I am cleaning this filthy floor," she said.

"I thought I made my wishes clear in the matter of your presence here."

"And so you did. I am not to order your servants. Therefore, I have no choice but to clean the floors myself."

He raised his eyes heavenward and prayed for patience.

"Miss Grant, you are not to clean my floors."

"You cannot wait to see the back of me, you mean," she said, putting her hands on her hips. "And so you shall after I have achieved my objective."

"To drive me mad?"

"To set your house in order so you may marry. My cousin's wishes were quite specific."

"Your cousin wanted me to marry *you*." There it was, out in the open.

"Which is absurd, of course," Miss Grant said quickly. She did not meet his eyes. "I can think of no match more ineligible. Why should you marry a female with no relatives who would own her and a sullied reputation besides? It was Cousin Sophie's kindness that led her to believe such a thing would be possible."

Blindness, more like. Why should a young, pretty, capable woman settle for marriage to a man a decade older than she?

"We are agreed on that, at least," he said in some relief. "So, where am I to find this entirely hypothetical lady who is to be my wife?"

"Here or there," Miss Grant said. "Marriage-minded ladies are as thick on the ground as apples in autumn."

"Lord, you sound just like her," he said in exasperation. He had often heard Mrs. Tilden say the same. His poor wife had barely been put in the ground before Mrs. Tilden started nagging him to marry again.

"Sir Michael, you are hurting me," Miss Grant said in a strained voice.

He looked down at his big, rough hands, which still tightly grasped her arms.

He released her at once, and she promptly dropped to her knees and seized the rag with which she had been cleaning the floor. "Stop that, I say!" he shouted.

Her head snapped up at the abrupt order.

"I should like to know who is going to do it, if I will not," she said resentfully. "These floors are filthy. You do not seem to have a single servant in residence whose responsibility it is to clean anything."

"The village girls come in every two weeks to turn the place out. They are due to arrive any moment, in fact."

"Village girls," Miss Grant said. Her eyes lit up. "Strong, healthy village girls. Excellent. And I suppose I can give *them* orders, since they are not spoiled retainers who have grown old in your service."

"Do as you wish," he snapped. He supposed he would *never* be rid of the troublesome little baggage otherwise. Perhaps she would bully the village girls for a time, be satisfied the place was clean, and go away. With luck, she would be in his carriage and headed back to the village by midafternoon, and he would be left in peace.

His ears pricked up at the sounds of girlish laughter and clattering pails. The village girls had arrived.

"Here they are now," he said in some relief at the prospect of leaving these innocents to Miss Grant's tender mercies.

Miss Grant's eyes lit up, and the girls fell back slightly when she advanced upon them.

"Good morning," she said. "I am Miss Grant." She singled out one of the girls. "You. Finish mopping the floor." Startled, the girl dropped to her knees and reluctantly took the sodden rag from the pail. "The rest of you, follow me," Miss Grant said as she led them from the room. "First we will turn out the parlor. There is dust thick enough to write one's name in on every table."

Michael deliberately avoided the eye of one of the girls, who gave him an imploring look as she followed in Miss Grant's powerful wake.

Better you than me, he thought heartlessly as he made good his escape.

CHAPTER 4

"Look at that," Catriona said as she pulled a chair forward to reveal the telltale coating of dust on the carpeting beneath it. All three village girls reddened in shame, as well they might. It was perfectly clear that Catriona was on to their ruse of making a few ceremonial swipes of the broom or dusting cloth on each visit to the house for an indifferent master and collecting their pay.

No more.

By the time Catriona and the village girls were finished, all the furniture in the parlor and Sir Michael's study had been dragged out and polished to a high gloss. The wood floors had been washed, waxed, and polished. The rugs had been carried outside and ruthlessly beaten on a line. By then, the sun was going down and the village girls were drooping. Their eyes were full of resentment, even though Catriona's face and arms were also sticky with an unappetizing paste made of perspiration, dirt, and dust, and her hair was as dank and dirty as theirs.

"Very good," she said briskly. "The house begins to look as it should. You did well. I understand you come every two weeks. I should like you to come every week from now on. And I should like you to come tomorrow, for we have not even begun on the other floors."

"Yes, miss," one of them said meekly.

"Now, let us proceed to the second parlor off the entrance. It appears not to have been used for years."

"Please, miss," one of the girls said with tears of fatigue in her eyes. "My mother has been expecting me home these past four hours. It is almost dark."

Catriona squinted toward the window and saw that it was so. She gave a sigh of resignation.

"I had no idea it was so late," she said as she rubbed the small of her pleasantly aching back. "Much has been accomplished, but there is still much to do. Go, then. Be back tomorrow, and a bit earlier, if you please. Tomorrow we will turn out the kitchen, dining room, and breakfast room, and we must have it all put back together in time for Mrs. Muir to cook Sir Michael's dinner."

"Yes, miss," the girls chorused, and practically ran from the house.

"You will never see those girls again," Mr. Timms said with cheerful spite from behind her. "They are bone lazy."

"Not today, they were not," Catriona said, rounding on him. "And if they performed their duties in a perfunctory manner before, why did *you* not put them through their paces?"

"*I*, miss?" Mr. Timms said, drawing himself up to his full height, which was just about to Catriona's eyebrows. "It is beneath my dignity to concern myself with such."

"Much is beneath your dignity, it appears," Catriona said as she put her hands on her hips. "How *could* you permit your master to live in such squalor?"

"The master lives as he chooses. *I* have nothing to say in the matter."

"You are the senior member of the staff here," she said. "Do you do *nothing* save answer the door and bring Sir Michael the post?"

"I polish the silver," he said with a sniff, "as is my duty. And I count it."

"*Do* you? Show me."

He looked as if he might like to object, but then he ushered her into the butler's pantry off the kitchen and revealed to her the near-blinding glory of no less than four sets of meticulously polished silver in their gleaming mahogany cases.

"Heavens, it is stunning," she said in disbelief. "There is enough here to serve several hundred guests."

"The late mistress was fond of entertaining," he said. "She brought it all from London when she married Sir Michael, as she did me." A reminiscent smile lit his face. "I worked for her family and was promoted to butler when she took me from her father's household to serve Sir Michael's upon her marriage."

"That is the Renaissance Lily pattern," she said reverently as she reached out but did not quite touch one of the exquisitely wrought knives. She remembered in time that every inch of her was filthy.

"It was her pride," the old man said. He cocked his head at Catriona. "You know your silver, do you, miss?"

"I grew up in London," she said evasively.

"Were you in service there?" he asked. He smiled at her quick, startled look. "Your speech is genteel enough, but no lady of my acquaintance would work as hard and long as you did today. She would not know how."

"We are all in service, in one capacity or another, are we not, Mr. Timms?" she asked.

"Yes. We are," he said, pointedly. "Do not think I am blind to the fact that this house has been left to go to rack and ruin. I tried, at first, to keep up appearances, but Sir Michael would not have a house full of servants, disturbing the silence with which he surrounded himself when the mistress died. We feared, at first, that he might die, too."

"What nonsense," Catriona said impatiently. "A perfectly healthy person does not die from grief. One does the best one can. One survives. I should know."

"You were fond of Mrs. Tilden," the butler said.

"Yes. I was," she said.

"She was a redoubtable lady. She would be pleased to see the parlor looking as it does, but Sir Michael will not thank you for it."

"I do not do it for *him*," she said. "Thank you for showing me the silver."

She left the butler's pantry to find a glowering Sir Michael blocking her path.

"I expected you to be long gone to Dumfries by now," he said. "Timms, did I not order you to have the carriage ready for her?"

"I dismissed it," Catriona said, fully aware that she looked as if she had been dragged through a bush backward and smelled to high heaven as a result of her exertions. Sir Michael, in that exasperating way of men, had also put in a long day's labor with the horses and his crops, but *he* smelled rather pleasantly of leather and horse. His dark hair was windblown, which only made it a more dramatic frame for his lean, handsome face and solemn dark eyes. "It took rather longer to finish the parlor than that, and you would not have liked me to leave the furniture standing out in the hall and the floor half cleaned."

"There is still some daylight left," he said pointedly. "Timms, order the carriage again."

Mr. Timms turned to obey.

"I cannot go to Mrs. Wilkins like *this*," Catriona said. She felt her cheeks go hot at Sir Michael's long inspection of her from the rat's nest of her hair to her scuffed and dirty shoes. "Allow me to preserve *some* modicum of pride."

"I concede your point," he said. "Very well, you may stay tonight. But tomorrow, you must go. Do you understand?"

"I understand," she said.

With that, she left the room. Although her body

ached, she forced her tired frame to hold her head and shoulders erect. Only the prospect of a hot bath kept her from drooping like one of those languishing females she despised, even though she knew she would have to draw the water for herself and sustain the glowering disapproval of Mrs. Muir as she heated it on the stove.

Sir Michael quickly wiped the smile off his face when he caught Mr. Timms looking at him with an expression of utter incredulity at Miss Grant's capitulation.

"There. She will be out of the house by this time tomorrow," Sir Michael said with satisfaction. "And then we shall be comfortable again, Timms."

"Heaven be thanked for it," the old man said, although he looked doubtful.

The next day, Sir Michael came into the kitchen to find Mrs. Muir in attendance. As he started to seat himself at the table, as usual, she shooed him away.

"Your place is set in the breakfast room, Sir Michael," she said gruffly. "*She* is already there."

He would have objected, for he was in a hurry to get to the horse barn, but he snapped his mouth shut before any words could escape. It was Miss Grant's last day in the house, so he could afford to humor her. Tomorrow, all would be back to normal, he told himself.

He found her already seated at the table, eating a bowl of porridge. She got up to pour him a cup of tea, although he tried to wave her away. There was toast in a silver rack he could not recall seeing before. Bacon and ham rested on a platter at his elbow. A dish of buttered eggs was before him.

Out of sheer stubbornness he was tempted to tell her to take it all away and bring him bread and cheese, but it would take a braver man than he to tell Mrs. Muir that her labors had been for naught.

His stomach growled. Loudly. Which made it impossible for him to declare he was not hungry.

At the homely sound, Miss Grant gave him a sly smile and poured herself a cup of tea. It gave him a pang to see, poised in Miss Grant's hands, the silly little rose-painted teapot his late wife had brought to the house upon their marriage. It had been stored away all these years, but Miss Grant or Mrs. Muir had unearthed it.

He remembered his late wife's airy, inconsequential chatter as she went about her day. Her gaiety. Her spontaneous laughter.

By contrast, Miss Grant's manner was matter-of-fact, and she said nothing until he spoke first. Well, the least he could do was be civil to the woman. She was leaving today, after all.

"Still eating your oats, I see," he observed.

Miss Grant looked up at him, all blue eyes and fair hair twisted in a knot at the back of her head. She was wearing a brown gown that should have looked plain, but served only to provide a dignified setting for her youth and beauty.

"Oats are most nutritious," she said seriously.

"Spoken like a good Scottish miss," he said. "Are you sure you have no Scottish ancestors?"

"None," she said. "I am English to the bone, but Cousin Sophie would have told you that."

"So she did," he acknowledged.

She looked down at her bowl for a moment.

"Does it disturb you to find a woman in your wife's place at your breakfast table?" she asked as she regarded him with a look of sympathy. "If so, I can take my breakfast in the kitchen."

"No, it does not disturb me," he said, after he had thought about it for a moment. "Perhaps it is because no two women could be more unlike."

She raised her eyebrows.

"I assume that was *not* a compliment. I have heard how you doted upon her from Cousin Sophie."

How odd it seemed for someone to talk of his wife

before him. His friends, relatives, and staff had tiptoed all about the subject of his late wife for years.

"No insult was meant," he told her. "I merely spoke the literal truth. My wife was small and dark, where you are somewhat taller and fair. She rarely joined me for breakfast. She preferred biscuits and chocolate in her boudoir long after I had eaten and gone about my work."

He could feel the disapproval emanating in waves off his breakfast companion.

"You think her lazy, I suppose. A bad wife," he said ruefully. It seemed strange to talk about her. He had not talked about her for so long.

"I would never be rude enough to say so," she said quickly.

"It is too late now to pretend you have delicacy of mind, my girl." He smiled. Actually smiled. And from the look on her face, he could tell that she was as surprised by this as he was.

Some say memory fails after time, but the image of his Clarissa remained fixed in his mind.

His pretty wife used wear a frothy dressing gown from one of London's most exclusive dressmakers for her breakfast, which she usually had served to her in the beautifully appointed bedchamber that she insisted upon calling a boudoir. Occasionally, she invited him to share her breakfast with her at a small table in her sitting room, and at those moments he felt as privileged as if he had been granted an audience by a queen. All the while she made pretty conversation in her musical voice and smiled at him with her soft, pink lips.

Mrs. Tilden used to say that Clarissa, though decorative, was a vain, silly creature, and no wife for a sensible man. But that was before his wife had died. After that, like everyone else, Mrs. Tilden did not speak of her at all in his presence for fear of breaking his heart further.

"I suppose she permitted you to go off into the fields with nothing but bread and cheese for your breakfast," Miss Grant said in disapproval. "In my way of thinking, that is no way to care for a husband."

He had to laugh at that.

"Oh, you are wrong," he said. "My wife did me the very great favor of allowing me to decide for myself what I would or would not have for breakfast. She did whatever she liked with the house for the most part, and I did whatever I liked with everything else—including myself."

The little baggage had the gall to give a little sniff of disapproval.

"Do you mean your *wife* chose those dreadful draperies in the dining room?" she said in disbelief. "And those dark, oppressive furnishings?"

Michael blinked.

"Well, not in the dining room, no. The furnishings there have been in my family for several generations, and my wife honored my wish to retain them. As for the draperies, what is dreadful about them? They keep out the light, just as they are supposed to do."

"Precisely my point," she said. "Everything is so dark and dreary in there. It looks like the setting for one of Miss Radcliffe's novels. One imagines a rotting corpse could very well enter through those doors, wailing and keening and threatening to carry one off to its crypt— *not* an image conducive to proper digestion."

"My dear Miss Grant," he said in disapproval. "You have a taste for lurid literature. I never would have thought it of you."

Her face turned scarlet. He might as well have accused her of practicing all sorts of perversions.

"It was Cousin Sophie who had a taste for such books," she said loftily. "She had a standing order from one of the bookstores in London, and a parcel came every month. She would laugh herself into stitches over the things."

He could not help giving a long, sentimental sigh. He missed Mrs. Tilden's acerbic humor.

"No wonder your spirits are so low if you must take your evening meal in such a depressing room," his companion said.

"My spirits are none of your concern, Miss Grant," he said in his most forbidding voice. But did Miss Grant, so masterfully put in her place, have the grace to blush and apologize for her familiarity? Ha! Not she.

"Cousin Sophie has made them my concern," she said, leaning forward in her vehemence. "If that were *my* dining room, I would take down all those heavy draperies and let the sun inside."

"Much to the detriment of the upholstery," he said dryly.

"No great loss," she said. "Your ancestors obviously had a taste for horrors."

"But the rest of the house was refurbished when my wife came here as a bride. Nothing would do for her but the very best," he said wryly. "The bills nearly beggared me."

"True. The colors and furnishings were likely considered very elegant twenty years ago, but they are sadly outmoded now."

"You would have the house all done up in the French empire style, I suppose," he said.

"Even that has been out of mode for years," she said with raised eyebrows. "How long has it been since you were out in society?"

"How long has it been for *you*, my girl?" he asked pointedly.

Her face schooled itself to blankness.

"Two years. Anyone will tell you so," she said, rising. "But I am an avid reader of the society pages because of Cousin Sophie's love for gossip. And your neighbors are not so out of the world that they do not aspire to fashion. Edinburgh is not so very far away, after all, and anyone may have furnishings shipped directly there from London. I am surprised your daughters will allow your house to fall to bits around you. Did they not plague you to refurbish the place before they were married?"

"They would have objected quite strongly to having their mother's house changed in any way, I assure you," he said.

"I hesitate to say this for fear of seeming callous," she said, "but the poor woman has been dead these eighteen years. The house is *yours*."

Michael surprised her, and himself, by giving an abrupt, mirthless laugh.

"You looked and sounded exactly like your Cousin Sophie just then," he said. "She has said the same to me over and over in the years since my wife's death."

"She thought you should have married again and had more children years ago."

"I tolerated Mrs. Tilden's interference in my affairs because she was my wife's relative and of such years that she commanded my respect and courtesy," he said. He felt his jaw tighten as if it were a vise. "I will *not* tolerate yours."

She should have dissolved into a little puddle of embarrassment. Instead, she smiled.

"Obviously you are one of those men who dislike conversation in the morning," she said, rising. "If you will excuse me, I have matters to see to."

"Your packing, I trust," he said, rising as well. "Let me wish you godspeed on your journey."

There. He could not be more direct than that. Timms had been entrusted with a money purse for her and told to order the carriage to take her away as soon as her belongings were packed.

Once outside, Michael took a deep breath of the autumn-scented air and went off to the barn with the

feeling that the weight of the world had been lifted
from his shoulders. By the time he returned to his
house, Miss Grant would be gone and his domestic life
would have settled down to its usual placid pace and
he could be comfortable again.

CHAPTER 5

After spending an anxious morning in the horse barn presiding over the difficult birth of a foal, Sir Michael entered his house at midday, expecting to find it quiet.

Instead, a ferocious din of clattering pails assailed his ears as soon as he opened the door, and the breakfast room, where he was in the habit of finding a simple bowl of stew, a half loaf of bread, and a hunk of the ever-present yellow cheese because Mrs. Muir knew he liked a bit of something this time of day, was full of sturdy young girls raising a fine dust with their cleaning.

"Timms!" he bellowed. The butler came scurrying into his presence.

"I told you she was to be gone by midday," he shouted. "What are they doing here?" His arm swept in an agitated arc toward the girls. "It is not their day."

"*She* told them to come back. They are turning out the kitchen."

"Oh, good Lord. Mrs. Muir will have had an apoplexy by now. If she has not committed murder instead."

Sir Michael skidded into the kitchen, fully expecting to find Miss Grant unconscious on the floor from a blow to the head with a kettle or Mrs. Muir laid out on the floor with limbs twitching in an apoplectic seizure. Instead he found a sight so stunning that he stood gaping, with his mouth opening and closing like that of a landed fish.

"You are a miracle worker if you have managed to

cook any kind of digestible meal on such an ancient stove," Miss Grant was saying as she made a note on a list. Mrs. Muir sat contentedly next to her with a teacup in front of her. "I will speak to Sir Michael at once about replacing it."

"If you can convince him to replace the old thing, you will have my gratitude, miss," the cook was saying. "Will you have another biscuit?"

"Thank you. They are very good. As soon as we complete the inventory I will speak to him," Miss Grant said after she had taken a delicate bite of the biscuit and chewed. "I must say I am pleasantly surprised by the larder. You have done your work well, and with precious little encouragement from your master."

"Sir Michael never notices what he eats," Mrs. Muir complained. "I could set a stewed rat with an apple in its mouth before him, and he wouldna notice."

"He has certainly noticed that there is no midday meal waiting for him in the breakfast room," Sir Michael grated out.

"Oh, Sir Michael!" squeaked Mrs. Muir. "It is not so late, surely."

"It is. Where is the bread and cheese?" He gave a wry look toward the bare stove. "And there is no soup, I collect."

"That is my fault," Miss Grant said.

"Make no mistake," Sir Michael said wrathfully. "I know *exactly* who to blame for this state of affairs. *You*, madam, were supposed to be gone from the house by now. I thought I had made my wishes perfectly clear in this regard."

"So you did."

"Timms. Did you not give her the money? Did you not order the carriage?"

"I did both, Sir Michael," the butler said with a sigh of exasperation.

"If I did not want your charity when Cousin Sophie

died, I certainly do not want it now," the disgraceful baggage said calmly. "And so I have told you. What I want is to make a decent home for you, as I promised her."

"And after you complete this orgy of cleaning and arranging, will you leave me in peace?"

"It depends. Cousin Sophie said I was to stay in my post until I was relieved by a new, competent housekeeper or your second wife, whichever arrived first."

"And I am to pay you a wage, I suppose."

"Certainly. I will not come cheap, but then competent staff never does. We shall prepare bread, cheese, and tea for you at once. A more substantial repast shall be set before you this evening. I would be grateful if you would set aside some time for me today so I may tell you what will be required to bring the kitchen up to snuff."

"The kitchen . . . There is *nothing* wrong with this kitchen. Everything was fine until you came here and started mucking about with it."

"Only a *man* would think so, but I am making allowances for you because you have been preoccupied with your horses and your crops, and your depressed state."

"My depressed state . . . My state was perfectly comfortable until you came here to plague me."

"I have come here to be your salvation, and that of your permanent staff. Have you not noticed that the knees of Mr. Timms's livery are so shiny you can practically see your face in them and your poor cook has been struggling to prepare digestible meals for you on a stove so antiquated it is a wonder it has not blown up in her face?"

"That will do," Sir Michael snapped.

"Every chimney in the house smokes," Miss Grant continued as both Timms and Mrs. Muir stared to see her override the master. "The hangings in the servants' quarters are practically in shreds."

"There are no servants residing in the servants' quarters," Sir Michael pointed out, irritated with himself at once for lowering himself to debating the matter with her. "Mrs. Muir has quarters near the kitchen because the stairs are too much for her arthritic knees, and Timms sleeps . . . Where is it you sleep, Timms?"

"On a cot in the butler's pantry," he said, flushing a little in embarrassment and favoring Miss Grant with a resentful glare. "The stairs are too much for my knees, too, and the old servants' quarters are too cold. It seemed a poor economy to have a fire down there, when this floor is perfectly warm because of the fire from the kitchen—"

"You may sleep anywhere you wish, for all I care," Sir Michael said with an impatient sigh. "It makes no difference to me. There is plenty of room."

"Well, it *should* make a difference to you," Miss Grant snapped. "No wonder his back aches after sleeping on that hard little cot. Two servants who have grown old in your service have a right to decent beds in which to rest themselves at night."

"Who are you calling old, missy?" Timms said forbiddingly. "I've still a good day's work or two left in me, I will have you know."

"My cot is perfectly comfortable, Sir Michael," said the old woman.

"Compared to the beds in the servants' quarters, it is," the incorrigible Miss Grant conceded. "Every one of them is musty with damp. I would not be surprised if vermin have made nests in the mattresses, they smell so nasty."

"I had no idea," Michael said slowly, horrified that he had neglected his servants so. "No idea at all."

"You had much to think about after the missus died," Mrs. Muir said kindly. "With two little mites left on your hands."

"That was eighteen years ago," Miss Grant said.

"It is unnecessary for you to remind me," Michael said through gritted teeth. "I know to the day when my wife died."

"Of course you do," Miss Grant said. "Everyone says you were quite devoted, although that is hardly an excuse for being a negligent master now."

"I am not a negligent master," he shouted. He hit his fist against the wall for emphasis. His eyes watered with the pain, but he would not whimper in front of this woman and his own servants.

Both Mrs. Muir and Timms backed away, wide-eyed.

"Do not be afraid," the insufferable Miss Grant said kindly to them. "Sir Michael will not hurt you. It is hunger that is making him snappish."

"I am not snappish," he snapped.

"As you say, Sir Michael," the maddening little baggage agreed in the soothing tone one reserves for madmen and small, cranky children.

Michael locked his jaws together to keep his ire inside.

He *never* lowered himself to losing his temper with his dependents. Only a blackguard shouted at persons who were not permitted to shout back. And Miss Grant, heaven help him, seemed determined to be one of his dependents.

"Miss Grant, I shall speak to you later," he said, introducing calmness into his voice by sheer force of will. "You will then give me an accounting of whatever you think needs to be done to the house to bring it up to your standards, for I hope Mrs. Muir knows I do not really want the stove to blow up in her face."

"Thank you, sir," Mrs. Muir murmured.

"There. I knew you could be reasonable if you chose," Miss Grant said, looking pleased and triumphant.

"But the moment this household is up to snuff, you are to leave, do you understand me?"

"At that time my work will be done, providing you marry or hire another housekeeper," she acknowledged, "and I shall take myself off to some watering hole to seek employment as a companion to an elderly invalid. It would suit me, the seaside, I think."

"You might marry instead."

"I think not. Husbands are much more difficult to manage than helpless little old ladies," she said with a straight face.

She was probably right, he thought. He knew that if she were *his* wife, he would be strongly tempted to beat her.

"Since *that* matter has been settled to our mutual satisfaction," he said awfully, "I will go to my study, since I trust it is still intact, and await Timms, who, if he chooses to remain in my employ, will do well to bring me bread and cheese within the next five minutes."

"At once, sir," Timms said quickly.

Sir Michael turned to stalk stiffly away in all his dignity, but not before he saw the smug smile light Miss Grant's blue eyes.

She had *won*, blast her!

If he had been a fanciful person—which he certainly was not—he would swear he heard the delighted cackle of the late, lamented Mrs. Tilden's most wicked laughter ringing in his ears.

CHAPTER 6

Marguerite, Lady Redgrave, practically mowed her sister's butler down in her eagerness to ruin her elder sister's day.

"Oh, do get out of my way, man," she snapped at the fellow when he leaped aside with surprising nimbleness for a man his age. "I know my way to my sister's parlor perfectly well."

"I regret to say, my lady, that Mrs. Walbridge is not yet receiving visitors—" the man said as he attempted again to bar her way.

Marguerite frowned at him. She had no patience with officious lackeys. Dorothea might be the elder, but Marguerite outranked her socially, a fact she had no intention of letting anyone forget. Which meant she did not have to take any sauce from a mere butler.

"I am not an ordinary visitor," she said haughtily. "I am your mistress's sister, as you very well know. Summon Mrs. Walbridge at once. I have come on a matter of grave importance. And I shall have tea in the parlor while I am waiting. And perhaps a sweet biscuit or two."

The butler drew up all stiff in outraged dignity, but he could hardly present further objections without giving offense, so he went off to do her bidding.

It was quite half an hour before her sister made her appearance, and by then an impatient Marguerite had drunk two cups of tea and eaten five biscuits. Dorothea was not one to rush her toilette merely because her only sister announced that she had come on a matter of life and death. Dorothea did not set foot from her dressing room until she was perfect from the top of her glossy, dark curls to the toes of her aristocratically narrow, expensively shod feet. Normally Marguerite respected her elder sister's pride in her appearance as quite one of her best qualities, but not today.

"Dorothea!" she gasped when her sister came into the parlor. She rose to her feet in her agitation. "The most dreadful thing! What do you think Father has done now?"

Dorothea gave Marguerite a quelling look and turned to face her butler.

"That will be all, Richards," she said majestically.

"Very good, madam," the butler said, and left the room.

"Now, Marguerite," Dorothea said with a sigh. "What has got you in a pucker this time?"

"Father has got a young woman living with him, that is what!"

"A young woman? *Our* father?" Dorothea gave a pretty little laugh. "You must be all about in your head. What would Papa want with a young woman?"

Marguerite rolled her eyes.

"Well, what do you *think?*"

Dorothea gasped and wrung her hands in agitation.

"You are mistaken. You *must* be mistaken. Papa would *never*—"

"He is a *man*, is he not?" Marguerite said with a bitter, cynical laugh.

Dorothea merely stared at her, aghast.

"And who do you think it is?" Marguerite continued. "It is that connection of Mrs. Tilden's, the one the old lady was always going on and on about in her letters. That Miss Grant." She started pacing the length of her sister's handsome carpet. "I always thought she was a sly one, with her yellow hair and her butter-wouldn't-melt-in-her-mouth ways."

"She is much too young for Father," Dorothea said. "There must be some mistake."

"There is no mistake. I had a letter of Mrs. Pritchett, who lives not far from Mrs. Tilden's house. The insufferable woman is laboring under the delusion that we are social equals merely because we were friends when we were children. She has kept up the connection, no doubt, because she hopes I will take her up, which I certainly have no intention of doing."

"What has Mrs. Pritchett to do with Father and this woman?" Dorothea asked with a huff of impatience. "Do strive for *some* coherence, my dear."

"It is being said in Dumfries that Mrs. Tilden actually left Miss Grant to Father in her will! And Mrs. Tilden was in the ground exactly a fortnight when the hussy packed her bags and presented herself on Father's doorstep, demanding to be taken in—which he promptly did, if Mrs. Pritchett is to be believed."

"What a faradiddle! It is all Eliza Pritchett's foolishness, for the girl was always a silly, gossiping ninnyhammer."

"And so I thought, sister, until I got Papa's letter this morning. He *confirms* it! Miss Grant is living in his house as his *housekeeper*, or so he says."

"His housekeeper," Dorothea repeated. "If it were any man but Father, I would call *that* a pretty euphemism for quite something else. Father is the very soul of honor."

"But *she* is likely not," Marguerite fumed. "You mark my words. She intends to trap him into marriage, and Father, being, as you say, the very soul of honor, is vulnerable to her schemes."

"He has not *looked* at another woman since our mother died," Dorothea scoffed.

"How do *you* know? You have not been to Scotland since your marriage two years ago. He could have a dozen so-called housekeepers in residence for all you know."

"Do not adopt that accusing tone with me, Marguerite. *You* have not been to Scotland in some time, either."

"But you are the elder. It is your responsibility to make certain Papa is not being taken advantage of by some marriage-minded female," Marguerite said.

"You have just as much time as I have," Dorothea said. "What is keeping *you* from going to Scotland to keep an eye on Father?"

"My responsibility to my husband, of course. The social obligations are endless. I am quite worn to a thread. It is not easy being the wife of a viscount."

"Nonsense. Your duties cannot be *very* onerous, since the dowager viscountess refuses to relinquish any of her prerogatives and still keeps her precious boy in leading strings," Dorothea said dryly. Marguerite felt hot color stain her cheeks. Indeed, living under her mother-in-law's roof had been quite trying during the short tenure of her marriage.

"You know nothing of the matter," Marguerite said as a sop to her pride. She suspected Dorothea knew all too well that her lavish storybook wedding had not culminated in the idyllic marriage she had anticipated. However, Marguerite truly did adore her husband, and she knew in her heart that he returned her regard. After all, the old witch could not live forever.

"One of us must go to Scotland and see what can be done about Papa and this woman," Dorothea said with a sigh of resignation. "I suppose it must be me since I am the eldest. I must confess, I would not mind rusticating a bit. Nothing very interesting is happening in London this season, and I am rather cross with Edward. I believe he has taken up with a mistress."

"Dorothea!" Marguerite exclaimed. "We are not to know such women exist."

"It is hard *not* to know when he will consort with her in Hyde Park before all the *ton*," her sister said bitterly. Her lower lip started to quiver.

"There, there," Marguerite said as she put her arm around Dorothea's shoulder. She knew all about

Dorothea's husband and his mistress, for Marguerite's husband had confirmed the rumors, but she would not have been the instrument of her sister's disillusionment for the world. "I am certain she is merely a passing amusement. All men stoop to such folly at times."

"Does your precious Henry?" Dorothea sniffed.

"I do not think so," Marguerite said, "but in a way you are more fortunate than I. Edward will probably discard his little ladybird as soon as you are with child and he has the responsibilities of fatherhood to occupy his mind. Until then, she need not plague you overmuch. He will take care that you are never in one another's company, and your acquaintances will take care never to mention her name in your presence. I, on the other hand, am married to a man who is firmly under his mother's thumb. I live under her roof—she makes it perfectly clear that *I*, the wife of the present viscount, am the interloper, and not she. I have to endure her presence at every meal. I have to tolerate her criticism of my clothing, my friends, and my taste in furnishings. The only escape I will ever have from her is with her death or my own."

Dorothea gave her sister a speculative look.

"It appears neither of our husbands value us as they ought," she said slowly. "It is time to teach them a lesson."

"What do you mean?"

"I mean, we should *both* go to Scotland to see what fine mess Father has got himself into with this Grant woman."

Marguerite gave a shudder.

"You mean both of us go to Dumfries? That backwater? Do you not remember what it is like?"

"Perfectly," Dorothea said with a grimace. "But dull as we may find Dumfries and Papa's dreary old horse farm, it may be worth enduring a trip to Scotland to put a scare into our complacent husbands. We have been constantly at their beck and call since we married them. They will see how they have been taking us for granted and treat us with more respect when we return. They can hardly object if we want to pay a visit to our aging father."

"Aging father, indeed!" Marguerite scoffed. "Papa is not yet forty, and a fine figure of a man."

"True, but no one else knows that. He made a brief appearance in London for each of our weddings, and he has not left his dreary old farm since. We can invent an illness for him. No one would consider it odd for us to go to his sickbed."

"I hate to lie to Henry," Marguerite said.

"Well, we cannot very well tell everyone that we are going to Scotland to keep Papa from making a shocking misalliance with a young woman. *That* would certainly make us look ridiculous."

"What if our husbands insist upon accompanying us?"

"They will not. They dislike the country as much as we do."

Marguerite had to admit that her sister's suggestion was brilliant, and not only because it was their duty to put an end to their father's liaison with this unworthy female.

Marguerite could well do with some time away from her mother-in-law, much as it would pain her to be separated from her husband. Moreover, as a viscount's wife, she would be one of the most important women in Dumfrieshire County. After having her self-esteem battered by her husband's mother throughout the duration of her marriage, Marguerite had no objection at all to showing off her fashionable London gowns and her jewels to an awestruck bucolic audience.

"Very well," Marguerite said. "I shall go home and tell my maid to pack at once."

CHAPTER 7

Catriona Grant presented herself in Sir Michael's study at precisely seven o'clock, the hour he had bade her to do so.

It was a dark, intimidating room, with a heavy mahogany desk, thick velvet draperies the color of burgundy wine, and glass-fronted bookcases full of leather-bound tomes. When he was in this room, no one dared disturb him, for this was where Sir Michael kept his ledgers and conducted estate business. This was where he summoned his recalcitrant managers, stewards, and other business associates to give an accounting of their unsatisfactory behavior, and the personality of the room was so strong that before he even opened his mouth to enumerate their iniquities, they cowered.

Unfortunately, though, this infernal female had caused the village girls to pull the curtains back and open the windows so the pleasantly fecund fragrances of an autumn evening filled the room and the twittering of night birds in the trees outside added its music to the ambiance. A side table held a flower-filled silver vase that Michael vaguely recognized as having been a wedding gift from a long-dead relative. He had found the papers in a desk drawer.

She and those giggling females from the village had been snooping into every nook and cranny of his home over the past week, unearthing all of the objects that reminded him painfully of that fleeting, effervescent presence that had been his fragile wife. He had been coming across these things for days—the candlesticks, the flower-etched crystal bowls, the handsome mantel clocks—the mere sight of which had been like daggers into his heart after his wife's death. Clarissa had prized pretty things so much that he had ordered Timms to pack them all away because he could not bear to look at them in the fullness of his grief.

He found they did not pain him now. Their presence merely annoyed him because it was Miss Grant who had caused them to be brought forth into the light.

"There, I knew that silver vase would be just the thing for your study," she said, looking pleased as she gazed with satisfaction about the room. "Attractive but still dignified. Do you not agree?"

"No, Miss Grant," he said wearily. "I do not agree. But I know better than to ask you to take it away, because if I do, you will only set something even more objectionable in its place."

"Quite right," she said, smiling. "Admit it. This is a much more pleasant room now."

"The flowers likely will make me sneeze," he said, just for the sake of being contrary. "And the open draperies will fade the furnishings."

"A good thing, if you ask me," she said, shaking her head at him in disgust. "These furnishings could do with a little fading. How you managed to get any work done in such a dark, musty room is beyond me. When was the last time you had it aired out?"

"Never, to my recollection, nor have I required it."

"How like a man! As for your sneezing, if you could endure this room with all the dust in it that the girls cleared out today, a few flowers are not going to bother your tender nose."

Michael gritted his teeth and absolutely *refused* to let her put him into a passion, even though he dearly would have loved to wrap his hands around her swanlike neck and squeeze until her facile little pink tongue turned black to punish her for cutting up his peace.

The stove had been ordered from Dumfries and installed in the kitchen, which forced him to subsist on cold meals for several days. The day after it was in place, the women had gathered every piece of soiled linen in the house and commenced an orgy of washing and bleaching and fussing that set his teeth on edge.

To his chagrin, he did have reason to be grateful to her, and his sense of honor required him to acknowledge his debt to her at once.

"I owe you my thanks, Miss Grant," he said.

"You certainly do," she agreed at once. "This house was a disgrace, but it is well on the way to being brought up to snuff. Another few weeks, and it will be quite tolerable."

"Not for that," he snapped.

"No? What have I done, then, to incur your obviously reluctant gratitude?" she asked with a teasing smile on her face.

"It is not a joking matter," he said, goaded by her flippant tone. No one else in his life *dared* make light of him. Still, he had to persevere. "For bringing my neglect of Mrs. Muir and Timms to my attention. It shall be remedied, of course."

"I am delighted to hear you say so," Miss Grant said. "As it happens, I have already seen to it. There are two small bedrooms on the ground floor that I have made ready for them. They seem to be very comfortable there, even though both of them objected at first, saying it would not be fitting for them to occupy such rooms."

Well, he could imagine she made short work of such objections!

Michael eyed Miss Grant with disfavor, even though he had intended to order her to do that very thing.

She had a positive talent for taking the wind out of his sails.

"I shall procure new bedding for them, of course, and for all the other beds as well, for what you have now is in a deplorable state. The sheets are so thin with wear and age that I am surprised the wind did not blow holes in them when they were hanging on the lines. I assume you have a household account in Dumfries that you will make available for my use. The store owner probably will require a letter from you authorizing me to purchase goods on it."

She stepped over to the bookcase, ran a casual hand along his books, and inspected her fingers. Looking for dust, no doubt.

"It shall be done. *Will* you be seated so I may do so?" he said irritably.

"With pleasure," she said as she disposed herself in a chair. "You had only to invite me, you know."

"My apologies," he said stiffly as he also sat down. "I am not in the habit of entertaining ladies."

"Do not worry your head about that. I am hardly a lady. I am your housekeeper."

"I know very well from Mrs. Tilden that you are of gentle birth, or I would not have permitted you to serve as her companion. She would tell me nothing of your family, however."

Her eyes hardened.

"Such a disclosure would have been irrelevant. I no longer have a family."

"As you wish," he said. "I did not summon you here to precipitate another argument."

"Why did you summon me here, then?" she asked.

Why, indeed? When she was looking at him with that expectant look on her face he could not remember. Oh, yes. To order her to move Mrs. Muir and Timms to more comfortable quarters, which she had already done without his permission as if it were her house rather than his.

For him to say this, though, would be to make himself ridiculous.

More ridiculous.

A week ago, he had felt himself a rational man in control of his destiny. Now he was a buffoon being ordered and herded about by a masterful female.

"I will give you that letter of credit in the morning," he said, rising. "I assume you also will want the carriage to go into Dumfries and make your selections."

She rose gracefully to her feet, and it pleased him that she recognized dismissal when she heard it.

"Yes. I will. Thank you, Sir Michael," she said formally. Her mouth was unsmiling, but he had the uncomfortable feeling she was laughing at him. "Sleep well."

Michael gave her a sour smile as she turned and left the room.

Sleep well. Not bloody likely with *her* in the house.

He had turned back to his accounts but was interrupted yet again when Timms practically skidded into the room. Michael frowned. Blast the woman! She was right. His livery *was* shiny at the knees.

"Sir Michael! Your daughters have arrived," Timms said, practically wringing his hands in distraction. Pleasure warred with consternation on his usually stern face. "Where we are to put them, I do not know."

"Calm yourself, Mr. Timms," Miss Grant said from behind him. "The girls began turning out the bedchambers before they left today. You do have two presentable rooms for them, although whether they are the ones Sir Michael's daughters would prefer, I have no idea."

Miss Grant stood aside to admit his daughters into the room.

Michael felt his heart expand, just looking at them.

Both had dark, glossy curls and sweet, delicate, fairy-like features like those of his late, lamented wife. As children, they were enchanting. As grown women, they were a bittersweet pleasure.

They always had been beautiful to his eyes, even—
or maybe especially—when they ran clattering through
the house, laughing, in braids and bare feet on sum-
mer days when they were little girls. Now they were exquisite, just like their mother, who had delighted in
all the most frivolous little trifles that London shop-
keepers had to offer for her adornment. It had been
so long since they had paid a visit to him that at first
he could only devour their beloved faces with his eyes
like a starving man.

"Papa!" cried his little Marguerite from the doorway,
and Michael opened his arms wide to receive her. But
then she remembered that she was a married woman
now, moreover a viscount's wife, and effusive shows of affection were beneath her dignity. "You are looking well,
Father," she said composedly as she took his hands in
hers and gave them a brief squeeze.

"As are you, my dear," he said, admiring her beautifully tailored traveling costume of dark blue and her
dashing hat. He turned to his other daughter, who was
no less beautifully turned out in green. Lord, they were
pretty! He was so proud of them! "And Dorothea, my
sweet." Dorothea, whose dignity was apparently not as
high as her younger sister's, gave him a warm hug.

"You smell just the same," she said with a sigh. "Tobacco
and bay rum."

"But has something happened to send you from London in such haste?" he asked, looking from one to the
other.

"Can your daughters not pay you a long overdue visit
unless it is a catastrophe of some sort?" Dorothea asked
playfully.

"We missed you," Marguerite said.

"And I have missed you," he said, pleased. He sobered.
"Did you receive my letter? We lost your mother's Aunt
Sophie some weeks ago."

"I know," Dorothea said as she pressed his hand. "I am

so sorry. We were much attached to her." She glanced at his erstwhile housekeeper. "As were you, Miss Grant. You have my sympathy."

"Thank you," Miss Grant said, and Michael saw wariness reflected on her face. "Do permit me to show you to your rooms."

"That is right," Marguerite said. How such a short woman managed to look down her nose at the considerably taller Miss Grant amazed Michael. It must be something that came with the title of viscountess. "You are a sort of housekeeper here, are you not? I had a letter of one of my friends."

Ah, thought Michael. That *is what they are doing here.* They wanted to save him from being caught in Miss Grant's womanly coils. She hardly had designs on *him,* he could assure them. She merely wished to take over his house and make his life miserable.

"It is a pity you did not come sooner," Miss Grant said coolly. "My cousin would have enjoyed a visit from you. She spoke of you often, and with great fondness."

Dorothea had the grace to look ashamed, but Marguerite faced her critic boldly.

"My social obligations as Lord Redgrave's wife are extensive," she said. Miss Grant, being a stranger, would not recognize her anger as stemming from guilt, but Michael recognized it at once. "I cannot go bounding off into the country for every little thing. But I would not expect you to understand."

"Every little thing," Miss Grant repeated softly. "No. I am afraid I do not."

"At any rate," said Dorothea, "it has been a long journey, and I would be glad to be shown to my room. If you would be so kind, Miss Grant."

"Certainly," Miss Grant said with an inclination of her head. "If you will follow me, ladies."

Michael let out all his breath at once when the women

were gone from the room and exchanged a look of commiseration with Timms.

"Now the fat is in the fire, Sir Michael," the butler said glumly.

"We are in for some rare entertainment now," Michael said. He lifted the brandy decanter suggestively. "Will you join me?"

"Sir Michael?" Timms said, practically goggling at him. "It wouldn't be fitting." His look at the decanter was longing, however.

"I know it is irregular," Michael said, taking Timms's feeble objection for assent. In all his years of service, master and butler had never shared a drink, but these were extraordinary circumstances. The three of them under his roof at once. It made a grown man want to quiver. He handed Timms a glass and hoisted his own.

"To the ladies," Michael intoned. Timms gave him a rueful smile and lifted his glass. "Perhaps they can succeed in rousting Miss Grant where we could not. If I were a gamester, I confess I would not know where to lay odds."

CHAPTER 8

It was not yet dawn when Dorothea was rudely awakened from a sound sleep. She put her hands over her ears to keep out the infernal clattering of those giggling peahens from the village whom her father's unwanted housekeeper was putting through their paces in the hall.

Gritting her teeth, she put on her dressing gown and stalked into the hall in her bare feet.

"Miss Grant!" she cried.

The plainly dressed blond woman emerged from one of the other rooms and raised an inquisitive eyebrow.

"Mrs. Walbridge," she said pleasantly enough, although her blue eyes were wary. "In what way may I serve you?"

"You may stop making all this racket at once," she said. "I told you yesterday that decent people do *not* awaken their guests with their incessant cleaning."

"I beg your pardon, Mrs. Walbridge," she said. "I thought starting at dawn was preferable to stopping at eight o'clock at night. We have to make up for at least ten years of your father's benign neglect. I understand that was when his last housekeeper died, and he never replaced her."

"For good reason," Dorothea said pointedly. "Can you not clean somewhere else until a civilized hour?"

"Certainly," Miss Grant said with a sigh, for all the world as if it were Dorothea who was being unreasonable. "Come," she added to the village girls, who already were looking exhausted. Miss Grant, it was obvious, was a harsh taskmistress. She led her small feminine army away.

Dorothea gave a small, smug smile of triumph and started back for her bedchamber. Then the pounding began overhead.

"What on earth is *that*?" cried Marguerite, also dressed in her dressing gown, as she came from her room. "It sounds as if there were elephants above us."

"It has something to do with Miss Grant, if I am not mistaken," Dorothea said sourly. "We have *got* to be rid of that woman!"

"My sentiments exactly," Marguerite said with a sigh. She looked around. "I must say the house looks better, though."

"Marguerite!" Dorothea said as she put her hands on her hips.

"It *does*! Papa was letting it all go dreadfully downhill." Dorothea gave a long sigh.

"I suppose it is my fault. As the eldest I should have made sure Papa's house was taken care of."

"What utter nonsense," said Sir Michael as he came down the hall dressed in the rough clothes he wore when he intended to spend the day with his horses. He gave Dorothea a kiss on the cheek. "I had no intention of letting either of my daughters stay behind to manage my household. It would have been a dreadful waste of a great deal of expensively acquired beauty and charm." He rolled his eyes upward, where Miss Grant and her minions must have been engaged in jumping up and down on the floor and throwing furniture against the walls from the sounds of it. "Alas, it seems I am to be managed, after all."

"Forgive us, Father," Marguerite said. He quirked an interrogatory eyebrow at her. "When we heard that you had retained Miss Grant as your housekeeper, we thought . . . Well, the letter from Mrs. Pritchett was—"

"Ah, Mrs. Pritchett," he said knowingly. "Now I know

why I am suspected of lascivious designs on Miss Grant. Mrs. Pritchett is the busiest gossip in Dumfries. And she has the filthiest mind. Believe me, my dears, I have no great liking for Miss Grant. A female who is determined to drive me mad is not my idea of a comfortable mistress."

"Can you not give her a sum of money and send her on her way?" Marguerite asked.

"Mrs. Tilden left her to me in her will." He smiled thinly at his daughters' expressions of disbelief. "I tried to pay her off, but she refused to go. Your aunt charged her with the responsibility of preparing the house for my taking of a wife. Mrs. Tilden worried that I would grow old all alone. Now Miss Grant feels that she must take me in hand or be hounded by Mrs. Tilden's wraith for all eternity."

Dorothea felt ashamed.

"We have neglected you," she said. "This is all our fault."

"You have been establishing your own homes," he said, putting his hand under her chin and lifting it so he could look into her eyes. "That is what a young woman should be doing instead of plaguing a perfectly contented man with her fussing and nagging. I wish an eligible suitor would come forward and claim *her*."

"Highly unlikely," Dorothea sniffed. "How is she to meet anyone? She has been living with our aunt for two years, and now she is determined to spend her time keeping house for you. You never entertain, and the Dumfries hostesses have long given up on inviting you to their parties because you never attend them."

"Waste of time," Sir Michael muttered as he proceeded down the hall. "If you will excuse me, I must go to the stables. I am long overdue."

"It is *your* house and *your* stables," Marguerite said as she placed herself in his path. "You may be late if you wish."

Sir Michael put his hands on her shoulders and kissed her on the cheek.

"That's my imperious little viscountess," he said fondly. "While I am gone, try to think of a way to rid the place of my overzealous housekeeper. I shall be forever grateful."

"And after she's gone, you will fall back into your slovenly male habits, I suppose," Dorothea said archly.

"Of course," he said with a jaunty wave as he went on his way.

Marguerite narrowed her eyes at Dorothea, who looked rather as if she had snabbled up the last lobster patty at a dinner party when no one else was looking.

"I know that look," Marguerite said. "You have an idea."

"A brilliant idea. We must persuade Papa to have a hunt party."

"He will never do it," Marguerite said. "He hates having guests."

"He will agree when I explain to him that it is the only way to get Miss Grant married and off his hands. We are going to invite all the eligible men in the neighborhood. Surely one of them will be attracted to her."

"The housekeeper?" Marguerite's expression suggested that Dorothea had taken leave of her senses. "Why should they?"

"Because we are going to dress her decently and pass her off as a family connection at this party. Papa will give her a dowry, and there is an end to the problem."

"Miss Grant will not agree," Marguerite said with a sigh. "Pity. A party would be lovely. We shall go mad here without *some* entertainment."

"She will agree readily enough when we explain to her that the purpose of the party is to introduce Papa to prospective wives."

Marguerite laughed out loud and gave her sister a hug.

"What a clever woman you are! So, we shall tell Papa we are having this party to find a husband for Miss Grant, and we shall tell Miss Grant the purpose of the party is to find a wife for Papa. I am proud to call you my sister."

"Thank you," Dorothea said, accepting this tribute as her due. "Now, let us ring for our maids and have them fetch our morning chocolate so that we may put our scheme into motion."

"A ball!" exclaimed Sir Michael when his daughters outlined their outrageous plan for ridding his house of Miss Grant.

"Not just a ball, Father," said Dorothea as she perched upon the arm of his leather chair the way she used to do when she was an engaging child of six. "A hunt party. You must invite all the men in the neighborhood. And the ladies, too, of course. We must not make our intentions *too* conspicuous."

"Subtlety, thy name is Dorothea," Sir Michael said dryly. "This seems a great deal of bother."

"How badly do you want to be rid of her?" Marguerite asked.

"Very badly, indeed," he said. "All right. You may have your party."

"Excellent! How long has it been since you rode to the hounds, Father?"

"A silly occupation for grown men," Sir Michael said. "I would not waste my time."

"Do not worry about a thing, Papa," Dorothea said. "Marguerite and I will arrange everything. We will not require your assistance at all except as an escort for the two of us and Miss Grant when we go to Edinburgh for our shopping expedition."

"Edinburgh! Are you mad? In the middle of the harvest? What on earth for?"

"For gowns, fans, dancing slippers, and kid gloves, of course," Marguerite said, laughing. "You can hardly expect Miss Grant to attract any kind of suitor in her present condition."

"Her present condition? What do you mean?"

"Her clothes, Father," Marguerite said. "Have you noticed her clothes?"

"I have not noticed much about her at all," he said. "You know I know nothing of feminine fashion. I leave that sort of thing to you."

"Then believe us when we say that Miss Grant will not do."

"Perhaps a new ball gown, then——" he conceded.

"At least two morning gowns, a traveling costume for that happy day when we see the back of her, and a ball gown in addition to an evening gown for dinner parties," Dorothea said firmly. "Does she ride?"

"I have not the least idea," Sir Michael said. "Nor do I care."

"If she does, she will require a riding habit."

"Very well," Sir Michael said, "but why must you go all the way to Edinburgh to procure these things when there are perfectly competent dressmakers in Dumfries? You are hardly purchasing a trousseau for a royal princess."

"Hardly, but we will require new gowns as well, and *we* can hardly appear at our own ball in the handiwork of a country seamstress," Marguerite said loftily. "I have my husband's dignity to uphold. He is a member of the House of Lords, you know. The least little thing can do him untold political damage."

"And you, Father, do not own a set of evening clothes that is not a disgrace," Dorothea said.

"How do you know?"

"I know *you*," Dorothea said archly. "Come, Father.

Will it not be worth a few moments being prodded about by a tailor to rid yourself of Miss Grant's tyranny?"

"Lord, yes," he said vehemently. "She is always nagging me for new hangings for the drawing-room windows and new linens. She is as bad as a wife. Now she is determined to choose new livery for poor Timms."

"Well, it is about time," Marguerite said. "Only I should think it is the place of your daughters and not your housekeeper to choose livery for your staff."

Dorothea's brow wrinkled prettily.

"Speaking of upper servants, Father, did you not have a valet the last time we were here?"

"He left my service to accept a more advantageous post," Sir Michael said. "I saw no reason to replace him. I never pay calls or receive them if I can help it. Except for the duke's stablemaster who came one day to look at a horse on the duke's behalf, no one except Miss Grant and the two of you has come near the place for months, and that is the way I like it."

"The duke is in residence at Drumlanrig Castle?" Marguerite said quickly. Michael could all but see her dainty ears prick like those of a pretty fox. "Of all the wonderful luck!"

"We must call upon the duke without delay," Marguerite said. "It would not do to be backward in any attention."

"You can hardly march up to the gates of Drumlanrig Castle and ask to see the duke," Sir Michael said in dismay. "And if you think I am going to leave my work to go with you, you are greatly mistaken."

"No, but Lady Constance may well be there," Marguerite said, preening a little. "It would hardly be inappropriate for us to call on her."

"Lady Constance?" Sir Michael said. "I do not believe I remember the lady."

"Of course you do. She is the duke's wife's niece, who

often acts as hostess for him now," Marguerite said coyly. "And she certainly remembers you."

"Ah. She who married Lord Buxton, who is deceased these three years," said Sir Michael as his mind's eye provided him with the image of a good-looking woman with aristocratic features and auburn hair.

"Lord Buxton was quite fond of Henry, and he took him up as his protégé when they were both in the House of Lords, I understand. Lady Constance always invites Dorothea and me to her parties in London," Marguerite said. "How could we neglect her now when she is staying practically in the neighborhood? It would be so rag-mannered."

Dorothea got that just-snatched-the-lobster-patty look on her face again, and Marguerite raised her eyebrows at her.

"We must, of course, invite the duke and his guests to our party," Dorothea said slowly.

"Invite anyone you please," Sir Michael said with a sigh. "I am very busy tomorrow, but I am at your disposal to go to Edinburgh the day after. Will that suit you?"

"Excellently well," Dorothea said as she kissed his cheek. "Thank you, Father." She gracefully slid off the arm of her father's chair and walked across the room to take Marguerite's arm. "Come, Marguerite. We must prepare for the trip to Edinburgh."

"What is it?" Marguerite said as soon as they were out of their father's hearing.

"Lady Constance," Dorothea said with a smug smile. "She would be *perfect* for Father."

"What a charming idea!" Marguerite said. "She is beautiful, rich, and she flirted with Father in the most ladylike way when he was in London for our weddings, for all that he did not seem to remember her at first."

"I must say things are coming along quite nicely," Dorothea said with a great deal of self-congratulation in her voice. "If all goes well, we will have Papa married off to a lady whose marriage will cause us to become the connections of the Duke of Buccleuch." The smile hardened on her face. "And when that happens, Miss Grant will have no excuse to stay here."

CHAPTER 9

Dorothea and Marguerite cornered their quarry in the kitchen, where Miss Grant and Mrs. Muir were having a cup of tea. The village girls had left and preparations for dinner had not yet begun, and so the house was blessedly quiet.

"Lady Redgrave, Mrs. Walbridge," Miss Grant said as both she and the cook rose to their feet. "Is there something you require?"

"Not at all, not at all," Dorothea said pleasantly. "My sister and I simply would like a word with you."

"Of course," Miss Grant said in perfectly civil tones, although her eyes narrowed in suspicion. "If you will excuse me, Mrs. Muir. I will be back directly to discuss the menus with you."

The cook nodded in assent, but when Dorothea would have ushered Miss Grant from the room, Marguerite turned back.

"Since we are in residence, it would be more appropriate for you to apply to Dorothea or myself for approval of the menus, Mrs. Muir," Marguerite said.

"I meant no offense, Miss Marguerite. Or, my lady, I should say," Mrs. Muir stammered. "It takes a body some getting used to. I keep forgetting you are a lady grown. And you, too, Mrs. Walbridge."

Marguerite gave the cook an affectionate pat on the shoulder.

"Come now, Mrs. Muir. You can call me Miss Marguerite, if you wish."

"It doesna seem long ago that I was chasing you and Miss Dorothea out of the kitchen for snatching the pies I had just made for dinner," the cook said with a sigh.

"Turn your back on your pies today," Dorothea said, "and we would do so again." When Marguerite gave a sniff, Dorothea teased, "Yes, even you, my Lady Redgrave, for all the airs and graces you give yourself."

"I am very partial to a fresh-baked pie," Marguerite admitted with a small smile.

"I shall bake an apple pie just for you, sweeting," Mrs. Muir said warmly.

"I shall look forward to it," Marguerite said. She gave Mrs. Muir a coy smile. "And if you would just give Dorothea and me a peek at the menus each day—there is no reason to trouble Miss Grant with such things."

"As you please, Miss Marguerite," the cook said.

"Come along, Miss Grant," Dorothea said as she took the housekeeper's arm.

"In what way may I serve you?" the woman said stiffly when the three of them were in the parlor and Marguerite had closed the door.

Dorothea showed all her teeth in a smile meant to be reassuring, but Miss Grant looked defensive, just the same.

"My father intends to have a hunt party and ball in three weeks' time," Dorothea said, "and my sister and I hope to enlist your assistance in making the arrangements."

"A party?" Miss Grant said skeptically. "Sir Michael? How ever did you talk him into such a thing? And why?"

Marguerite gave her a smug smile.

"We are his only daughters, and he probably feels that after we have come so far to pay him a visit, he owes us some entertainment."

'It is important for the family to keep up appearances in the neighborhood, of course," Dorothea said smoothly.

"Important to *whom?* You will never tell me that Sir Michael gives a rap about his social standing in the neighborhood," Miss Grant said. "I have lived with Mrs. Tilden for two years, and during that time Sir Michael was a frequent visitor. To my knowledge he has never shown the least interest in entertaining his neighbors."

"Miss Grant," Dorothea said, giving her a straight look. "Do you or do you not wish to discharge your obligation to Mrs. Tilden and my father?"

"I do, of course," Miss Grant said. "Unfortunately, your father is the most stubborn, obstinate—"

"That will do," Dorothea said. "Did it not occur to you that the only way that you will be able to leave this house is if either Marguerite or I move back into it—which I assure you we have no intention of doing—or Father remarries?"

"We mean to invite every respectable lady of Papa's age in the neighborhood to this party," Marguerite said.

"Do you expect me to believe," Miss Grant asked, "that you told your father that he should have a party to invite every husband-hunting woman in the neighborhood to his home so he can take his pick of them, and he *agreed?*"

"No," Dorothea said coolly. "We told him the purpose of the party was to find a husband for you."

"A husband for—I do not want a husband!"

"Why not?" Marguerite asked. "They can be quite charming when they choose."

"Do calm yourself, Miss Grant. You will not be expected to take a husband if you do not want one," Dorothea said. "We merely told Papa the purpose is to find a husband for you so that he would agree to have the party."

"And why should I agree to this ridiculous scheme?" Miss Grant asked.

"Because you want to be free, do you not?" Dorothea

asked. "Free to go to the seaside and rent a little cottage of your own?"

"That would be heaven," Miss Grant said with a sigh. "But I must seek employment."

"Not if Papa marries," Marguerite said. "If he does, you will be free of your obligation to him. He would not send you out into the world without a penny to your name, and you know his new wife will not want a young housekeeper in her new home. Papa is extremely grateful to you for your care of Aunt Sophie. Upon his marriage, he will give you a handsome sum to establish yourself to discharge that obligation, I promise you."

"And you will have earned it," Dorothea cut in when Miss Grant opened her mouth to make an objection. "For this is to be quite an elaborate party."

"We are going to invite everyone who is anyone," Marguerite said, "including the Duke of Buccleuch. He is in residence at Drumlanrig Castle. And I suspect Lady Constance, one of his late wife's relatives who would be a perfect wife for Father, is in residence at Drumlanrig Castle as well."

"So, if you truly want to be rid of this obligation to our father," Dorothea added, "you will do all you can to support Father's belief that this party is being created to find you a husband."

"I detest being the sort of scheming female who thinks of nothing but trapping some vulnerable male into marriage," Miss Grant said.

"But you will not be," Dorothea pointed out, "for all you have to say is no, after all. Once Papa is married, all you have to do is be gracious as you collect the sum Papa is sure to settle upon you. And you will be free. Is that not what you want?"

Miss Grant looked as if she was about to protest, but thought better of it.

"Of course," she said. "It is what I have always wanted."

"There, then," Dorothea said comfortably. "All you have to do is put yourself in our hands."

"Yes, do not worry about a thing," Marguerite said. Her eyes were gleaming. "The first item of business is to take you shopping. In Edinburgh."

"Hardly necessary," Miss Grant scoffed. "The clothes I have are quite adequate for a woman who has no intention of attracting a husband."

"But Papa's are not for a man who has any intention of attracting a wife," Marguerite said with a sly smirk. "Unless we somehow contrive to get him to Edinburgh and into the hands of a good tailor, he will appear in the ballroom in one of his disgusting old coats from twenty years ago."

"Very well, then," Miss Grant said with a sigh. "When do you wish to go on this shopping expedition?"

"The day after tomorrow," Dorothea said at once. "There is not a moment to be lost. My dear Miss Grant, I hesitate to wound your vanity, but your hair is in desperate need of some attention. Was it Mrs. Tilden's maid who had the cutting of it?"

"I cut it myself," Miss Grant said defensively. She appeared to be grinding her teeth. "I have not been in a position of late to become skilled in the current mode of hairdressing."

"Poor, poor Miss Grant," Marguerite said. Miss Grant looked at her rather sharply, apparently in the belief that she was being sarcastic, but Dorothea could tell Marguerite spoke from pure sympathy from all the innate goodness in her heart. She put a friendly arm around Miss Grant, who tried very hard, Dorothea could tell, not to flinch. "Do not worry. Dorothea and I know *everything*."

"Two hundred pounds! You cannot be serious," Michael blustered as he gave his daughters his most intimidating stare. It was wasted entirely, however, because the minxes had been wrapping him around their little fingers since they were in leading strings. "The woman is not going to London to be presented to the *ton*."

"And it is a good thing for your purse," Marguerite said, "for that would cost you a great deal more."

"True," he said with a sigh. "I could have built a barn or two and added a herd of breeding stock to my stable with what I spent launching the two of you into Society. I do not believe Lord Wellington spent as much to equip his army for the battle with Napoleon."

Marguerite gave a pretty little laugh and sat on the arm of his chair to put her slender arm around his shoulders. She smelled of rosewater.

"You know you do not grudge a penny of it," she said.

"No, my little viscountess. I do not," he admitted. "But Lord Redgrave would have wanted to marry you if he had first seen you wearing rags, or he's a gudgeon who doesn't know a diamond of the first water when he sees one."

"True," Marguerite said smugly. "But happily, it was not necessary. Miss Grant, now, she is going to require a great deal of work if we are to get her out of the house. And when we have brought some unfortunate gentleman to the sticking point and she balks at breaking her precious promise to Aunt Sophie to mollycoddle you into madness, you will confide to her that you intend to offer for some eligible lady and there is no reason why she cannot seize her happiness. And then you may be comfortable again."

Michael had to laugh at the look of eagerness on her face. Marguerite was never more absurd or appealing than when she was trying to be clever. Still, his daughters' plan to rid his house of Miss Grant was just outlandish enough to work. At the worst, this precious plot would provide enough entertainment for his worldly daughters to keep them with him a bit longer. Lord, how he had missed them when they went off to London to seek husbands without a backward look.

"It might be worth the expense, at that," he said.

"There is not a moment to be lost," Dorothea insisted grimly. "The woman is a disgrace. Her hair is so dowdy I am filled with shame at the thought of anyone connecting her with our household. And her hands! They need attention at once. We shall have my maid and Marguerite's take her in hand tonight, for it will take the combined labors of both of them to make her presentable enough to be seen in the shops of Edinburgh, let alone in good society."

"Good heavens," Michael said, taken aback. "I do not think her appearance is as bad as all that."

"How can you say so?" Marguerite exclaimed in disbelief. Dorothea looked just as startled.

"Well, it seems to me that she is of somewhat pleasing looks," Michael said cautiously. "Certainly I have seen women more ill favored than she, and *they* manage to find husbands."

"And we shall find one for her," Dorothea said comfortingly. "You may leave everything to us, Father."

CHAPTER 10

Catriona stared in astonishment at the line of carriages readied for the trip to Edinburgh.

"Are we staying a month?" she asked wonderingly.

"It is plain that you have never traveled with Dorothea and Marguerite," Sir Michael said as he looked up from where he had been whispering soothing words into the ear of a large brown horse. "I suspect the entourage they require for their comfort on even the most simple journey is more extensive than that of the queen and all her daughters. It makes me think their mother was of royal blood, as her family legend suggests. They are wonderfully spoiled, my daughters."

Catriona's mouth dropped open, and she ran forward. Sir Michael's eyes widened in surprise, but he relaxed when he realized she only wanted to pet the horse's head. For a moment she looked as if she were going to pet *him*, or worse. It confused him when he identified the emotion that assailed him when he realized her true intention.

Incredibly, it was disappointment.

"Oh, what a beautiful animal," she cried. "So big. So muscular." She ran her hand across the sleek flanks. She licked her lips. "So powerful."

"You know your horseflesh, Miss Grant," he said in pleased surprise.

"This is not one of those dainty, mincing creatures

who would blow away in a good wind," she said. "Is he one of yours? I do not believe I have ever seen his like."

"He is a Hanoverian," Sir Michael said proudly as he ran a practiced hand over the horse's coat as well. When he did so, his hand brushed Catriona's. Both drew back immediately at the contact of human flesh on human flesh. Sir Michael cleared his throat. "It is a relatively new breed, established by King George II at Celle. My horses were much in demand as cavalry remounts in the late war."

"With good reason," Catriona said as she looked into the horse's mild yet intelligent brown eyes. "I will wager you are well up to the weight of a mountain of a man, are you not, my beauty?" She pursed her lips, almost to kiss the horse, he was so wonderful. "*You* will not flag and wilt because of a little hard work."

"Am I correct in assuming you ride, Miss Grant? If so, I would gladly mount you—"

At that moment, young Lady Redgrave came to a halt in her approach to the carriage and gave a gasp of utter horror. Catriona felt her face grow hot as she realized what Sir Michael had been saying as his daughter came within hearing of their conversation.

"Get away from him this instant!" Lady Redgrave shrieked. She stepped forward and grabbed Catriona's arm. "Dorothea, she was petting Father's horse," she called to her sister. "We cannot go to the shops in Edinburgh with her reeking to high heaven of horse."

Catriona let out all her breath at once. Sir Michael gave her a rueful look full of humor. The viscountess had been so horrified by her familiarity with the horse, not her precious father.

Mrs. Walbridge, however, had narrowed her eyes to slits as she looked from Catriona to her father.

"We cannot have that," she said with a hard look at Catriona. Between the two of them, the sisters hastened Catriona away to one of the carriages. "You will ride with us, of course, so we may brief you according to your role."

"My role?" Catriona asked. Involuntarily, she looked to Sir Michael for enlightenment, but he only shrugged.

"Yes, we have decided that we will represent you as our cousin by marriage, which is true in a way, although no one needs to know the precise degree of relationship is as remote as it is," Mrs. Walbridge said. "We can hardly announce to the world that we are having a party for the purpose of marrying our father's housekeeper off." She gave a slight grimace of distaste. "You may as well begin to address us by our Christian names at once so we may all become accustomed to it."

"I had thought I was to ride in the second carriage with your maids," Catriona said, surprised. "You cannot want my company on such a long journey, Mrs. Walbridge."

"On the contrary, my dear *Catriona*, there is much we want to learn about you," Dorothea said mildly, though her eyes were hard. "And you are to call me Dorothea, mind. It behooves my sister and me to keep you under our eye at all times. Otherwise, how are you to go on?" She patted Catriona's hand.

"But will you not be dreadfully crowded?" Catriona said.

"Not at all," Dorothea said graciously. "Papa always rides, no matter what the weather. I suspect it is because he knows perfectly well that he appears to great advantage on horseback, for all that he affects to be dead to vanity."

"Now you have caught me out," Sir Michael said gaily as he mounted the powerful horse. He gave the ladies a jaunty sweep of his hat. Mrs. Muir came out from the house with a basket of dainties for the delectation of the master's daughters. Catriona knew very well it would be a grave impertinence for her to venture to take a crumb, for all that she was now on a Christian-name basis with dear Dorothea and Marguerite.

"I have made a plum cake, for I know it is your favorite, my lamb," the cook said to Marguerite. She gave a startled look of apology. "Or, my lady, I *should* say."

"One of your wonderful plum cakes!" Marguerite exclaimed as she placed a kiss on the old woman's cheek. "How kind! 'My lamb' will do perfectly well, my dear Mrs. Muir."

It was at moments like this that Catriona suspected that Sir Michael's snobbish daughters had hearts after all. Their affection for the old servant did them great credit.

As soon as the door was closed, Dorothea let out a long sigh of relief, as if she had been newly released from prison. Before Catriona knew what she was about, she took her hand.

"Much better," she said skeptically as she examined Catriona's fingernails. "And did you use the Denmark lotion, as I suggested?"

"I did," Catriona said. "Although why I must—"

"Tut, tut, Catriona," Marguerite said wisely. "You consider yourself the supreme authority when it comes to the ordering of our father's house, but in matters of female adornment, our word is *law*."

That evening, although Sir Michael had been eager to press on and get the irritating necessity of procuring new clothing for himself and his female companions over with the sooner, his daughters insisted that ladies of their position could hardly arrive in Edinburgh half asleep and all dusty with travel after having spent a hideous night cramped in their carriage when a tolerable inn was available for their comfort.

"I suppose it will do," Dorothea said as she looked about the lobby of the hotel with her nose in the air. "Father, you must procure a private dining room, of course.

You can hardly expect us to dine in the taproom with the other inhabitants of the inn."

"Certainly not," Michael said, lips twitching, as he went off to make the arrangements.

"And do order the dinner yourself, Father," Marguerite added. "Otherwise, we shall find ourselves faced with greasy sandwiches and cabbage or something equally vile."

"Yes, Cousin Michael," Catriona added. "And do not forget to order a sweet. Strawberries and cream would do nicely, followed by pâté de foie gras and lobster patties."

Michael gave a hastily smothered snort of surprised laughter as Catriona turned an expression on him that was Marguerite to the life at her most languid.

"No, Cousin Catriona," Marguerite said kindly. "The pâté and lobster patties go *before* the sweet. And I doubt if either will be available in such a place. Still, Father, you could ask."

"I will do so," Michael said as he gave Catriona a look of reproof. "We will dine at seven o'clock, if that meets with your approval."

Dorothea gave an anxious look at the handsome mantel clock.

"I suppose we can be ready if we hurry. Where have our maids got to?"

"They are directing the men in the disposal of your luggage," Catriona said.

"Catriona, do be a dear and see if you can keep them from dawdling," Dorothea said. "That leaves us only an hour to freshen up and dress for dinner. It is a mere country inn, but one never knows what distinguished persons may be among one's fellow travelers, and so it will not do to relax one's standards."

"Certainly," Catriona said with a wry look at Michael as she went to do his daughter's bidding.

"And perhaps some champagne," Marguerite added

to her father. "It need not be of the most expensive vintage, but I would dearly love a bit of reviving sparkle after spending all day in the coach. I think we deserve a bit of indulgence after the pace you set on the road."

"I shall do my poor best, my little viscountess," he said affectionately.

Catriona was surprised to find herself alone with Sir Michael when she arrived in the private parlor for dinner, even though it was some five minutes past the appointed hour.

"Good evening, Cousin Catriona," Sir Michael said as he rose from his place on the sofa.

"Good evening, Sir Michael. I would apologize for being late, but it seems Mrs. Walbridge and Lady Redgrave are late as well."

"I hope you are not too hungry," he said, smiling. "I confess to practicing a bit of subterfuge. I actually reserved the room for seven o'clock, but ordered dinner for half past seven, for if I had told my daughters half past seven, they would not have arrived until eight o'clock, and they cut up stiff if one presumes to begin without them."

"Did you manage to bespeak the pâté de foie gras?" she asked.

"There was none available, alas."

"Pity. I suppose there will be no lobster patties, either."

"Sadly, no. But there will be strawberries and cream. And champagne, although not of the very best vintage."

"If I may ask, how did daughters of yours become so spoilt, Sir Michael? I cannot believe they dined on pâté de foie gras and champagne or kept you waiting hours for your dinner as they primped and fussed with their clothing when they lived with you."

"You must blame their husbands in some small part," he said, "although I will admit I indulged them rather more than was probably good for them. They are the very image of their mother, with all her daintiness and delight in fashionable life. I feared when they were young they might have inherited her delicate health as well, but, thankfully, they are as strong as they are beautiful, much as they try to hide it behind a carefully cultivated languor."

"They are very beautiful," Catriona said, "and accustomed, it is plain, to getting their own way. I thank heaven that it is my duty to manage *you* rather than them, for that is by far the easier task."

"I am afraid that it is you who will be managed, Catriona, if I know my daughters," Sir Michael said.

"We shall see about that," Catriona murmured.

"Ah, here is the champagne," Sir Michael said as a waiter appeared with the wine at the doorway. "Leave it. I shall open it myself. You may serve dinner when the rest of my party arrives." The waiter surrendered the bottle and retreated. "I would offer you a glass of champagne, but Dorothea and Marguerite will be dreadfully put out if the wine is flat by the time they arrive."

"It does not matter," Catriona said, "although I do admit to being a bit peckish. Perhaps when your daughters have brought me up to snuff, I will be more willing to starve for the sake of my clothing."

"I must say you are being very good-natured about this," he said suspiciously.

"Well, I am getting rather long in the tooth. If I am going to marry, it had better be soon, as Mrs. Walbridge has repeatedly warned me, although, to do her justice, she has expressed the matter with a great deal more delicacy than I have."

"She would," Michael said proudly. "Lord, they are a pair of charmers, are they not?"

"Charmers," Catriona said wryly. "Precisely the term I would have chosen."

He laughed.

"It will not be so bad as that. You should be pleased that all of your rather excessive cleaning will not go to waste. At least the neighbors will be impressed by it, while it is quite lost on me. And after the girls have their little party, they will go off after they have done their best to marry you off and thus provide for your future."

"You know as well as I that I will not marry as long as your future is not settled."

"Can it be they have not told you that they intend to marry me off to a suitable lady, one who will not only increase my consequence in Society, but theirs?"

"The most excellent Lady Constance," Catriona said. "Rich in her own right and connected most advantageously by marriage to the Duke of Buccleuch. I have had the lady's pedigree explained to me in excruciatingly thorough detail. What does surprise me is that they have told you."

"They have told me that the purpose of the party is to find a husband for you, but I know my daughters. Do not be deceived by their youth and high spirits. Inside these pleasing forms beat the hearts of the oldest, most manipulative busybodies in the kingdom, convinced that they can ensure the happiness of everyone they love if they can somehow trick them into dancing to the tune of their piping."

"I hardly think they want to ensure *my* happiness."

"They are, however, quite determined to ensure *mine*, and finding a suitable husband for you is not inconsistent with this. Their plans are always perfectly benevolent. Otherwise, they would throw you off the cliff into Solway Firth and make an end of it."

"I am to be grateful for their machinations, in fact," Catriona said, amused in spite of herself. "Well, I cannot say I am not. I have not been outside Cousin Sophie's house in Dumfries for anything except to accompany her to card parties and church services for two years. And I have not had fine new clothes since before that.

How fortunate it is that you are willing to stand the reckoning in order to indulge your daughters. I gather you are doing this for them rather than for me."

"Correct. But I can well afford to purchase a gown or two for you and throw a party for the neighbors. Once you are married and off my hands, and regardless of whether my ring is on Lady Constance's finger, my darling girls will return to their adoring husbands happy women. I have learned from long experience that it is impossible to break my little fillies to bridle through sheer force. One must let them have their heads for a bit first."

"You," Catriona said, "are a very strange man."

Sir Michael grinned.

"Never doubt it, Catriona," he said. "The easiest way to brush through the business is to let them think they are getting their way. Then, when they are congratulating themselves that they have pulled the wool over our eyes, they will go quite tamely into harness." His smile grew as the door to the dining room opened to admit two visions of loveliness in violet and yellow brocade, respectively.

"How lovely you look," Sir Michael said as he walked to his daughters and kissed their hands in turn, which made them giggle and flutter their eyelashes at him. "Well worth waiting for."

"Are we dreadfully late?" Marguerite asked without a trace of apology.

"Not at all, my little viscountess," he said. He looked up at the waiter, who was standing in the open doorway. "Ah, there you are. You may serve the first course, if you please." The man bowed and withdrew. "So, my dears. Let us have some champagne and toast the future success of our enterprise."

"We were afraid that if we were too late, we would not get any," Dorothea said with a light laugh.

"Nonsense. Your tardiness has given Cousin Catriona and me the opportunity to have a little chat." He smiled at Catriona with such charm and goodwill that she blinked in surprise. He handed her a glass of champagne and her hand tingled where their fingers met. "I believe now we understand each other," he added in a tone that was almost . . . intimate.

"Yes, I believe so," she said. To steady herself, she took a big gulp of champagne and choked on it. Sir Michael pounded her briskly on the back. "Go slowly, my girl. You are not accustomed to spirits. Are you all right now?"

"Perfectly," Catriona said as she took another sip. "This is good."

"Tolerable, merely," Marguerite said with a superior air.

"But quite drinkable," Dorothea added kindly. "You did well, Father."

"You relieve my mind," Sir Michael said. "Ah, here are the oysters. There was no pâté to be had, I am afraid."

"Oysters?" Catriona said with a sidelong glance at him.

"You are thinking of their hypothetical properties to stimulate seduction. All nonsense, of course. Do try some." He laughed. "Come, come, Catriona. Do not be a coward."

At that, Catriona gave him a look of defiance and opened her mouth to accept the half shell that he held in his hand. He placed it to her lips and tipped the half-jellied, half-liquid contents down her throat.

"All at once, now, there's a good girl," he said softly.

"Do not tease her, Papa," Dorothea said in shrill disapproval. "You know very well that most persons are repelled by the taste the first time."

What a bumpkin they thought her.

Catriona savored the rich taste of the oyster meat for a moment in her mouth before she slowly chewed and swallowed it, all the while gazing into Sir Michael's eyes.

"Sublime," she said softly as she smiled at him. She lowered her voice intimately. "There is something so very . . . voluptuous about the flavor and texture of oysters, is there not?"

She enjoyed the look of surprise and consternation on

his face as he drew quickly away. Good. That would teach him to play games with her. He was flirting with her to give his daughters something to think about, of course.

What surprised Catriona was how very good at flirting he appeared to be. Perhaps he had not lived like a cloistered monk at Dumfries all these years after his wife's death, as everyone thought.

"I am still perfectly willing to mount you, if you wish, Cousin Catriona," he said.

Dorothea and Marguerite choked on their champagne. Sir Michael, who Catriona was beginning to think was quite a rogue, bent an innocent look on them and rose to stand behind them so he could pat them both on the back. Catriona noticed that his touch was considerably lighter than it had been when he pounded on *her* back.

"That is very kind," Catriona said sternly as he turned an unrepentant look on her. "But do not trouble yourself. I will not have much leisure for riding horses with all the party preparations."

"Nonsense. Dorothea and Marguerite intended to purchase a riding habit for you. You may as well get some use from it. I have some very gentle horses in my stables."

"I do not require a gentle ride," Catriona snapped from sheer pride before she realized what she had said. Heavens. She was as bad as *him.*

"I thought not," he said, grinning.

Dorothea and Marguerite exchanged another look.

"I hope you have something of more substance than this to set before us, Father," Dorothea said a bit too loudly.

"I do beg your pardon, love. I am quite remiss in my duties as host." He walked to the door and spoke to the waiter. "We are ready for the soup."

CHAPTER 11

"Just *what* did you think you were doing?" Catriona demanded when she and Sir Michael met over the teacups the next day in the taproom. Of course, it would have been vastly improper for her to go there alone, but when she received his note very early in the morning to meet him there in order to break her fast, curiosity and a high sense of injury would not allow her to refuse.

She was accustomed to beginning her day with a hearty breakfast, and she assumed taking her morning meal under the escort of her employer, moreover a man who was supposedly her cousin, was perfectly acceptable. Perhaps high sticklers like his daughters would not approve, but she hardly aspired to their standards of nicety. Nor would they know about her tête-à-tête with their father unless Sir Michael or Catriona herself chose to confess it to them. She had no doubt they were still asleep and would not ring for their maids and their morning chocolate with sweet biscuits for at least another hour.

"I do not believe I know what you mean, Cousin Catriona," he said with a twinkle in his dark eyes. He looked unforgivably pleased with himself.

"I begin to think that manipulation and making mischief are not qualities your darling daughters inherited entirely from their mother," Catriona said. "I refer, of course, to your outrageous flirting with me last night. As you know very well. Those suggestive remarks were the outside of enough, and before your daughters. You are perfectly willing to mount me, indeed. They did not know how to look."

"They did not, did they?" he said, looking ridiculously pleased.

"You should be ashamed of yourself," Catriona said in disapproval.

"Oh, come now," he said as he nudged his sturdy earthenware cup forward as a signal. She pursed her lips and filled it with tea from the rather ugly, angular pot before them. "You enjoyed the game as much as I. You do not require a gentle ride, do you?"

"Nor do I," she said, raising her chin in challenge. "I am equal to anything your stable has to offer."

He gave a short laugh.

"You are a bruising rider, I have no doubt. I thought as much. Where did you learn to ride?" he asked pleasantly.

He made the question sound casual, but his eyes were rather too alert for one engaged in making idle conversation.

Oh, no, you don't.

"At a very young age," she said, smiling right back at him. She turned her attention to a waiter who chose that moment to come to their table, and enjoyed the way Sir Michael's eyes widened when she ordered eggs, thin toast, bacon, potatoes and a bowl of porridge for her breakfast.

"I will have the same and a portion of sirloin," Sir Michael added when she was through. His eyes held an expression of genuine respect in them. "My late wife," he said when the waiter had gone, "could not abide more than chocolate and sweet biscuits in the morning."

"I am reluctant to speak ill of the dead, but it is no wonder that she was plagued with sickness," Catriona said. "Of course, I have always been blessed with rude good health, as my own mother used to say. She was a dainty woman in the style of your daughters, and I got the impression that my vulgar sturdiness was an embarrassment and a reproach to her."

"This is the first time I have heard you mention any member of your family except for Mrs. Tilden," he said. "Where did your people come from?"

"I have no people," she said, annoyed with herself for saying so much.

"You are mistaken. You now have Dorothea, Marguerite, and myself," he said lightly, and lifted his cup as if to toast her.

"There you are," cried Dorothea in accusing tones as she and Marguerite accosted them in some haste. Marguerite was somewhat out of breath as she drew to a halt before them. "Here Marguerite and I have made haste to dress so that we may be on the road in good time to reach Edinburgh before midday, and you are lingering over your breakfast."

"I did not expect you to arise before noon," Sir Michael said, unabashed. "Do seat yourselves and have some tea. Between us, Catriona and I have ordered enough food to feed an army."

"I never can abide a big meal in the morning," Marguerite said with a fastidious sniff as the waiter began laying an astonishing number of dishes on the table. "And my darling Henry would have an apoplexy at the thought of his wife having breakfast in a common tap-room."

"Then we shall not tell him. Sit and keep us company, darling," Sir Michael said as he took the carving knife in anticipation of slicing off some pieces of sirloin.

"Oh, very well," Dorothea said with a sigh of resignation.

Catriona noticed that the ladies did manage to force down a buttered egg or two between them as well as a good portion of the bacon and toast.

"We shall visit the dressmakers' shops right after we are installed in the hotel," Marguerite said as she ran a fastidious eye over Catriona's only traveling costume of black wool. "And we must do something about that hat. No one wears hats in that style anymore."

"As you please," Catriona said. She was rather tired of the hat herself, and she was perfectly aware that the traveling costume was a bit threadbare around the edges.

Dorothea fixed her father with a stern eye.

"And you, Father, must see a tailor without delay. I shall inquire at the shops as to which is the best in Edinburgh."

"If I must," he said glumly. "You know men's evening clothes are all alike, and they never go out of fashion."

"Trust me in this, Father," Marguerite said, "They do, and yours have."

"I bow, as always, to your expert judgment in the all-important matter of fashion, my little viscountess," he said affectionately. "I will visit the tailor without delay."

"And we must see to hiring a new valet for you."

"Nonsense. I am perfectly capable of dressing myself."

"That is beside the point, Father," Marguerite said earnestly. "No gentleman can be without his valet."

"I had a valet," Sir Michael said glumly. "He left me, if you will remember. And the one I had before him died. I have come to the conclusion that valets are more trouble than they are worth."

"It presents a very off appearance, Papa," Dorothea pointed out. "And we must make the best possible impression at your party. Appearances are so very important. Marguerite and I have our positions to uphold. We would die of shame if the *ton* were to find out that our father does not employ a valet. You would not want to embarrass us, would you?"

"And shall Catriona have a lady's maid to make her smart as well?" he asked.

"She would agree with me that her present situation in life would make the hiring of a maid ridiculous," Dorothea said. "*She* is not a baronet. You are. I hope you know I mean no offense in saying so, Catriona."

"None taken," Catriona said cheerfully.

"Precisely," said Marguerite. "Our maids can easily see to Catriona's needs after we are dressed for the party, of course."

"Well, I believe we have all eaten enough," Dorothea said, rising. "This inn is quite out of the way, but we cannot take the chance that some traveler will recognize us and the gossip reach London that we were seen in a common taproom."

"You are with your father," Catriona said. "Where is the harm in that?"

"You will pardon my saying so, I am sure, Catriona, but behavior that seems acceptable to one of your background is far from being acceptable for us," Marguerite said. "Dorothea and I will wait by the coach." She exchanged an uneasy look with her sister as she watched Sir Michael gallantly assist a suspicious Catriona to her feet. The incorrigible man! He was still flirting with her to annoy his daughters. "Catriona, you will not want to linger behind, I am certain, while Father settles the bill."

She and Dorothea managed to position Catriona between them, as if to remove her physically from their father. Catriona looked back at him once and noted that he had the gall to look amused.

"Her figure is not too bad now that we have her out of that dreadful traveling costume," Dorothea said critically as she walked slowly around her supposed cousin as Catriona stood in her chemise before the mirror in the dressmaker's shop.

"Perhaps we should put her in gray. It would be very handsome with her coloring," Marguerite said. "And a hat in gray, too, of course."

Catriona was becoming weary of being discussed as if she were not present.

"I hate gray," she said.

Dorothea looked at her as if a rock had spoken.

"I beg your pardon, cousin?"

"I do not like gray. It is dreary. You will never convince Sir Michael that you are doing your best to find me a husband if you start decking me out in funeral colors."

"Gray is not a funeral color. It is dignified. It is elegant," Dorothea said. "It is suitable."

"I notice neither of *you* wear gray."

"What color do you want for your traveling costume then?" Dorothea asked with a sigh.

"Blue," she said. "It will look better with my coloring than gray."

"You must depend upon my sister and me to be a better judge of such matters than you," Marguerite said.

"Miss would look very well in blue," the dressmaker ventured to point out.

"I beg your pardon?" Marguerite said, looking shocked that the woman would dare question her sister's taste.

"Miss is too young and attractive to wear gray," the seamstress said. "That is a color for dowagers."

"There. You see?" Catriona said. "If Sir Michael is going to stand the nonsense for a new wardrobe for me, it may as well be something fit to look at."

"Very well. Blue it is," Dorothea said in exasperation. "But a darker blue. Light blue will show wear and soil."

"Quite right," Catriona said.

"Excellent. Now let us see some patterns for ball gowns," Marguerite said. She frowned when Catriona wandered over to a stand that had a collection of partially finished dresses on it. "Catriona, do pay attention."

But Catriona had lost her heart.

The gown was pink silk, and it had a bit of ruching about the hem to give it a lovely bell-shaped silhouette. The bodice was low, and there was an elegant artificial rose in white satin on each of the dainty puffed sleeves.

She couldn't suppress a little whimper of pure desire from escaping her lips.

"It is so beautiful," she breathed.

"That gown," Dorothea said, "obviously belongs to someone else, for it is in the later stage of completion." She tried to draw Catriona away, but Catriona could not bring herself to release the tiny sleeve of the gown from her worshipful fingers. "Catriona, you must let go."

The dressmaker cleared her throat.

"If you will permit me to say so, Lady Redgrave, Mrs. Walbridge," she began.

"Yes?" Dorothea said with a look so intimidating the woman almost quailed.

"The gown was made for a customer who decided not to purchase it after all, so it is for sale."

Catriona, to her abject embarrassment, gave another little whimper.

"It looks like it belongs to an opera dancer," Marguerite sniffed.

"I want it," Catriona whispered.

"No," Dorothea said firmly. "The gown is made of *silk*. Quite unsuitable for an unmarried woman, moreover, if you will forgive me saying so, one in your particular circumstances." Eager to distract Catriona from the forbidden ball gown, she showed her a pattern card. "Now this would be just the thing made up in a softer color, light green, perhaps, or yellow. Or white."

Catriona was still mesmerized by the pink dress.

"Cousin Catriona," Marguerite said kindly. "We would not want the gentlemen at Father's party to get the wrong idea."

"The wrong idea," Catriona repeated blankly.

"That your virtue is not as perfect as it should be," Dorothea said.

"Because I chose to wear a pink silk gown? Do not be ridiculous," Catriona said.

Dorothea pursed her lips and turned to the seamstress, who was watching the exchange with great interest.

"I believe I saw a bolt of yellow muslin I should like to examine. Would you be kind enough to bring it here?" Dorothea asked the seamstress. When the woman was gone, she patted Catriona on the shoulder. "I hesitate to speak of such matters, but it is known that you came to Scotland to live down some scandal with a man. Do you think it wise to appear in Society wearing a gown that is in questionable taste? You have always been so modest in your appearance. Certainly you do not wish to give any-one cause to question your respectability. And surely you owe it to my father not to embarrass him under his own roof by decking yourself out like some rake's *chère amie*."

Catriona bit her lip. The gown *was* rather much, she had to admit. She would look conspicuous at the ball in the vibrant pink amid all the pastel hues of the neigh-borhood's fashionable ladies. And when she went to live with an invalid lady at the seaside, she would hardly be in a position to wear it.

"I suppose you are right," she conceded, although she could not hide her disappointment.

Dorothea patted her on the shoulder.

"There. I knew you would make the sensible choice," she said, pleased. "We shall find you something just as pretty, I promise you." She indicated the pattern card again. "This would be very elegant in cream with a bit of lace trim."

"Yes, it is quite nice," Catriona said as she tried to con-jure up some enthusiasm.

Throughout the afternoon, her deceptively dainty-looking patronesses led her inexorably from shop to shop until Catriona was certain she had covered every square inch of the great city of Edinburgh on foot.

By the end of the day she was the proud owner of several pairs of handsome shoes including a pair of white dancing slippers, a pretty chicken-skin fan, a cream velvet opera cloak, several pairs of elegant silk stockings, and a beaded yellow reticule. She also had been fitted for the new dark blue walking costume, a number of muslin morning gowns, an evening gown, and a ball gown, but Catriona could not get the vision in pink silk out of her mind.

"There, are you not pleased?" Dorothea said in tones of congratulation.

Catriona smiled at her.

"Yes, I thank you," she said. "I have not had new clothes for so long. I feel quite indulged."

"It was a very great pleasure," Dorothea said warmly. "And I was most pleased to find this chicken-skin fan for myself. It is quite as elegant as any I have seen in London, and at a fraction of the price."

"A fruitful day, indeed," Catriona commented.

"The pink silk would have been a dreadful mistake," Marguerite said kindly. Catriona supposed she did not mean to rub salt in the open wound of her desire.

"Indeed," she said lightly. "Pink silk! I would have looked quite ridiculous."

"Too true," Dorothea said. "Do not worry. You will be quite one of the most elegant ladies at Papa's party."

"Next to Dorothea and myself, of course," Marguerite said archly.

CHAPTER 12

"Lady Constance! How charming!" cried Dorothea as her party encountered the duke's relation and her maid in the tearoom at their hotel. "It was not so very long ago that we met in London."

"Indeed," the dashing, auburn-haired matron replied. "And how do I find you, dear Mrs. Walbridge? I distinctly remember catching you in my rose garden teasing my cat the last time we were in London."

Catriona smiled politely and could not, for the life of her, imagine the sophisticated Dorothea lowering herself to any activity so mundane as teasing a small domestic animal in a garden.

The lady turned to Marguerite and took her gloved hand.

"And here is dear Lady Redgrave. How delighted my late husband would have been to see Redgrave settled with such a sweet, lovely wife," she said with a sentimental sigh.

Marguerite beamed at her, but her expression dimmed when Lady Constance turned toward Catriona with an inquisitive look on her face. Catriona watched Lady Constance's eyes swiftly inspect her clothing and dismiss her at once as a nonentity, but she smiled briefly in a noncommittal way that told Catriona that she wasn't certain whether she was someone marginally worthy of her notice or a maid. It was the sort of look that would prompt a less

strong-minded individual to want to apologize for daring
to breathe the same air as her betters.

"Lady Constance, may I present our cousin Catriona
Grant, who is staying with us at present at Papa's estate,"
Dorothea said smoothly.

"A pleasure, Miss Grant," she said regally. "Do you stay
long in Dumfries?"

"My plans are undecided," Catriona replied.

"Interesting," Lady Constance murmured as she gave
Catriona another of those swift inspections. "And how is
your father, my dears?"

"You may judge for yourself, for here he comes," Marguerite said as she turned to greet Sir Michael. "Papa,
look who is here." Sir Michael swept the elder lady a bow
and took her hand briefly.

"Lady Constance! How delightful to see you," he said.
His eyes narrowed at her speculative look. "What nonsense have these little minxes of mine been telling you
about me?"

"Sir Michael! I am glad to see you," she said. "I am having a small card party in my suite tonight for my Edinburgh friends. You have become quite the despair of all
the Dumfries hostesses, I'm told, but I shall ask you and
your daughters to attend in person so you will not dare
refuse, not with your daughters here to add their pleas
to mine. It shall be a social triumph, luring the elusive
Sir Michael to my little party." When he would have
protested, she held up one dainty, gloved hand. "I will
not listen to your excuses, so you may as well save your
breath. I shall expect all of you this evening." Her smile,
when she turned to Catriona, did not reach her eyes.
"And you, too, of course, Miss Grant."

There was that condescension again. The wretched
woman was doing it on purpose, Catriona had no doubt,
to put her in her place.

"I thank you, my lady," Catriona said, "but I am afraid
I am very dull at cards."

"You must do as you please, of course," Lady Constance said indifferently. She turned and contrived rather neatly to cut Catriona off from the group as she, Sir Michael, and both his daughters formed a conversational foursome to discuss people Catriona did not know. She murmured an apology and would have inched away to escape to her room, but Sir Michael's hand suddenly shot out and grasped her wrist.

"Where are you going, Catriona?" he asked. "You have not yet had anything to eat or drink."

"I am not hungry."

"You may keep us company, then," he said as he led the way to a table with her wrist still imprisoned in his large hand.

"Papa," Dorothea said, imperfectly concealing her annoyance at his inexplicable insistence that Catriona join them. "Catriona must be quite tired after all that shopping. She will want to rest."

"I have never heard of a bit of shopping wearing out a healthy young female," he said. He sounded almost paternal. "I hope you enjoyed yourself, Catriona."

"Very much," she said. "I am afraid you have been very generous."

"Have I?" he said with an arch smile. "It is the least I can do to repay your generosity."

"*My* generosity?" she asked, surprised.

"In caring for my wife's aunt so devotedly," he said. He noticed Lady Constance's look of inquiry. "Catriona came to stay with Mrs. Tilden two years ago when her health failed. She was in her nineties, and when she died recently, Catriona came to stay with us. I am exceedingly grateful to her for making Mrs. Tilden's last days comfortable."

"It was a pleasure," Catriona said.

"And now Catriona is in search of someone new to manage," Sir Michael said humorously.

"I quite see," Lady Constance said with a regal nod of

her head. "Now that Mrs. Tilden is dead, she will need to stay with you until she finds a new situation. Perhaps I know someone who is in need of her services."

"You are kind," Catriona said, offended by being spoken of as if she were a *thing* in want of disposal. "But I beg you not to put yourself to such trouble."

"Actually, Lady Constance, we thought that Catriona might marry," Sir Michael said.

"Ah. Hence the new clothes. Very generous of you, I must say. I suppose you might try to find someone for her," Lady Constance said with just the slightest tone of skepticism in her voice. "She is well past her first bloom, but quite presentable still. A gentleman with several children from a previous family to rear might be persuaded to marry her."

"You relieve my mind, Lady Constance," Catriona said through gritted teeth.

"And how did your shopping excursion go, Father?" Dorothea interjected with a repressive look at Catriona, who obviously resented Lady Constance's presumption in assuming *she* had the right to an opinion on Catriona's supposed marital prospects.

"Quite successfully," he said with a sigh. "I am now— or will shortly be—the possessor of several coats tight enough across my shoulders to please even your sartorial standards, my dears. The tailor held up my old coat with two fingers as if its existence offended him."

"How many coats did you purchase, Papa?" Marguerite asked.

"Three. And a great many other garments, as well," he said. "The wretched man would not let me out of the place until I did so. I shall go back to have them fitted on Tuesday, and then we may go home, I thank the Almighty."

"But, Papa, our fittings are going to take at least a week."

"Quite right," Lady Constance said with a nod of approval. "One cannot rush the fittings."

"I have a feeling one can if one is willing to pay handsomely enough," Sir Michael said shrewdly.

Catriona finished her tea and set the teacup before her very carefully, for in her present mood she would have enjoyed watching it shatter on the decorative little table.

"If you will excuse me," she said, "I would like to put away my purchases."

"Of course," Lady Constance said with a sweet, insincere little smile. "Do let me wish you luck, Miss Grant, and do not despair. I am certain we can find some man for you."

"You are kindness itself, my lady," Catriona said, smiling back just as insincerely.

"That one has an impertinent tongue," Lady Constance said as she watched Catriona leave the room with her head held high.

"But a good heart underneath it all," Sir Michael said. "She did nurse Mrs. Tilden quite devotedly."

"And received a salary for this, I presume," Lady Constance said. "The girl has no reason to feel herself ill used, and I hope you are not laboring under the misapprehension that you are under a crushing obligation to her merely because she gave satisfaction in her position."

"On the contrary, she expects nothing from me," Sir Michael said, "except a post as my housekeeper, and that because Mrs. Tilden put the idea in her head that she owed it to me to take my household in hand."

"I had heard something about a will, but it was so ridiculous that I dismissed it out of hand as a wild tale," Lady Constance said.

"If it seemed a wild tale, you heard the right of it," Sir Michael said glumly.

"The old lady must have been senile," Lady Constance exclaimed.

"Not at all. Mrs. Tilden just had a great love of ordering people about," he said. "She did leave the girl a small legacy, and I have every intention of adding to it so she will not want for a decent dowry if she chooses to marry."

"And she does have Aunt Sophie's emerald ring and ruby brooch," Marguerite said in a tone of resentment. "The settings are old fashioned, but the stones are good."

Sir Michael gave her a straight look, and she colored before his gaze. He knew well that his daughters resented the fact that Catriona had received Mrs. Tilden's most valuable jewelry.

Lady Constance's eyes narrowed.

"Servants are notorious for gaining the confidence of their employers and influencing them to give them valuables that should rightfully be bequeathed to their relations," she said.

"No," Michael said firmly. "Catriona would never do such a thing. I offered her money to start a new life, and she refused. She is the least mercenary person of my acquaintance."

"She is the least mercenary or the most devious," Dorothea said. "Why should she accept a purse and go away when she could stay and possibly become Lady Stewart?"

"Oh, do be serious!" Michael exclaimed. "I am certain she has no such design."

"Papa," Dorothea said with a sigh. "Men are so naïve."

"I confess, I had the same suspicion of Cousin Catriona's motive in insisting it was her duty to take Papa and his household in hand," Marguerite said. "No doubt it was she who put the notion into Mrs. Tilden's head."

"I would not suffer such a creature in my house for a moment," Lady Constance said.

"Well, I can hardly turn her out after the service she has rendered to this family in caring for Mrs. Tilden," Michael said. "I think you are mistaken if you think Catriona intends to make up to me. For one thing, she takes a positive delight in vexing me with all her plans to transform my house into a vision of cleanliness and inconvenience. For another, I fail to see why a young woman of more than passable looks should settle for a husband ten years her senior."

"At the risk of turning your head, Sir Michael," Lady Constance said carefully, "a woman could certainly do worse."

"I think she could and *should* do better," Sir Michael said.

"Exactly!" Dorothea said triumphantly. "Which is why Marguerite and I have been under such pains to persuade Papa to have this party and introduce her to the neighborhood's bachelors."

"A party! I do hope I will be invited," Lady Constance said. "I so enjoy a party."

"Of course," Sir Michael said glumly. "It seems everyone of note in the kingdom is to be invited."

"Excellent! I will be delighted to give you any assistance in my power to help you marry off your Miss Grant creditably," Lady Constance said with a gleam of mischief in her fine eyes. "Before she leaves Edinburgh, I promise you, she will be ready to take her place in Dumfries circles as quite the belle of the county."

"I am not quite prepared to stay in Edinburgh as long as all that," Sir Michael interjected with no small amount of alarm.

"Marguerite and I have already made great progress," Dorothea said, "in choosing a new wardrobe for her. You will find her quite transformed when you see her next."

"Which will avail you nothing unless you can do something about her bossiness," Lady Constance said.

"Lady Constance, it has been a very great pleasure," Sir Michael said, rising. "I will leave you now. I have much to do before your card party tonight."

"Much to do, Papa? How is that possible when you are away from home and staying in a hotel?" asked Marguerite.

"I must write to my steward, since you have informed me that we must stay in this place longer than I had planned. Autumn is a critical time to be away from the farm," he said.

"You and your old farm," Marguerite said with a pretty pout of reproof.

"Never mind, my dear," Lady Constance said cheerily to Marguerite as she gave Sir Michael an airy wave. "Your father, much as we enjoy his company, will be quite in the way. We are to talk of fashion, you know, Sir Michael, and mysterious female arts designed to beguile some hapless man into taking the vexatious Miss Grant off your hands."

"Mysterious female arts? Knowing Catriona, she will scorn to employ them," Sir Michael said, "but I will leave you to it."

"Yes, take your old pessimism away," Lady Constance said as she waved him on quite cheerfully.

"He has a point, you know," Dorothea said with a sigh once her father was gone. "Miss Grant can be most stubborn."

"It becomes clear," Lady Constance said, "that someone with a stronger will than hers must take her in hand." She preened herself a little. "It will be a challenge, to be sure, but before I am through with your little Miss Grant, she will know to a nicety how to tempt a gentleman."

CHAPTER 13

Catriona's eyes narrowed in suspicion when the three fashionably dressed ladies bore down on her with determined smiles fixed on their faces. She was sitting in her room eating her breakfast on a tray, for her employer's daughters had given her quite a stern little lecture the day before on the grave impropriety of having breakfast in a common taproom for a lady of marriageable age. More importantly, her behavior would reflect on *them* since she had arrived in Edinburgh in their company, a catastrophe to be averted at all costs.

"My dear Miss Grant," Lady Constance exclaimed. "We were about to go out, and we could not go without you."

"I fail to see why not," Catriona said with raised eyebrows as she sipped her coffee.

Lady Constance regarded the remnants of Catriona's rather substantial breakfast with unfeigned dismay.

"Good heavens, my good girl! Surely you do not eat all of *that* in the morning. If so, we must contrive without delay to find you a husband."

"Perhaps I am not quite awake and all my faculties are thus still somewhat muddled by sleep, but I fail to see what one thing has to do with the other."

"It is plain that you will run to fat before you are thirty, which will make the task of marrying you off quite impossible."

"You alarm me," Catriona said mildly as she took a

defiant bite of toast liberally smeared with strawberry marmalade.

"I take leave to tell you now, young woman, that gentlemen do not appreciate sarcasm, especially in the morning," Lady Constance said.

"I do beg your pardon," Catriona said wearily. "But it is you who have invaded my bedchamber before I have barely swallowed my tea."

"There is no time to be lost," Dorothea said. "We are to have the first fittings for our new clothes this morning. Since Papa is adamant about returning to Dumfries within the week, he sent a message to the dressmaker offering her a princely sum to have our gowns ready in time."

"But what about my breakfast? I have not nearly finished."

"Yes, you have. We shall tell a footman to have it removed on the way out," Lady Constance said with a sniff at such vulgar evidence of Catriona's appetite. "One cannot be too careful about vermin." She broke off and eyed Catriona critically. "Good heavens, girl, is that black ensemble the only one you have for town wear?"

"It is," she said. "If the three of you wish to reconsider being seen with me in public, I shall excuse you. I can always go to the dressmaker's alone."

"Such a tongue you have, missy," Lady Constance said with a sigh. "It is clear we shall have our work cut out for us."

"*You*, Lady Constance? You will pardon me for asking, but why should you lend your efforts to the transformation of this sow's ear into a silk purse?"

"Sir Michael is an extremely kind gentleman," Lady Constance said as her cheeks colored delicately. She cast her eyes down modestly. "How could I fail to be of service to his family?"

"You want to marry him yourself," Catriona said.

"You are a forthright young woman, are you not?"

Lady Constance said. "We shall have to break you of that, I am afraid, for gentlemen do not appreciate such directness in a female. But you are correct. Now that his daughters are married and my sons are established creditably, there could be no impediment to our marriage."

"My father and Lady Constance would be perfect for one another," Dorothea said fondly, "only Papa has been slow to recognize it, burdened as he was with us until we married, with the farm, his old horses, and now you."

"I had the impression that you barely knew one another," Catriona said in disbelief.

"True, we do not meet often since Sir Michael has become quite estranged from social life since his wife died, but we used to meet quite often," Lady Constance said stiffly.

"So you see, Catriona," Dorothea said, "Mrs. Tilden's making him responsible for you, though kindly meant, merely placed an impediment in the way of Father's happiness. Lady Constance would be a splendid match for him in every way."

Catriona laughed in their affronted faces. She could not help herself.

"You have plotted his downfall between you," she said. "You underestimate Sir Michael if you think he will succumb to such manipulation. I have never met such a hardened bachelor in all my days."

"And you are, of course, intimately acquainted with many bachelors," Lady Constance said snidely. "As for your age, it is best when a female reaches a certain number of years not to be so quick to make reference to it."

Catriona's amusement died abruptly.

"I fail to see why my past or, more to the point, my future is any of your business, Lady Constance," she said.

Lady Constance threw up her hands.

"You must rid yourself of this habit of such plain speaking," she said. "I am of half a mind to give up on you."

"Do," Catriona said. "You must see that I am quite hopeless."

"Nonsense. A few new clothes and a curb on that sharp tongue of yours, and the business is done." Lady Constance's eyes gleamed with the challenge.

"He is not the marrying kind," Catriona said.

"All men are the marrying kind with the proper incentive," Lady Constance said, preening herself a little.

"I long to call you Mother," Marguerite said soulfully as she put a soft, pampered hand over Lady Constance's.

"And I could not have two more charming daughters," Lady Constance said. "I was blessed by the Almighty with four strong, handsome sons, but I have always longed for a daughter. And now I will have two."

"All we need," Dorothea said, "is to throw Papa and Lady Constance together on a regular basis, and love will take its course."

"The day they agree to wed, I am out of his house," Catriona said. "So it is not necessary, after all, for me to go through this farce of finding a husband."

Marguerite gave her a mischievous look.

"No, not at all," she said, "unless you *want* to relinquish all the pretty clothes and furbelows that Dorothea and I have been at such pains to choose for you. Admit it, Catriona. You *want* these things. I saw the lust in your eyes."

Catriona threw one hand up in surrender.

"You do not fight fair, Marguerite."

"I do not fight at all," Sir Michael's daughter said with a roguish smile. "Why should you not have some new clothes to take to your precious little cottage at the seaside? Why should you not enjoy yourself at Papa's party and meet some of the bachelors? No one will hold a pistol to your head and *make* you marry anyone. You can make a few pleasant memories and take some beautiful gowns with you, satisfied in the knowledge that you have helped my father find an amiable wife to give him comfort in his old age and run his household as well as Aunt Sophie could have wanted. Is that not the intent behind her last wish? For Papa to be happy, and for you to have the future you want?"

Catriona thought of the many pretty garments the sisters had chosen for her, of the hats, the kid gloves, the charming light blue kid half boots, and was weak.

"Dear Catriona, do say you will help us bring Papa and Lady Constance together," Dorothea said.

"I will not stand in your way," Catriona said shrewdly, "but when we go for our fittings, I want to try on the pink silk gown if it is still there."

Dorothea threw up her hands.

"All right, you may try it on if you want to torture yourself to such an extent," Dorothea conceded, "but we will *not* purchase it for you. If we do, everyone will think you are someone's—" She broke off as she groped for a word she could use in feminine company.

"Opera dancer?" Marguerite suggested.

"Marguerite! You are a genius!" cried Catriona. "I will become an opera dancer. Then I can have the pink silk gown after all."

"Do not be silly," Lady Constance said crossly as she herded the young women from the room. "Pink silk gowns, indeed."

The afternoon was half gone and Dorothea, Marguerite, and Catriona had failed to meet Sir Michael at the tea shop, where they were to enjoy some refreshment and take his carriage back to the hotel. After cooling his heels for the better part of an hour, he set off for the dressmaker's shop on foot. He knew the address well, for it was the most modish shop in Edinburgh and Miss Cumerford was the only dressmaker outside London his daughters would permit to make clothes for them.

Miss Cumerford herself stepped forward at once when he arrived at the door and practically genuflected in delight at seeing him. He surmised from this that his daughters had ordered so many clothes for themselves as well as Catriona that the bill was likely to stop his heart when he saw it. His daughters, though married, would still expect him to stand the nonsense for this excursion.

"Sir Michael, what an honor!" she said. "Your daughters have just completed their fittings, and your charming cousin is just trying on one more gown."

"Papa!" cried Marguerite, giving him the conscience-stricken smile of one confident of forgiveness. "Are we so dreadfully late that you had to come in search of us? I am so sorry to put you to such trouble."

"No trouble at all, my dear," he said as he put one arm around her shoulders and kissed her on the forehead, careful not to disarrange the frivolous little pouf of veiling over her stylish curls. "And there's my princess," he added as he put his other arm around Dorothea. "Have you been enjoying yourselves?"

"Hugely," Dorothea said. "We have found the most wonderful things. We knew you would want us to have them." She gave him a coy little look. "I am afraid we have been putty in Miss Cumerford's hands."

"Not quite," the seamstress said ruefully as she gave a little moue of reproof. "Not all of my protestations have prevailed in convincing you not to break your pretty cousin's heart."

Sir Michael raised his eyebrows and would have asked for further enlightenment, but just then he heard Lady Constance's masterful voice emit from the other room.

"Enough of this nonsense, girl," she was saying. "The gown is vastly unsuitable."

"I know," Catriona replied. "Just let me enjoy it for a little while."

"Unsuitable, is it?" Sir Michael said. "Come out, Catriona! Let us have a look at it."

Lady Constance, hearing his voice, rushed into the room.

"Shame on you, Sir Michael!" she said, although she was simpering at him. "I will not have you encourage the girl in her folly."

Catriona herself stuck her head into the room from the doorway, but the gown under discussion remained invisible to him.

"That is enough, missy," Lady Constance said sharply. "Change out of that gown at once!"

"Catriona," Sir Michael said, not liking Lady Constance's unkind tone, "if you really want the gown—"

"It is exceedingly impractical and expensive besides," Lady Constance said. "She could have two other gowns for what this one cost."

"I am afraid she is right, Sir Michael," Catriona said quite cheerfully. "I merely wanted to try it on, and I have, so now I am content."

"There," Dorothea said warmly. "I knew you would see reason."

"I will be just a moment," Catriona said as her head disappeared from sight.

He looked thoughtfully after her, but he was distracted from the matter when Marguerite slipped her arm into his.

"I am famished," she declared. "We do not deserve it, Papa, but I hope you are going to take us back to the tearoom and treat us to some refreshment."

"Of course, my little viscountess," he said, patting her arm. "Lady Constance, you will join us, I trust?"

"I would be delighted," that lady said graciously as she took Sir Michael's free arm and smiled up into his face. He returned the smile but was distracted when Catriona came back into the room and stopped, as if transfixed, in the doorway as she stared at Michael and Lady Constance.

"There you are, Cousin Catriona," he said, smiling kindly at her. "The ability to change costumes quickly is an art that I have always prized in a lady. Do come along. We are to have tea and little cakes so that you may recruit your strength."

"Excellent," she said. "Not *too* many little cakes, I'm afraid, or Miss Cumerford will have to let out the seams of our gowns before they even leave the shop."

"Miss Grant," Lady Constance said despairingly as she led the way out of the shop, followed closely by Dorothea and Marguerite.

Michael raised his eyebrows at Catriona as he gestured for her and his daughters to precede him and Lady Constance from the shop.

"Are you enjoying your first visit to Edinburgh, Catriona?" he asked.

"Very much," she said as she waved farewell to Miss Cumerford, who smiled dotingly after them.

CHAPTER 14

By Friday, Miss Cumerford and Sir Michael's tailor had delivered most of the new clothes and, thus burdened with finery, Sir Michael's coach was ready for the journey back to Dumfries.

It was not a surprise to Sir Michael that Lady Constance intended to accompany them on part of the journey, for she, his daughters, and Miss Grant had been as close as inkle-weavers for the past week in Edinburgh. *Ah, well,* he thought tolerantly, *women are never happier than when they are plotting some man's downfall.* They had no idea he was well aware of their plans for him and Lady Constance. How well it would suit his daughters to be related by marriage to Charles Henry Montagu Douglas-Scott, fourth Duke of Buccleuch and owner of Drumlanrig Castle, which was without dispute the most impressive estate in Scotland.

The present duke was a good man, well liked and courted assiduously by every hostess with pretensions to fashion, including Sir Michael's own daughters, who would be delighted to refer casually in conversation to "our relation by marriage, His Grace, the Duke of Buccleuch." Much as his daughters loved him, Sir Michael had no doubt that they would cheerfully sacrifice his freedom in order to move into the more august social circles that Lady Constance and the duke occupied.

They were made in their socially ambitious mother's very image, bless them.

The two of them approached him at that moment with Lady Constance and behind them a small army of servants carrying portmanteaux, trunks, and bandboxes.

"Are you ready to set out, Papa?" Dorothea asked, for all the world as if it were *he* who had been keeping *them* waiting.

"Whenever you wish, princess," he said, smiling at her.

"What is keeping that girl?" Lady Constance said with a frown toward the hotel.

At that moment, a blond vision in cream and russet appeared in the doorway, and his jaw dropped.

"There you are," Lady Constance snapped. "Don't dawdle, girl."

"Yes, Lady Constance," said the vision with Catriona Grant's voice.

Sir Michael blinked.

Who was this tall, slim, exquisite creature? A charming and extremely frivolous confection of straw, tulle, and cream-colored artificial roses crowned her blond, up-swept hair. Whatever he had paid for this ensemble had been well worth it.

"I would be glad for your assistance, Sir Michael," said Lady Constance with an edge to her voice.

"I beg your pardon?" Michael said as he tore his eyes away from Catriona.

"Your *arm*, if you please," she said.

"Oh, of course. Forgive me." He assisted her into the carriage and turned to help his daughters in as well. He looked around. "Is Catriona not riding with you?"

"It would be far too crowded for four all the way to Dumfries," Lady Constance said. "Miss Grant will ride in my carriage with the three maids."

"Poor Miss Grant. Is it right to banish her to ride with the servants?"

"Actually, Father, she *is* a servant," Dorothea said. "She is hardly family merely because she is some distant connection of Aunt Sophie's."

Michael glanced at Lady Constance.

"Lady Constance knows all," Marguerite said. "And she will do her best to help us find a husband for Catriona." She squeezed the elder lady's hand. "So kind."

"Yes. So kind," Michael said skeptically. He stepped back and rapped once on the roof of the carriage to signal the driver to depart. Still holding the reins of his horse, he walked to the second carriage, where Catriona was about to enter with the maids.

"Oh, miss, I could not," Lady Constance's maid was saying. "It would be vastly improper."

"Why on earth not?" Catriona said. "Lady Constance will never know. And neither will Mrs. Walbridge or Lady Redgrave. We will brush all the evidence away before we arrive. If you will not have one, then out of civility I cannot have one, either, and that would take all the fun out of my petty larceny, would it not?"

"Plotting mutiny, Catriona?" Michael asked as he took her elbow and helped her into the coach. When he did, an object that she had hidden close to her body bumped his hip. "Ah, what is this?"

"I managed to procure a basket of biscuits and fruit from the kitchens, and I am prevailing upon my companions to share it with me," she said. "So do not be surprised when you see it enumerated on your bill. I hid it from Dorothea and Marguerite, for they would be horrified if they knew I intended to eat fruit in my new clothes. No doubt they would confiscate my prize and gorge on it themselves after they had given me a stern lecture. I trust you will not betray me."

"I am as silent as the grave," he vowed, "or I will be if I can prevail upon you to part with an apple for my horse."

"Done," Catriona said at once as she reached into the basket. "And a biscuit for his master."

"Thank you, Catriona," he said as he accepted the small, dainty biscuit. It was too pretty to eat, but it looked so delicious that he popped it into his mouth all at once. He closed the door, nodded to the smiling maids, and rapped the top of the carriage to send it on its way. Then he tossed the apple into the air, caught it, and offered a bite to his horse.

He watched as the two carriages and baggage coaches swept out of sight with the four females who, he had no doubt, were going to make his life entirely too interesting until this precious party they insisted upon having was over.

As he tossed the apple core over his shoulder and mounted his horse, a thought so surprising crossed his mind that it caused him to make a clumsy business of an action that was as commonplace for him as climbing out of bed in the morning. His horse's head turned slightly as if to make sure that it was his master, and not some interloper, seated upon him.

In Sir Michael's breast rose an emotion that he had not experienced in so long that he almost didn't recognize it.

It was anticipation. Of the party. Of having his daughters plot and scheme around him again. Of having the pleasure of watching pretty Catriona Grant find her feet in Dumfries society.

It would be, he told himself firmly, like having another daughter to establish creditably.

As he set his horse at a brisk pace to overtake the carriages, he told himself that it was as a daughter he thought of her. The brief, thrilling quickening of his heart that he had felt when he first saw her in her fine new clothes was nothing more than the appreciation of a man with not quite one foot in the grave for any female of youth, beauty, and charm.

She was closer to his daughters' age than his, he reminded himself. She was a responsibility and a temptation, but she was not for him.

He would find her a good husband who would give

her children and the position in society that all females craved. Failing that, he would help her become established as a contented spinster in the little seaside community she often talked about.

He would not burden Catriona with a husband many years her senior when she could aspire to marital prospects more suitable to one of her age and temperament. Mrs. Tilden had trusted him with Catriona's happiness. He would not fail either of them.

Michael tried persuasion. He tried reason. When those failed, he tried arguing. All to no avail.

"How excessively uncivil of you, Sir Michael! One would think I had proposed your returning to Dumfries by way of Siam," Lady Constance said with the pretty, trilling laugh that often punctuated her conversation when she was attempting to disarm her opponents by making their petty arguments look foolish. They were stopped at an inn to change the horses and fortify themselves before they embarked upon the next leg of the journey. The party was to have divided so that Lady Constance could go west to Castle Drumlanrig and Michael, his daughters, and Catriona could proceed south to his estate near Dumfries. Now, it seemed, the ladies between them had decided on a different plan. "I merely propose that you make a short detour to Drumlanrig Castle so that my kinsman, the duke, may thank you properly for your care of me. Would you really expect me to travel alone for the last leg of my journey? *Anything* can happen to a defenseless woman on the road. Highwaymen. A sudden rainstorm that would leave her stranded on the road and prey to any danger."

"It would be too bad of you, Papa!" cried Dorothea.

"Our dear mother, if she were still living, would be horrified," Marguerite said.

"Perhaps you can explain one of the mysteries of life

to me, Lady Constance," Sir Michael said. "I ask this for academic reasons only, since it is clear that I will comply with this proposal or risk having three females reproach me all the way to Dumfries."

"Two females," Catriona interrupted. He raised his eyebrow at her. "*I* would not reproach you. I think it is a silly idea."

"Only because it delights you to vex us," Marguerite said.

"Not true. There is too much work waiting for me at Dumfries if you are to have this party of yours in two weeks."

"Nonsense. A few invitations, a meeting with the cook, some flowers cut from the garden and the thing is done," Dorothea said airily. "Mr. Walbridge and I entertain often in London." She patted Catriona on the hand. "Do not worry about the party, Catriona. As hostess, I will arrange everything."

"*You* to be the hostess!" Marguerite exclaimed. "What makes *you* think that *you* are to be the hostess?"

"Why, I am the elder and much more experienced in entertaining guests than you are, my dear," Dorothea said loftily. Her smile hardened. "I would be surprised if the dowager Lady Redgrave allows you to have any say whatsoever in the arrangements at Redgrave House."

"It would make a very odd appearance to all the neighborhood if you were to be the hostess," Marguerite said just as loftily. "Unless you have forgotten, *I* am the wife of a viscount. That gives me precedence over you. Is that not true, Lady Constance?"

"I see no reason why you cannot both be hostesses," the elder lady said. She turned to Sir Michael and gave him a flirtatious little rap on the wrist. "But you, sir, were about to ask me a question."

"Was I?" he asked, bemused. Then he remembered where he was before the younger women began their squabble. "Ah, yes. I was wondering, Lady Constance, why the danger to a lady traveling with two stout foot-men and a maid *from* Edinburgh is fraught with so much more peril than the journey *to* Edinburgh by a woman intent upon visiting the shops."

"There are times, Papa, when you have no sensibility at all," Marguerite said as she embarked upon her third biscuit.

"None whatsoever," he agreed. "I am waiting for your answer, Lady Constance."

The elder lady's lips quirked in amusement.

"The truth, as your infallible gift for logic has already discerned," she said, "is that the peril is exactly the same."

"There now! An honest woman," Sir Michael said as he impulsively took her hand and kissed it.

"Except for the reluctance to part with such charming company so soon," she continued as she favored both Dorothea and Marguerite with fond smiles.

"Ah, check and mate," Sir Michael said. "My congratulations, Lady Constance. You have neatly vanquished all of my objections."

Both Dorothea and Marguerite gave little crows of delight.

"Thank you, Papa," Dorothea and Marguerite chorused.

"I knew you were too kind a gentleman to refuse," Lady Constance said approvingly. She included Catriona in her benevolent glance. "You will enjoy Drumlanrig Castle, Miss Grant. It is quite beautiful, and just now the duke has several bachelors staying with him, for the shooting is quite the best in Scotland."

Sir Michael burst out laughing.

"And what know you, my lady, of shooting?" he asked.

She laughed back at him.

"Nothing, of course. Only the word of his grace, who is inundated with sports-minded friends whenever he comes to Drumlanrig. He can barely escape to London in time for the season."

"Most gentlemen, my lady, would not refer to tolerating London with all its noise as an escape," Michael said. "It is only for ladies and their fervent devotion to gossip and the shops that London is an escape."

"You paint all women with the same brush," Catriona objected. "*I* do not prefer the noise of the city."

"Well, that makes you superior to all of us, doesn't it, dear?" Marguerite said tightly.

"I am certain I said nothing to indicate such a ridiculous sentiment," Catriona said with upraised brows. "We are all equal in the eyes of the Almighty."

Lady Constance put one white, pampered hand to her throat.

"My dear girl," she said, "I do hope you are not one of those tiresome persons who is going to bring the Deity into every conversation. If so, you will find yourself bereft of society at every gathering, I promise you. As for believing everyone is equal in the eyes of the Almighty, you cannot believe such twaddle."

"Certainly not," Catriona said. "Forgive me. It was a momentary lapse."

"You are forgiven, dear girl," Lady Constance said charitably. "I believe we are all a little weary. That is why it is an excellent idea to break our journey at Drumlanrig."

"Very true," Sir Michael said, forbearing to point out to the geographically creative Lady Constance that Drumlanrig was not precisely on the way to Dumfries and stopping there would mean that the travelers would be compelled to add at least thirty miles to their homeward journey. "And I will say that Lady Constance is perfectly right. Buccleuch does enjoy some of the best shooting in the country."

"All the pretty birds," Marguerite said reproachfully.

"And the ladies should be grateful for them, my sweet," Sir Michael said, "for they are far better bait in attracting unsuspecting bachelors than any of the delightful feminine arts husband-hunting predators find it in their power to employ."

"Sir Michael! Why did you not tell me this before?" Catriona cried. "I would have had Miss Cumerford trim my hats with more feathers."

CHAPTER 15

Catriona stared at her first glimpse of Drumlanrig Castle as it swept into view from the road, for never had she seen such a beautiful place. Constructed from pink sandstone, it featured a horseshoe staircase that swept to the first floor, a bell tower, and stone carvings over the windows.

"It is magnificent," she said to Lady Constance upon alighting from the carriage as Marguerite and Dorothea tried very hard not to look impressed. "Are you certain the duke will not mind if we stop here?"

"His grace is extremely hospitable," she said complacently. "He will be delighted."

The front door opened, and Charles Montagu Douglas-Scott, the Duke of Buccleuch, aged five-and-forty, came out of the house wreathed in smiles. He held out his hands to his cousin, who took them, and smiled at Dorothea and Marguerite.

"Welcome, Constance," he said. "How kind of you to bring such pretty ladies to my house."

"Good afternoon, dear Charles," she said, "may I present Sir Michael Stewart"—the gentlemen bowed to one another—"his daughters, Lady Redgrave and Mrs. Walbridge, and their cousin, Miss Grant. His Grace, the Duke of Buccleuch. Sir Michael and his party were kind enough to escort me here on their way to his estate near Dumfries."

"Your Grace," murmured the three ladies as they curtsied before him.

"Delighted," he said, looking pleased. "Do come in and have some refreshment after your journey. I have a horse of your breeding, Sir Michael. A splendid hunter and jumper."

"Yes, Your Grace. One of my Hanoverians," Sir Michael said as he and the duke drew back to allow the ladies to precede them into the house. To his annoyance, he noticed that of the four swaying, feminine forms before them, the duke's eyes rested longest on Catriona's, for she followed the three others. The veil of her hat in back gave a tantalizing view of the long, graceful nape of her neck.

"Yes. A chestnut. Perhaps you would like to put him through his paces tomorrow before you return to Dumfries. I would be honored if you and your party would stay for the night."

"Thank you, but I am eager to go home. The harvest, you know."

"Nonsense, Sir Michael," said Lady Constance, who was blessed with excellent hearing. "You cannot expect these young ladies to get back into the coach as soon as they have arrived, without an instant of rest. Surely you can depend upon your steward to see to your old crops."

"Papa, please!" cried Marguerite. "I would enjoy seeing more of this wonderful castle."

"As would I, Father," Dorothea added. "His grace is so kind to invite us."

The duke gave a bow of his head in acknowledgment.

"Shall we consider the matter settled?" the duke suggested to Sir Michael. "Do indulge this old bachelor and his guests with the sight of your daughters' pretty faces over the dining table. And Miss Grant's, too, of course."

"I rather imagine your guests will be put out to find they have to rig themselves out for dinner since the ladies will be present," Sir Michael said, "but how can I refuse? My girls will plague you with questions about the castle and your lofty ancestors, I warn you."

"The ancient Douglas stronghold," murmured Catriona.

"Quite right," the duke said, smiling at her. "Are you a scholar of Scots history, my dear?"

"An amateur only," she said demurely. "I have lived in Scotland only two years, but I quickly fell in love with its beauty and its tragic history."

Dorothea and Marguerite gave Catriona twin looks of horror and Michael hid a grin, for he knew there was nothing his girls found more dull than someone who prosed on and on about dusty old historical persons and places.

"Tragic, Miss Grant?" the duke said.

"Culloden, you know," she said.

"Um, yes. Do step into the house, Miss Grant," he said as he offered his arm, "and enlighten me further."

"Did you see the way she monopolized the duke over the tea table?" Dorothea whispered furiously to Marguerite later, when they and their father stood waiting for the housekeeper to conduct them to their rooms. The duke seemed to have conceived a fancy for Miss Grant, as she appeared to be a fountain of knowledge on various illustrious Douglases, Scotts, Montagus, and past Dukes of Buccleuch and of Queensberry, for their host was also the fifth duke of that Scottish peerage.

"It was not well done of her," Lady Constance said disapprovingly. "Since his wife died, poor Charles is continually pursued by women. It must be most annoying for him."

"He did not look annoyed to me," Sir Michael pointed out. "Perhaps his grace would like to make the girl his second wife and take her off my hands."

"What a silly thing to say," Dorothea huffed. "Then she

would take precedence over us all, and that would be intolerable."

"The Duke of Buccleuch take Miss Grant to wife? What an extraordinary idea!" Lady Constance said.

"Ah, here come the rest of the fellows," said the duke, who had been pointing out a portrait of historical interest to Catriona at some distance away when several other gentlemen entered the room. "You are finished shooting all the birds on my estate, are you?"

"Yes! You have not a one left," a tall, handsome man said cheerfully. "I hope you are going to introduce us to these pretty ladies."

"With pleasure," said the duke. "Sir Michael Stewart of Dumfries and his daughters were kind enough to escort Lady Constance from Edinburgh. Lady Redgrave and Mrs. Walbridge, you see before you my young friend and cousin, Mr. Walter Montagu, and his friends, Mr. Robert Wieland and Mr. Justin Sandhurst. And here is also Miss Grant, Sir Michael's relation by marriage."

Oddly, Catriona seemed to have conceived a passionate interest in the pattern of the draperies, for beyond one startled look at the gentlemen she had kept her back to them. She turned at the sound of her name, for good manners really left her no choice, and Michael was surprised when Mr. Montagu rushed across the room to take both of her hands in his.

"Lady Catriona! Can it be you?" he cried. "I have looked . . . That is to say, I was surprised when you disappeared so suddenly from London several years ago. No one seemed to know where you got to." His brow furrowed. "And why are you being introduced as Miss Grant? Are you traveling incognito?"

"If I were, you certainly have put paid to that!" she said tartly. "I have not been known as Lady Catriona for some time, and I do not wish to be addressed by that name now. As for where I have been, I have been here, in Scotland, nursing my cousin, who has since died."

"Nursing your cousin?" he said, perplexed. "I do not understand—"

Catriona made a hasty gesture to silence him, and Michael could see her color was high.

"I am sorry, Mr. Montagu," she said abruptly. "The matter is painful for me, for I was very much attached to my cousin."

"Of course," he said at once. "Forgive me."

"If you do not mind, Your Grace, I should like to go to my room now. I imagine all of us would," she said.

"Naturally you will want to rest before you change for dinner," the duke said. His eyes darted from her to Mr. Montagu, but mercifully his manners were too polished to permit him to ask for an explanation of this extraordinary scene. He caught the eye of the housekeeper, who was standing just inside the room. She stepped forward to lead the guests to their rooms.

"But, Lady Catriona—Miss Grant, that is," the young man blurted out. He forgot himself so much as to catch her hand in his as she passed him on the way to the doorway. "Is that all you have to say to me? I thought we were friends, you and I."

"I will thank you to unhand me, sir," Catriona said between her teeth, but Mr. Montagu refused to release her.

"Walter?" the duke said, looking displeased. "Miss Grant does not wish to be detained."

"My apologies," the young man said at once, and released her.

A flurry of knocking sounded at the door not five minutes after Catriona was installed in a bedchamber, and Marguerite and Dorothea came in. Their eyes were alight as they pounced on Catriona.

"Lady Catriona!" Dorothea cried. "Do forgive us. We had no idea your father is the Earl of Grantham. We just had the whole from Mr. Montagu."

"Your father is richer than the duke himself," Marguerite said. "Why did you not tell us who you are?"

Catriona gently extricated herself from Marguerite's grasp on her hand.

"Because I am not that person any longer."

"Lady Catriona—" Dorothea began.

"Please do not call me by that name, Mrs. Walbridge," Catriona said. "The Lady Catriona who left London two years ago no longer exists."

"You cannot mean that," Marguerite said. Her pretty face was flushed with embarrassment. "And to think we made you ride in the coach with our maids!"

"Think nothing of it," Catriona said with a faint smile. "I did not mind at all."

"But this is wonderful news," Dorothea said excitedly. "People will be clamoring for invitations to our party just for the honor of meeting you. It will be a sensation."

"Mrs. Walbridge, I beg of you—"

"My dear Lady Catriona," Dorothea said, "you must call me Dorothea. Are we not cousins?" She frowned. "*Are* we cousins?"

"Very distantly, but yes," Catriona said. "I beg you not to make a fuss about this."

"Not make a fuss! How can we not?"

"Well, if you do," Catriona said dryly, "you are going to be late for dinner. The first bell has already sounded."

"Oh, dear heavens!" cried Marguerite, alarmed. She took Catriona's hand. "Come, my dear. You must help me decide which of my gowns to wear. And I will have my maid dress your hair."

"Well, *I* shall lend you my emeralds to wear with your green evening gown," said Dorothea, not to be outdone in the matter of fawning over the rich earl's daughter.

CHAPTER 16

"I cannot tell you what a relief it is to learn of your real identity," Marguerite said to Catriona, who was now decked out in Dorothea's emeralds and wearing the light green evening gown Sir Michael's daughters had chosen for her in Edinburgh. "We have been so silly, Dorothea and I. We thought you had set your cap at Papa!"

She and Dorothea laughed gaily to show Catriona just how ridiculous this idea was.

"We thought we were protecting our father from a fortune-hunting little hussy," Dorothea said. "I hope you can forgive us for being less than welcoming, Lady Catriona."

"I am not—" Catriona broke off, deciding she might as well save her breath. "There is nothing to forgive."

"Your hair is such a lovely color. And your eyes are such a clear blue. It is plain to anyone with eyes that you are of noble birth. Gentlemen must have been lined up at your father's doorstep for the privilege of courting you. Heaven knows you can look much higher for a husband than a man old enough to be your father," Marguerite said.

"Sir Michael would have had to be a *very* precocious child to be my father," Catriona said, growing weary of all this flattery. She liked Dorothea and Marguerite better when they were being all superior to her. "He is only ten years older than I, you know."

Dorothea and Marguerite went off into shrill gales of

laughter in appreciation of her excellent wit. Catriona's sense of humor had been much praised while she lived under her father's roof, and now she surmised it was to be so again. It had been quite a shock to learn two years ago that she was not perceived to be nearly so clever by those who were unaware of her pedigree.

"Mr. Montagu is a very handsome man," Dorothea said slyly. "Was he one of your suitors? I feel sure he never quite got over his infatuation with you."

"I am almost certain he is married by now," Catriona said dryly. "I certainly hope he has done so."

"Pity," Marguerite said, "but there are lots of fish in the sea." She gave a bright smile of anticipation. "We may look as high among the peerage of Scotland for guests as we choose for our party, for everyone will want to meet you."

"I dearly love to give a party," Dorothea said with a sigh. She gave Catriona a friendly little tap on the shoulder. "I cannot wait to return to Papa's estate to begin the arrangements. We will have you engaged and married before the cat can lick her ear."

"There is the second dinner bell," Marguerite said before Catriona could reply to this. "Come along, or we shall be late. You look lovely, Lady Catriona. Truly lovely."

"Thank you," Catriona said, perfectly aware that the most potent beauty secret any woman could have was the discovery of an earl or two in her family tree. "But I thought we agreed we were to be cousins, Cousin Marguerite."

"So gracious," Marguerite murmured.

Yes, she had missed this, Catriona admitted to herself. The bowing. The scraping. The pretty clothes. The admiring looks of the young men.

She set her head at a regal angle and swept down the hall with Sir Michael's daughters following in her wake like acolytes.

All the gentlemen turned with appreciative smiles on

their faces when the three young ladies entered the room. Lady Constance, Catriona observed, was already there, involved in what appeared to be close conversation with Sir Michael.

"You naughty girl," Lady Constance said as she advanced, dimpling, on Catriona. Catriona was tempted to look behind her to see who she could possibly be greeting with such warmth and enthusiasm. "What a sly trick to play on us all. Mr. Montagu has told us your secret."

"*Has* he?" Catriona said, unsmiling. "And just what has Mr. Montagu told you?"

"That you are the daughter of the Earl of Grantham, of course," Mr. Montagu said as he came forward to take her hand and place a kiss just above her knuckles. "And that your father has given it out that you have been staying with relatives, first in the country and then abroad. And all the time you were in Scotland."

"In my family, Scotland *is* abroad," Catriona said. "And I was staying with relatives. One relative, in fact. This is perhaps an awkward matter to bring up, but I am estranged from my father. We have not spoken in years. I have no doubt that he has forgotten my very existence."

"I do not know your father, Lady Catriona," the duke said, "but I feel sure he regrets your estrangement."

Catriona smiled at him.

"Your kind heart does you justice, Your Grace," she said. "No doubt a fond father like yourself finds the situation unfathomable. Let it suffice to say that harsh words were spoken on both sides that can never be rescinded."

"It is very sad," Marguerite said. Incredibly, tears sparkled in her pretty dark eyes. "I would miss my father very much if I were estranged from him."

"And he would miss you, too, my dear," said Sir Michael as he put an arm around his daughter's shoulders and kissed her temple. "Never doubt it." Marguerite turned shining eyes to her father's face and Catriona was touched by the tenderness she saw there. Sir Michael took his free arm and gathered Dorothea into the circle of his embrace as well. "I could never disown either of my girls, no matter what they had done."

"Your daughters are fortunate, Sir Michael," Catriona said. She gave a tight smile. "This is, perhaps, an inappropriate subject for his grace's drawing room. Surely he and his guests do not wish to hear my family business. In truth, the subject is an awkward one for me."

"Of course, my lady," the duke said. "Please forgive our vulgar curiosity."

"You are forgiven, of course," she said with a regal inclination of her head. It was odd, she thought, how these haughty little gestures never entirely left one. They merely slept beneath the surface, waiting to emerge.

"Let us discuss instead the hunt party we will have in a few weeks' time," Dorothea said brightly. "Your Grace, I hope we can depend upon you to join us. Lady Constance has already been kind enough to offer her advice and assistance."

"It would be an honor," the duke said with a slight bow.

"And Mr. Montagu, Mr. Wieland, and Mr. Sandhurst will join us, too, I hope," Dorothea added graciously. "And your wives, of course."

"I fear that three sad bachelors stand before you," Mr. Wieland said gaily. "Perhaps we will find the ladies of our dreams at your party."

"Bachelors? All of you?" Catriona asked, startled. She was looking, of course, at Walter, who gave her a small smile and a nod. She felt her heart pound nearly out of her breast. "Surely you were to be married, Mr. Montagu?"

"I was betrothed to Miss Macy when we met in London, Lady Catriona, but she decided she would be happier married to some other man."

Catriona's gaze fell to her hands. She hoped no one noticed the color that she could feel stinging her cheeks.

"I was an inattentive fiancé, I fear," he continued. "It seemed some other lady had stolen my heart, and I never had quite been able to forget her."

Marguerite clasped her hands together.

"Oh, how romantic," she said as she gave Catriona a sly glance. "And where is the lady now, the one who stole your heart?"

"She was lost for a while," he said, gazing soulfully at Catriona. "But perhaps I have found her again."

"Well, this is certainly interesting," the duke said, amused. The butler announced dinner. "Lady Constance? May I escort you to dinner?" He smiled paternally at Catriona and Walter. "By strict precedence, it is Sir Michael who should have the honor of escorting Lady Catriona into the dining room, but I feel sure he will surrender this prerogative to my cousin, who would be grateful for an opportunity to renew his acquaintance with her."

"By all means," said Sir Michael as he nodded to Marguerite, who, as the next most important lady present, happily accepted his arm. Dorothea walked between Mr. Sandhurst and Mr. Wieland.

"I looked for you everywhere," said Walter in an urgent undervoice so only Catriona could hear.

"Mr. Montagu, please," she said, just as quietly. "This is neither the time nor the place."

"You are just as lovely as ever."

"Well, there is always the time and place for *that*, I suppose," she said, smiling.

He gave a peal of laughter.

"Ah, how I have missed your delightful sense of humor," he said.

It seemed, Catriona surmised, that there was no help for it. She was destined to be a wit once more.

"You do understand that my father has washed his

hands of me," she said. "He has a new wife and has rid his life of this unsatisfactory reminder of his former marriage. It is quite unnecessary for you to greet my every remark with such fulsome appreciation."

Mr. Montagu touched her hand as if in sympathy, although she had asked for none. Miss Grant might have appreciated the gesture. Lady Catriona, who had made her appearance on this stage a mere hour ago, considered it an act of presumption.

"I had heard of the marriage," Walter said. "An actress, I understand. Her name is—"

"I know her name, and I do not want to hear it now," Catriona said.

"As you wish," he said, smiling for the benefit of their auditors. "I had no desire to offend you."

"The estrangement between my father and me is hardly the stuff of light social discourse," she said. "I do not wish to address the subject again."

"Of course. Forgive me."

Mercifully, they had arrived at the dining room table, and Walter seated her at her appointed chair, some places closer to the duke at the head of the table than the humble Miss Grant would have warranted.

Through the first course, she was aware of their eyes upon her. She was tempted to slurp the soup, just because Lady Catriona could do so and elicit no response other than bland smiles. Since she was now a generally acknowledged wit, they would probably laugh with appreciation. For a moment she was sorely tempted to test the theory, but she could not bring herself to do so.

Everything was so lovely—the roses from his grace's hothouse on the snowy damask cloth on the dining-room table, the glitter of crystal and the soft glimmer of candlelight, the sixteenth-century paintings on the oak-paneled walls, the two fireplaces adorned by wood carvings, the glitter of the ladies' jewels. The way all eyes turned to her as if the sun had risen whenever she spoke the merest commonplace.

Yes, she had missed this.

She had missed it very much.

Walter was seated next to her, and the duke cast paternal glances her way. The dear man obviously imagined that he was a benign conspirator in reuniting a pair of long-lost lovers. Did he imagine that in promoting this pretty romance he was helping his young relative obtain a fortune at no expense to himself? If so, he—and Walter—were doomed to disappointment.

Lady Catriona Grantham at the age of six-and-twenty had a dowry of sixty thousand pounds in addition to a large portion of the personal fortune she would have inherited at her father's death. Miss Grant at the age of eight-and-twenty had only a small legacy from Mrs. Tilden, whom the Earl of Grantham had considered beneath his notice as one of his poor relations until he had need of a place to which to banish his unsatisfactory daughter.

The earl washed his hands of Catriona when she embarrassed him by breaking off her betrothal to the man he had chosen for her and demanding that she be permitted to marry Mr. Montagu instead. And he washed his hands of her again when, after a year with Mrs. Tilden, he decided she had learned her lesson and ordered her to return to the bosom of her family. She refused to leave Cousin Sophie, whose health had begun to fail, and return to heel.

Catriona could not leave Cousin Sophie when the old lady needed her most, and her reasons were not entirely altruistic. Only in Cousin Sophie's house had she experienced true freedom. She could speak her mind. She could express her tastes without wondering if they were lofty enough to be worthy of her elevated status in Society. And when an acquaintance laughed at her jokes, she knew it was from amusement rather than a wish to court favor with the rich heiress or her rich father.

In other words, Miss Grant knew who her friends were; Lady Catriona had not the faintest idea.

How ironic that a year after the earl had banished his only daughter from his life for the unpardonable sin of aspiring to marry beneath her, *he* married an actress, practically off the stage. It had been the food of the gossip columns for days. Then the happy couple settled into their social niche—the earl was no less rich and influential merely because he had married a woman of inferior pedigree, after all.

The earl now had an infant son to replace the sad disappointment that was Catriona. No doubt a spare heir would follow shortly.

No, that dowry was gone. Perhaps she should tell Walter so he would stop being charming and debonair and eat his soup so she could eat her own. The lobster bisque was quite delicious, and she wanted to give it her full attention. She had not tasted lobster bisque in years. Lady Catriona had ingested lobster bisque practically with her mother's milk. Miss Grant found the creamy taste a rare luxury.

Yes. She had missed this. Definitely.

Dinner was served à la Russe, in courses, and the duck and its elegant accompaniment of pâté de foie gras made her eyes widen.

"I told the duke of all your favorites," Walter murmured. "You see, I remember everything about you."

Pâté de foie gras. The most divine substance known to man or woman.

"If there are strawberries with cream as well, I shall expire from sheer bliss," she said.

An appreciative twitter of amusement rippled along both sides of the table.

"From my very own hothouse," the duke said with a smile. "But first, perhaps, you will have a taste of the roasted chicken stuffed with green grapes and walnuts and served with a sauce of oranges and cherries."

"With very great pleasure," she said, "although if we do not leave your board soon, all the seams will have to be let out of the lovely gowns we just purchased in Edinburgh."

Amazingly, this vulgar remark, when uttered by Lady Catriona, ascended the heights of wit, and everyone laughed.

"How amusing, dear Lady Catriona," Dorothea gushed. "How I envy you your lovely figure."

Another ripple of appreciation started around the table with one exception—Sir Michael looked far from amused.

"Do not be silly, Dorothea," he snapped. He practically glowered at Catriona. "You are perfect exactly the way you are." He glanced at his other daughter. "As are you, Marguerite."

"Thank you, Father," Dorothea said, surprised by his vehemence.

"Well!" Catriona said, wondering what ailed the man. "Now that Sir Michael has determined that I am not perfect . . ."

"There are enough men fawning over you already," he said. "I have no wish to add to their number."

Eyebrows rose all along the table at this rudeness.

Oddly, Catriona found his candor quite refreshing, and she had been back in her old world for the space of only a little more than an hour.

"Sir Michael, I am desolated," she said, smiling. "I see that none of my arts will be of use in luring you to my court of admirers."

It was so easy, the seemingly careless banter that held a whisper of steel at its core.

"Montagu is attentive enough to make up for my absence," he said.

Silence greeted this remark. Walter seemed uncertain

whether to address this reference to himself or to ignore it.

"True," Catriona said. She smiled at that young man and had the satisfaction of seeing Sir Michael's frown deepen, but her smile hardened when she felt Walter's hand tentatively touch her knee. Still smiling, she rapped his knuckles with her fan so hard that the gesture could not be taken for flirtation.

"Beg pardon," he whispered and removed the offending hand from her knee.

"So I should hope," she whispered back.

"I lost my head."

"You are going to lose that hand if you do not take care."

Predictably, he laughed as if she were the keenest wit in Christendom.

Why had she not noticed two years ago that his laughter resembled the braying of a horse?

Now when Sir Michael laughed—*really* laughed—it was a deep, warm sound that came from the chest and made his eyes crinkle with good humor. *That* was how a man should laugh.

Sir Michael was not laughing now. He was listening to Dorothea, who was talking to him over Mr. Sandhurst, but Catriona suspected his sour expression had nothing to do with this violation of dining-table etiquette.

"You must invite Mr. Montagu and these gentlemen to pay a visit to us in Dumfries," Dorothea said. "I am certain Mr. Montagu and Lady Catriona would appreciate the opportunity to renew their acquaintance."

"They have been ogling one another for nearly an hour," he groused. "I would say the acquaintance has been renewed."

"Oh, Papa. Do not be such an old grump," Marguerite said. "It is a charming idea." She fixed her big, dark eyes on Walter. "I am certain it would be a charitable act to take him and his friends away from Drumlanrig before they deplete the entire feathered population of the duke's grounds."

"And I am certain the gentlemen would enjoy looking at your stud, Father," Dorothea added. "Papa's Hanoverians are quite famous."

"I should enjoy that," Walter said heartily as he gave Catriona's hand a squeeze under cover of the table. She quickly snatched her hand away, and as she did, she saw Sir Michael's eyes narrow. That caused her to favor Walter with a smile instead of a frown.

It was a wonder how all of Lady Catriona's old guile immediately asserted itself once the forthright Miss Grant had been banished.

CHAPTER 17

When Michael went into the breakfast room the next morning dressed for the journey home, he found only Catriona waiting for him, when it had been agreed that his daughters, as well, would arise early so they could set forth early for Dumfries.

Catriona looked up at him with a look of mild inquiry in her big, blue eyes when he crossed the room to loom over her. She was wearing a dark blue traveling costume with a wide notched velvet collar and a stylish hat set at a rakish angle on her blond curls.

How could he not have known she had been bred to every privilege? There never had been anything the least subservient in her manner toward him or any other person. Her carriage was aristocratic and her speech was impeccable. She had worn her simple gowns with the assurance of a queen. Dressed in fashionable clothing, she was extraordinary.

She raised one well-shaped eyebrow.

"Good morning, Sir Michael. May I pour you a cup of tea?"

Irrationally, her civil greeting made him furious.

"What you may do, young woman, is tell me what sort of a game you are playing! Since you are living under my roof, I have every right to inquire into your motives."

"I do not play games," she said, looking straight up into his eyes. "You know me that well, I should hope."

"I *thought* I did. That was before I learned that you gained entry to my house under false pretenses."

"False pretenses? Hardly. As for my motives, they are exactly what they always have been—to honor Cousin Sophie's wishes by putting your house in order. And to obtain gainful employment for myself. Nothing more."

"Did she know the truth about you?"

"Cousin Sophie? She knew the only truth that mattered, that I was in disgrace with my father and needed a temporary roof over my head. I brought with me a letter from my father, who really is her distant cousin, and a modest purse to pay for my keep. She thought at first that I was with child and needed a bolt-hole, for why else would a young lady be sent by her father to a distant relative? She even fussed over me for a time because she thought I was in a delicate condition." She gave a sad, reminiscent smile. "I believe she was disappointed when she learned the truth. Cousin Sophie was excessively fond of babies."

"And how long did you expect this imposture to last? I do not understand what you meant to gain from it."

"Perhaps, as your daughters suspected, I intended to trap you into marriage all the time," she said.

"You mock me," he said bitterly.

"I do not. Do stop looming over me in that threatening fashion. I am going to get an ache in my neck from looking up at you. You are not intimidating me in the least."

"A mere baronet hardly has the power to do that, has he, *Lady* Catriona?"

She gave a short laugh.

"You would be surprised how much power you have over me," she said. "All right. If you will not sit, I will stand." She rose, and before he could step back, she put her gloved hands on his shoulders.

"See here," he said in consternation. "What are you about?"

He could smell the faint floral scent of her perfume. It made him slightly dizzy. Then she put her hand on the back of his head to pull his face to hers and kissed him.

He should have drawn away, but he could not. She was all sweetness and fire as he plundered her soft, lush mouth.

When he broke off the kiss so they could breathe, they just stood looking at one another. Her eyes were shining like sapphires.

"Lady Catriona, forgive me," he said, horrified by what he had done. "That should not have happened."

Incredibly, she leaned back against her chair and smiled at him.

"You have been wanting to kiss me like that for two years," she said.

He opened his mouth to deny it, but he could not.

"I have done my best to hide it," he said. "I am almost old enough to be your father."

"You are not," she snapped. "And if you were, I would not care."

"You do not know what you are saying."

"I beg your pardon, Sir Michael," she said. "I know *exactly* what I am saying. And do not say that this is all so sudden, for it is not. You have been trying *not* to kiss me for two years. And I have been waiting all this time for you to lose the struggle."

"I had no idea you knew," he said. Oddly, it was almost a relief now that the truth was out.

"I knew because I felt the same. Why do you think I did not go back to London a year ago, when my father decreed that my period of banishment was over, my sentence was served and I could resume my career as a pampered young lady? London had no attraction for me when the two people I loved most in the world lived here. So he washed his hands of me all over again."

"Catriona, my dear. You cannot love me. You are young. You are beautiful. You are well born."

Anger blazed from her eyes. She was so glorious in her fury that he badly wanted to kiss her again. He stepped away and gripped the back of a chair so he could keep his hands off her.

"I knew that would be your reaction if you learned the truth about my birth," she cried. "I *knew* it! That is why I did not tell you. I thought that if I bided my time, eventually you would declare yourself to Catriona Grant, Mrs. Tilden's caretaker. There was not the remotest possibility that you would declare yourself to Lady Catriona Grantham."

"There was not the remotest possibility that I would declare myself to either one of you," he said. "Seduce a young woman in my employ? Only a cad would do so. Make a fool of myself by offering for an earl's daughter? Never. He would laugh in my face for the presumption, a man of my age."

"My father has nothing to say to the matter," she said, "but he would be a complete hypocrite if he dared look down on your suit because of your age or birth. His wife is an actress, after all. He certainly can afford to forget I exist now that he has a son."

Michael sensed the hurt in her voice despite her bravado and could not stop himself from cupping her soft cheek in his hand. He did draw the line at kissing her again, even though she leaned forward expectantly.

"Your father is a fool," he said, "and not for marrying a young woman. A man's son is his pride, but a man's daughter is his heart."

Her eyes misted.

"Oh, Michael," she said. "It is no wonder that I love you." She bit her lip. "I meant to give you time to become accustomed to the idea before I said it right out loud. You have a way of seeing into a person's heart."

"I am a father," he said gently. "What you feel for me—"

"Do *not* say it!" she cried as she put her arms around

his neck. "Do *not*! This is not a silly infatuation. I had a silly infatuation. It caused my father to send me to Scotland. What I feel for you is not the same. This is love."

"I am not one of your beaux that you can toy with," he said as he extricated himself from her.

"One of my beaux! What are you talking about? You have known me for two years. In that time I lived with Cousin Sophie, and after that I lived with you. Did you see any beaux dancing attendance on me in all that time?"

"You certainly made up for it tonight with Mr. Montagu, Mr. Wieland, and Mr. Sandhurst. The three of them were ogling you as if they were starving wolves and you—"

"The only one staring at me like a starving wolf at dinner, Sir Michael, was you."

"You are mad. They could not take their eyes off you."

"They could not take their eyes off Lady Catriona Grantham! Not me. Do you think any of them would give me a second glance if I truly were Miss Catriona Grant? I promise you that when the truth comes out that Lady Catriona Grantham no longer has a dowry of sixty thousand pounds, their ardor will cool as if a jug of cold water had been poured on it."

Michael had to put his hands behind his back to keep from touching her.

"I feel sure you are mistaken," he said, "but I am also sure your father would be eager to reconcile if you will give him a chance."

"It is he who would not give *me* a chance," she said wryly, "and I never thought to feel grateful to him. If he had not sent me to Scotland, I might have been married to another by now. And I never would have met you."

"But your father—"

Catriona put her hand on his.

"Sir Michael," she said softly. "Do you not understand what I am saying to you?"

"Of course I understand," he said, nettled. "You do me much honor, but I am too old for you."

"Marguerite's husband is at least ten years older than she is. And Dorothea's is not much younger."

"That is different. The girls *wanted* to marry them."

"Well, I should like to marry *you*, if you would be kind enough to ask me," she said smiling.

"You do not know what you are saying," he said softly, "and it is cruel of you to tempt me."

"Am I tempting you?" she said mischievously as she put her hands on his shoulders again.

He caught her wrists to put her away from him, but somehow he couldn't make himself let go of them.

"You know you are," he said, frowning even though she looked adorable and she bloody well knew it. "It is not well done of you."

Dorothea and Marguerite stepped into the room but came to a shocked standstill when they saw their father clutching Lady Catriona's wrists. He quickly released Lady Catriona and walked to them.

"There you are," he said in his most patriarchal voice. They were not much younger than Lady Catriona. Not really. What had he been thinking of to kiss her like that?

"Papa, we must be on our way," Marguerite said. He did not know whether to regret or be grateful for his daughters' tardiness. If they had arrived for breakfast at the agreed-upon time, he would never have kissed her.

"You have not had your breakfast," Lady Catriona said. Her voice sounded odd, and by the way his daughters' eyes narrowed, he knew they had noticed it.

"There is no hurry," he said. "We can wait until you have eaten."

"We had chocolate and sweet biscuits upon rising, as always, Papa," Dorothea said reproachfully.

Marguerite moved to his other side, and between the two of them, his daughters managed to separate him from Lady Catriona.

"Lady Catriona," Dorothea said. "I hope you will ride with us in the first coach and keep us company. Papa, of course, will want to travel on horseback."

Her pointed look at her father made it clear that this was not merely an observation. It was a command.

Lady Catriona gave a regal inclination of her head.

"It would be a great pleasure," she said.

"We must get right to work on the guest list for the party," Marguerite said. "Of course we must invite that charming Mr. Montagu." She looked at Lady Catriona from the corner of her eye. "He was most attentive to you last night. And he asked me if he might call on us in Dumfries."

"In Dumfries?" Lady Catriona said, frowning. "What on earth would he be doing in Dumfries?"

Dorothea gave a pretty tinkle of laughter.

"Calling on you, of course, you sly thing," she said. "What else?"

"I have not the slightest interest in Mr. Montagu, if that is what you are hinting," Lady Catriona said.

"Perhaps not," Marguerite said, "but the gentleman certainly is interested in *you*."

CHAPTER 18

It was just after dawn, and Sir Michael, Catriona discovered, had spent most of the night in the barn, where his most valuable mare had finally given birth to twin foals with the utmost difficulty. With barely enough strength to shrug himself out of his coat, he had stumbled into his study and collapsed into his favorite leather chair, where he promptly fell asleep and was snoring softly with his mouth open.

Catriona found him there, and she supposed it said much for the power of her affection for the stubborn man that she found the sight of him—even the rather gamey smell of him—endearing. There were little lines at the corners of his eyes made from laughter or squinting into the sun. His sensual, finely chiseled lips were drawn down at the corners in an exhausted frown.

How she wanted to lean over the back of his chair, kiss the top of his head, and put her arms around his neck.

As if he had heard her thought aloud, he smiled in his sleep. Then he opened his eyes and looked at her.

"Lady Catriona," he said, straightening at once. He blinked. "What are you doing up and about at this hour?"

"The question, Sir Michael, is why you have not yet been to bed."

"My mare—"

"Yes, I know all about your precious mare and your precious twin foals. I feel certain your stablemaster and grooms are taking splendid care of them all. Stand up. You must go to bed at once. You cannot be very comfortable here."

He shook his head.

"No time. I will rest here awhile, and then I must—"

"Go to bed," she finished for him. She grasped his hand and tugged until he got reluctantly to his feet. She fitted her shoulder under his so she could get her arm around his waist. "Come along, now."

He looked absolutely befuddled.

"What are you doing?" he asked. His voice cracked at the end of the sentence.

"Helping you to your bedchamber, since you are apparently too exhausted to get there under your own power."

"But my horses . . . and the harvest," he said groggily.

"You have taken care of your horses, your servants, your daughters, and me this age, Michael. It is time someone took care of you." Catriona guided him toward the door.

"I do not need anyone to take care of me," he said. "I am a grown man."

"For a grown man, you are using extremely poor judgment if you think you can stay up all night birthing foals and spend all day directing the harvest without so much as an hour's sleep. Have you forgotten that your guests will be arriving in two days?"

"Two days," he repeated vaguely.

"Yes, and I am afraid I cannot permit you to linger in your study. The village girls and I are turning it out along with all the rooms on this floor today. You would be very much in the way."

He frowned and jerked her to a stop.

"You already cleaned this room. I remember."

"That was weeks ago, before we went to Edinburgh," she said as she tugged him forward and after a moment he fell into step beside her. "It must be cleaned again before the guests come. And after that, we will start on the bedchambers, which is all the more reason for you to go to sleep now and arise at midday and take yourself out of the house so we can turn out your bedchamber and change the linens."

"I was insane to agree to this party," he muttered.

"Quite possibly, but it is too late to repine now," she said briskly. "The invitations went out as soon as we returned from Edinburgh, and the guests from farther afield are already on their way. Come along. No time to dawdle. I have much to do today."

He stopped again and peered into her face.

"You look like a housekeeper again," he said with a frown.

"That is because I *am* a housekeeper for the present."

"No. You are the daughter of the earl. And our guest."

"A guest!" she said with a laugh. "I am hardly that, and you should be grateful for it. Your daughters, despite their enthusiasm for entertaining on a grand scale, are of no use whatsoever in preparing a household for a large party. We cannot all be merely decorative, alas."

"It is hardly fitting for you to work—"

"Michael, we have been through all this," she said impatiently. "Just because I am the daughter of an earl does not change anything between us. I am still bound by my promise to Cousin Sophie to take care of you and your household until you marry."

"Too old to marry," he muttered.

"Well, then, I suppose that means I will be here forever," she said airily as she gave him a gentle shove to get him moving again.

They were about halfway up the stairs when Sir Michael stumbled and nearly sent them both tumbling. Only his grip on the railing and his desperate grab at Catriona at the critical moment saved them from disaster.

Catriona had closed her eyes and tensed her body for a fall only to find herself caught around the waist and encircled in one of Sir Michael's strong arms. He was supporting them both with the death grip of his other hand on the railing. When she looked up into his face, she saw hunger in his eyes.

"You are so beautiful," he said.

At last, she thought with relief as she raised her lips in anticipation.

He was going to kiss her. She just knew it.

Then the railing gave an ominous creak under his hand.

Instead of taking advantage of her vulnerable position and kissing her as she could tell he sorely wanted to do, he straightened so he was no longer dependent upon the railing for support and let go of Catriona as soon as he saw she was steady on her feet.

"You had better stand back from me," he said. "I am too heavy for you to support."

"You should have thought of that when you refused to hire a valet as Dorothea suggested," she snapped in her disappointment. The man was determined to be chivalrous, blast him!

"Don't need a valet," he said.

"Every gentleman needs a valet to keep his clothing and linen in order, to dress him for parties, and to help him to bed when he is in his cups or was foolish enough to stay up all night in the horse barn," Catriona said. "Unfortunately, there is no time now to hire one before the party."

"No," he said when she would have taken his arm again. "I can go up the stairs myself."

"Very well, then. I shall follow at a distance."

"You will go first."

He was afraid he would carry her along with him if he stumbled again, she realized, and her heart turned over. Dear Sir Michael. Always thinking of everyone but himself.

"As you wish," she said, since, after all, she had won the argument. He was on his way to bed, just as she ordered him. Once there, he threw himself across the bed, closed his eyes, and would have gone right to sleep if Catriona had not taken one of his boots and tugged it off.

"What are you doing?" he demanded in sleepy alarm.

"Do not worry," she said, as she tugged off the other boot. "Your footgear is all I intend to remove. Do take care with the counterpane. There is not time to launder and dry it before the guests come."

"Desist, woman," he said grumpily. "No one is going to see my bedchamber, I assure you."

"The ladies will want to see every inch of the house, according to Dorothea and Marguerite. You have not entertained in so long that all the world is longing for a peek at the place."

"What utter nonsense," he said thickly.

"Do not worry about it," she said as she smoothed a dark lock of damp hair from his brow and took advantage of his half-asleep state to brush a soft caress against his cheek. She even found his whisker stubble endearing. "I will take care of everything."

Michael awoke some hours later with a stiff neck and a deep sense of embarrassment. He was very much afraid that the rather strong barnyard odor in the room was emanating from him. Lady Catriona had, out of the kindness of her heart, guided his tottering, geriatric steps to bed and was nearly hurtled down the stairs to her death.

Had she been injured, he never would have forgiven himself.

And to compound his embarrassment, he had almost kissed her. She had been so beautiful. It had been heaven to have her in his arms again.

But she was young, well born, and he was certain that her father, the earl, would eventually come forth to claim and dower her so she could contract the brilliant marriage that was her destiny by birth and fortune. The deluded lady had somehow fixed upon him as a prospective bridegroom, but she would regret marrying him before the wedding cake had gone stale.

What could he offer her, really?

Two daughters who would fight her to the death for their share of the rather unremarkable Stewart family jewels that would rightfully belong to his wife.

A country estate over which to preside in Scotland, far from the fashionable parties and shops in London that ladies so delighted in.

The duty of caring for her husband through his doddering old age and last illness, just as she had spent the last two years caring for Mrs. Tilden.

Her position as Lady Stewart would be poor compensation for such inconveniences. She deserved a duke or an earl, at least. How could Michael allow her to throw herself away on him?

Michael pulled on his boots and decided to avoid for the moment the beguiling dilemma that was Lady Catriona by going out to the horse barn to see how the new mother and foals fared.

He forgot his resolve to avoid the woman who occupied most of his thoughts, however, when he heard a clattering from the adjoining room, his late wife's boudoir, which everyone in the household knew must *never* be violated. He threw open the door to find that this shrine to his lost wife was in the process of being flagrantly desecrated by the annoying female who was determined to drive him mad.

Never mind that last night—or rather this morning—he would have given his eyes for just one kiss from those soft, tempting lips. Now he could have cheerfully wrung her neck. He clenched and unclenched his hands to keep from doing that very thing.

"What the deuce do you think you are doing?" he bellowed at the women. All but one gave startled bleats of

terror and fled from the room. The remaining culprit
put her hands on her hips and faced him with narrowed,
belligerent eyes.

"I am giving this room a thorough cleaning, as someone should have done decades ago," Catriona bellowed
right back.

He clenched and unclenched his hands again. If only
she knew how close he was to committing violence.

"You have disturbed her things," he said, indicating
the table that had once held his wife's glass perfume jars.
The counterpane and linens had been taken away, and
her clothes had been taken from the wardrobe and
placed on the naked mattress. Among them were her
wedding dress and the negligee she had worn on their
wedding night. "How dare you?"

"For pity's sake, Sir Michael, even the bishop allows
the altar at Canterbury to be dusted now and again," she
said, completely unintimidated by his anger. "This excessive homage to your late wife is touching but rather
unwholesome, if you will permit me to say so."

"I will *not* permit—"

"You do no honor to her memory by allowing this filth
to settle on her earthly possessions. I expected it to be
dusty, but you would not credit the dirt and the cobwebs
and the dead insects. Her shoes are dried and brittle
from neglect, and her woolens are being eaten by insects. Her beautiful gowns are stiff with filth and damp.
And the linens and counterpane were a disgrace."

"You had no right—"

"It is the finest bedchamber in the house, and it
stands neglected and unused in all this time. Well, all
this sentimentality is very well, sir, but we must have
every spare room for guests. Do you have any idea how
many people your daughters have invited to this precious party?"

"I neither know nor care," he said, trembling in his

anger. "No other woman shall sleep in this room. I have made a vow on this, and I will not break it."

"No, you will not break it," the little harpy shouted right back at him. "Heaven forbid that a living, breathing woman should take the place of your dead wife. You would have to live and breathe again as well, would you not? And you would have to admit that your precious Clarissa was nothing but a weak, spoiled, shallow little fool who did not half deserve you."

Catriona put both hands over her mouth, too late to keep the terrible words from escaping. Sir Michael cast one hand out toward the door.

"You have crossed the line, madam. Leave my house."

Her eyes went wide.

"Leave your—just where do you expect me to go?"

"I neither know nor care," he said, turning his back on her. "Leave me, Catriona. Pack your things. I do not want to see you again."

"You do not mean this," she said softly.

"I do. Go now," he said.

With that, she bit her lip and fled from the room.

"And tell those girls to stay *out* of this room!" he shouted after her.

When she was gone, he sat on the bed and took his wife's pink cashmere bedjacket in his hands. It had been so soft and pretty when he purchased it for her. She had complained of the cold dampness of the winter nights, and this had made her happy. Now it was dull, and there were little holes in the sleeve. But when he buried his face in it, he imagined he could still smell her perfume.

Clarissa was gone. And now Catriona soon would be gone.

At last, he would have the pushy little baggage out of his house.

He was glad, he told himself determinedly. Everything would return to normal now. Once their wretched party was over, his girls would go back to London and their fashionable lives and he would have his solitary life back with no interfering females to distract him from his work and drive him to madness.

With a sigh of what he told himself was sheer relief, he doggedly began hanging his dead wife's clothes back in her wardrobe. And although it took a quarter of an hour, he lined her perfume bottles back on the vanity to fit the little circles left by their removal so that all looked the same again.

The bare mattress mocked him.

He looked about himself in dismay and wondered how he could have been so blind. The hangings and the carpet were gray with dust. The dressing table, wardrobe, and vanity table of which Clarissa had been so proud were dull, and the neglected wood was probably warped. The perfume bottles, despite his best effort to get them back in the same order as his wife had arranged them all those years ago, looked wrong.

He had vowed to keep the room exactly as she had left it only to see Catriona was right. It was not the same. It would never be the same. Catriona had pulled the draperies aside and opened the windows to let the unforgiving light of day enter the room. Now he could see it clearly: Clarissa's boudoir was not a tribute to her beauty or to his faithfulness. It had not been for a long time. It was a grotesque mockery of its former luxury and charm. The fastidious Clarissa, if she could come from heaven to revisit her old home, would be appalled by it.

She was dead, dead, dead. And if her spirit did still exist on some unearthly plane, the last place it would choose to visit was this house in Scotland that she found so remote and uncomfortable in life despite the fact that the man who adored her beyond all reason and still grieved for her sought to make a shrine of it to his lost love.

His wife was dead. His children were married and

would soon return to their husbands. He was lonely. He had been for some time, but not until now did he truly feel it.

Blast Lady Catriona! Thanks to her, his last comfort was gone.

CHAPTER 19

Fuming, Catriona packed every one of the beautiful garments Sir Michael's daughters had purchased for her.

Perhaps a better woman would have taken only the plain, practical gowns she had brought with her, but if she had to leave her benefactor's house on his whim, the least he owed her was a decent wardrobe. She had worked herself to the bone in his house for weeks, and she had not been paid a shilling for her pains.

"Where are you going?" asked Dorothea as she walked into the room with Marguerite right behind her.

"I have been banished for daring to desecrate your mother's sacred boudoir by proposing to clean it," she said bitterly as she folded a green muslin day gown.

"Where will you go?" Marguerite asked.

Catriona gave a shrug.

"I hope you are not going to pretend that you care. It would be unworthy of you," she said.

"No need to snap at Marguerite," Dorothea said coolly. "She was always the one with the tender heart. She is imagining you starving in a gutter, and with the slightest encouragement she will no doubt bestow a modest purse and her second-best coat upon you."

"But not you," Catriona said, amused in spite of herself.

"Not I," Dorothea said, "for I do not believe for a moment that you intend to starve in a gutter. You are going to go to your father, of course. It is what any sensible woman would do."

Catriona stared at her.

"Do not tell me you did not think of it yourself," Dorothea said in disgust. "Really, Lady Catriona, I had formed a better opinion of your powers of reason. I thought you were more clever than that."

"I will admit it seems the most sensible plan, much as it galls me to admit that is my intention. My father does not want me back. Not that I plan to give him any choice."

"Do not be ridiculous. Of course he wants you back, if for no other reason than to come over the generous father willing to take his penitent daughter back into the family bosom. You will have to swallow your pride, I expect."

Catriona gritted her teeth.

"I shall not find that very pleasant after vowing never to darken his door again," she said grimly.

Marguerite burst into laughter.

"No, you did not tell him so," she said, highly amused. "Even I would not be so melodramatic."

"I was much addicted to Minerva Press novels at the time," Catriona said dryly.

"Oh, I have *all* of them," Marguerite said. "In London. Once you are established in your father's house, you will call on me and I will lend them to you."

"Will you? Will you indeed?" Catriona asked, absurdly touched. "That would be very kind. I will be certain to leave my card."

Catriona felt her lower lip tremble. How ridiculous! Was she about to weep in sheer sentimentality because one of Sir Michael's daughters had made a tepid overture of friendship to her? She got control of her emotions by firmly telling herself that Marguerite only wished to ingratiate herself with the Earl of Grantham's daughter.

"Do so," Marguerite said cordially.

Catriona cocked her head at her.

"You do know, do you not, that I am in love with your father?"

"Of course we know it," Dorothea said. "We are not stupid. But I am sure you will agree that Lady Constance is a much more suitable match for him."

"It is true that she is past childbearing age and you need not fear that she will give birth to a son to cut you out of your inheritance."

"Oh, Catriona, you silly creature," Marguerite said. "Papa is so fair, he would never admit a preference for a son to his daughters. The boy would get this horrid estate and all his horses, and he is more than welcome to them, but Dorothea and I would get an equal share of his fortune. Papa would not have it any other way."

"Then what does Lady Constance have to recommend her as a stepmother that I do not?" Catriona asked. Oddly, she felt no resentment. She simply wanted to know.

"It is the sheer absurdity of the situation," Dorothea explained. "Can you see us being compelled to defer to a little brother as the head of the family after our father's death? Papa would have to appoint a guardian for the little fellow, and he would have trustees, and we would have to see to his education and all. Papa has never cared particularly about the title, nor do we. Now if he had been an earl, like your father, we could style ourselves as Lady Marguerite and Lady Dorothea. But he is a mere baronet, and baronets are as common in London as weeds are in a kitchen garden. The title will go to a cousin, one of whom Papa is quite fond, actually, so that is all right. And if the children of his new wife were girls, it would be even more ridiculous. In addition to finding husbands for our own daughters, we would have to find husbands for *them*."

"And there is the embarrassing gossip to be endured," Marguerite added. "Everyone would think he is a senile old man to marry a young woman in a vain attempt to recapture his youth, and they would *pity* us. It would all be so undignified. So, Lady Constance, you see, is really the best solution. And she *is* related to the Duke of Buccleuch and Queensberry."

Catriona shook her head in grudging amusement.

"I owe you a great debt," she said.

"For the clothes? Do not mention it," Marguerite said generously. "If not for our shopping excursion to Edinburgh, this visit would have been quite without amusement."

"Oh, I did not mean the clothes, although I am most grateful for them," Catriona said. "I mean for making me laugh. I certainly did not expect to laugh at all today."

"A pleasure," Dorothea said as she arched one shapely brow at her. She gave Catriona's bulging portmanteau a dubious look. "You will never get the half of them in there. Do permit me to lend you one of my trunks."

"I am not certain when I can return it," Catriona said.

Dorothea gave an airy wave of her hand.

"Do not worry about it, my dear."

"It is well worth the loss of a trunk to see the back of me?" Catriona suggested.

"See. I knew you were clever," Dorothea said approvingly.

It was well past polite calling hours when Catriona arrived at her father's town house in a hackney carriage.

"Good evening, Langley," she said to the majestic butler who answered the door, for all the world as if she had left the house for the space of only an hour instead of two years. "Has my father retired for the night?"

"No, Lady Catriona, he has not," Langley said without a blink of emotion, even though he had known her from a child. So dignified a retainer would hardly be so vulgar as to remark upon her prolonged absence. "May I take your coat?"

"Please," she said with a misty smile at him in gratitude for his introducing the semblance of normalcy to her homecoming. "I have a trunk and a portmanteau in the carriage. And the driver will have to be paid off."

"I shall take care of it at once, Lady Catriona," he said. "His lordship is in his study. Perhaps you will join him. If you wish, I can instruct the cook to assemble some sort of meal for you."

"I would appreciate it, Langley, thank you."

With that, she braced herself and went in search of her father. She had not written to tell him she was coming home for it was best, she thought, to take him by surprise.

When she opened the door to the study, however, it was she who was surprised.

She had expected to see him sitting alone and smoking a cheroot as he indulged in an after-dinner brandy. Instead, he was laughing back at a drooling infant he was dandling on his knee as a very pretty dark-haired woman looked adoringly at the both of them. Her stepmother, Catriona presumed.

She was a relatively famous actress, one whom Catriona had seen on the stage a number of times before she and her father had their falling-out.

"Catriona!" the earl exclaimed as he nearly unseated the infant.

"Father," Catriona said, tight lipped, although she hadn't taken her eyes off the woman.

"What are you doing here?" her father asked.

"Perhaps I should tell you in private."

"Permit me to introduce you to Elvira, Lady Grantham, your stepmother, and Christopher, your half brother."

Catriona exchanged a wary nod with Lady Grantham and gazed speculatively at the baby boy, who had been scooped into to his mother's arms and was gazing just as speculatively back at her.

"I hardly believed it when I saw it in the newspapers," Catriona said wonderingly.

The earl thrust out his chin in warning. Catriona could not help noticing he looked ten years younger than he had before she left his home.

"If you have anything to say about my marriage," he said with soft menace in his tone, "you will say it to me, and *only* to me." He put his hand on his wife's shoulder, and the woman ducked her head as if in embarrassment. Catriona could not help but smile. The woman always had been a very good actress, and she didn't believe for a moment she truly was embarrassed.

"You fell in love," Catriona said.

"Completely. Hopelessly. Forever," he said with a fond squeeze of his wife's shoulder. "Elvira was not always an actress. She came from good family that fell upon hard times, and in order to survive she—"

Catriona held one hand up to stop him from completing the hackneyed excuse. Lord, had the woman any pride or originality at all?

Not that it mattered.

"It is not for me to judge," Catriona said with a smile at her new stepmother. "So, you fell in love. How delightful."

"Now I know how great an injustice I did you in separating you from Mr. Montagu," the earl said. "I am delighted that you have come home at last. I have long wished to mend this rift between us, and if there is anything I can do to promote your happiness—"

"As a matter of fact, my dear father, there is," Catriona said thoughtfully.

"Anything. Just name—"

"Later," she said as she turned to her new stepmother. "What a delightful child." A baby brother. How amazing. She put a finger on the boy's soft cheek. "You will permit me to hold him, will you not? I have not known many children, but I think I could grow quite fond of this one." She took the baby in her arms at her stepmother's reluctant nod of acquiescence. "Yes, I could. Grow very fond of you," she said in a singsong voice that made the baby bounce and drool a bit more. "Do you know, Papa? I believe he has a great look of you."

"Do you honestly think so?" Lord Grantham said, pleased.

"That is just what I have been telling him, Lady Catriona," said her stepmother eagerly.

"Oh, I think this will be a jolly house from now on," Catriona said as she kissed the soft, dark peach fuzz on the top of the boy's head. "I am glad I came home."

"Then you will stay?" her father asked hopefully.

"But of course," Catriona said, smiling. "Anyway, I have no choice, for my employer gave me the sack."

"Your employer?" Lady Grantham said, blinking in confusion at the earl's daughter's use of such a vulgar term, just as if she had never heard it in her life. She was a treasure, her stepmother.

"I shall tell you and Papa all about it tomorrow," Catriona promised. "I hope I may have my old room."

Lady Grantham bit her lip in consternation.

"I am afraid we had it fitted up as a nursery," she said. "I know there are nursery apartments on the third floor, but neither of us could bear to be so far away from our darling little Christopher."

"You said you would not live under my roof again if you were starving," her father said defensively. "You are such a stubborn little chit, Catriona, how was I to know you did not mean it?"

"Never mind," she said as she patted his shoulder and hoisted the child further up on her hip. "I will stay in the rose guest suite. I always did fancy it."

Langley appeared in the doorway and bowed impartially between Lady Grantham and Catriona.

TO TEMPT A GENTLEMAN

"A meal has been laid out for Lady Catriona in the breakfast room."

"Thank you, Langley," Catriona said as she relinquished the infant to his mother. "I am quite famished. I do not suppose there are lemon tarts."

Langley permitted himself a wide, paternal smile.

"Cook has just now begun rolling out the pastry," he assured her.

Catriona gave a deep sigh of contentment.

"Mrs. Quiggley's lemon tarts. I so dreaded swallowing my pride to come here, but this has been the most wonderful homecoming imaginable. A new baby brother. I just cannot believe it. I am happy for you, Father."

"I am glad," her father said. Since his wife had left to take the child to the nursery, he confided, "I was afraid you would object in the strongest terms to my marriage."

"Not at all," Catriona said cordially as she slipped her arm into his and strolled with him toward the breakfast room. "After choosing an actress as your wife, you can hardly object to my choice of a husband."

"You have found Mr. Montagu?" His face lit up.

"Actually, I have. But I will tell you all about it presently," she said. "We must not keep the fatted calf waiting."

CHAPTER 20

Sir Michael gave a long sigh of annoyance as Dorothea and Marguerite came running into his study, wringing their hands and looking distressed. Ever since Catriona had gone, the house had been sheer chaos.

"Papa, what are we going to do? Pierre refuses to share a kitchen with Mrs. Muir," Dorothea cried.

"Then Pierre will have to go," he said calmly.

"Papa, can you not send her to some relations until the party is over?" Marguerite said.

"She has no relations. This is her home," he said.

"But we cannot *do* this without Pierre!" Dorothea said. "I have summoned him all this way from London, and now I must tell him to go back again? He will resign. I just know it." Tears sparkled on her lashes. "And Edward will be very vexed with me, as if it were not bad enough already."

"Well, you have been away from his house for weeks. Reason enough for your husband to be vexed, although I have been delighted to have the two of you to myself. I am surprised your husbands have not been here, demanding that you go home at once. They must sorely miss you. I know *I* have missed you in the time since you have been married."

Sir Michael smiled at his daughters and would have put an arm around each of their shoulders, but he was surprised when they both burst into tears and tried to throw themselves on his chest at the same time.

"There, there, what is the matter with the two of you?" he asked as he patted them on their backs.

"He does not miss me," Dorothea sniffed. "He has his . . . actress to keep him company."

"His *actress*!" Sir Michael said, frowning. "And you not married two years yet! Are you certain? He is not the man I thought him, or I never would have consented—"

"He was seen embracing her in Hyde Park," Dorothea said. "I thought leaving London and coming here would teach him a lesson, but he has not sent me one letter. And it has been *weeks*! He probably does not even know I am gone."

"Have you sent *him* any letters?"

"Of course not! I am the wronged party! He should have written long since to beg me to return to him!"

Michael took her by her shoulders.

"Dorothea, are you telling me you have left your husband?"

Dorothea's lips trembled.

"And he did not even notice," she said in a small voice.

Michael narrowed his eyes at her.

"I find it hard to believe you did not tell him you were leaving in the strongest and most histrionic terms imaginable," he said with a shake of his head. "You did have a blazing row, I trust?"

"Of course not," she said stiffly. "It is not for me to acknowledge the creature's existence. If he cannot be bothered to write me a letter when he comes home from his club to find me gone—"

"Does he not know where you are?"

"I left him a letter to tell him I was visiting you, of course—"

"And he did not find that suspicious?" he asked. "And I thought the two of you merely had come here to ensure that Catriona was not about to become your new stepmother."

"You knew?" Marguerite asked.

"Of course, I knew," Michael told her. "I reared the two of you. I know how you think. So, that is why *you* are here, is it, Marguerite? You just came along to keep Lady Catriona from becoming the mistress of this house?"

Marguerite hung her head.

"I thought not," Michael said, rolling his eyes. "Make a clean breast of it, my girl. Do not tell me that Lord Redgrave has a mistress, too."

"If only it were that," Marguerite spat out. "As I tried to explain to my sister, if one ignores one's husband's mistresses, they tire of them eventually. But his *mother*! The woman is intolerable. She criticizes my clothes, my taste in furnishings, my friends, and she will not so much as permit me to approve a menu when we entertain guests. And whenever I complain to Henry, he sides with *her*."

"Does he, now?" Michael said. "And why is that?"

"He says it is because I am too inexperienced to run a great household, and I will do well to learn at my mother-in-law's knee. *He* does not see what a tyrant she is, for she only shows him her sweet, cloying side."

"And does he believe your only reason for coming to Scotland is to visit your father?"

Dorothea must have heard the hurt in his voice, for she patted him on the shoulder.

"Papa, we have missed you most sincerely," she said kindly. "And if you would only move to a more civilized place, or even an uncivilized place closer to London, I am sure we would be forever visiting you."

"That is a comfort," he said wryly. "Well, do cheer up, girls. You did manage to drive off the pernicious Lady Catriona."

"No, Papa," Dorothea said. "*You* did that yourself."

"Not that we blame you," Marguerite said hastily. "It was the outside of enough for her to presume to touch Mama's things. I know Mama's boudoir gives you great comfort."

Michael thought about that.

"Well, as for that, I fear Lady Catriona was right."

"She was?" the two of them chorused.

To their surprise and Michael's own, he gave a bark of laughter.

"Do not look so dismayed. I am not about to go in pursuit of the woman and beg her to return."

"She has gone to her father, the earl," Marguerite reminded him.

"Yes, I knew that," he said, gritting his teeth. When he had learned Catriona left the house, he had been on the point of setting out to find her, certain so proud a young lady would have set out on foot for the next village to seek shelter. A hundred horrible things could happen to a young woman alone. He had only desisted when Dorothea and Marguerite admitted they had helped her pack her clothes and sent her off to London on the mail coach, which at first had relieved and then vexed him exceedingly.

"About Pierre—" Dorothea began.

"Yes, Papa. We cannot serve our guests meals cooked by Mrs. Muir!"

"Why not?" he asked. "She makes the best haggis in Scotland."

Dorothea and Marguerite both shuddered, as he knew they would.

"Papa, that is *disgusting*!" Marguerite said, wrinkling her pert nose.

Dorothea gave him a look that would curdle milk, and Michael threw up his hands in surrender.

"Very well," he said. "I shall go talk to the man."

"Offer him some money in addition to his salary," Dorothea suggested helpfully. "Pierre is very fond of money."

"I will, darling," he said with a squeeze of her elegant shoulders.

The girls left, but the butler lingered tentatively in the doorway.

"Yes?" Michael inquired. When the butler hesitated, he gave an impatient huff. "Out with it, man! Do you think I do not know when you have something to say after all these years?"

The butler raised his eyes to the ceiling.

"Do I understand that there will not be guests in the blue room, Sir Michael?" the butler asked. "The young ladies wish to assign the room to—"

"No, Timms," Sir Michael snapped. "There will be no guests in *her* room. I will speak to the young ladies myself."

"Very good, sir," Timms said with a long, accusing stare as he took himself off. The man had the gall to plague him with his silent recriminations over the manner of Lady Catriona's departure, even though at one time he would have been delighted to see the back of her.

As he himself would have been, he thought glumly.

When the butler was gone, Michael gulped down the glass of fine brandy he had intended to sip slowly by the fire and coughed when it burned all the way down. It felt *good*.

Then he realized that he would probably go to the blue room tonight and see if some chance wisp of her perfume lingered in the wardrobe.

It was pitiful. Just pitiful.

Even so, he sat in the blue room until almost dawn trying to conjure the comfort of her presence, and he barely made it back to his own bedchamber before the girls from the village were scheduled to disrupt the quiet of morning with their infernal cleaning and clattering.

"Papa, Papa! This is just intolerable," cried Marguerite as she ran into the barn where Sir Michael inspecting the health and progress of his precious twin foals. "The silly girls did no work at all. They were giggling so loudly that they finally woke us up. When we got dressed in a hurry and went out to see what they were doing, they just *stared* at us as if they expected us to give them direction!"

"Possibly that is because Lady Catriona rose before dawn and was dressed and ready with a schedule of tasks they were to perform each day," Michael said with what patience he could muster. "You are married women now. Do you not know how to direct your servants?"

Both girls looked affronted.

"*I* have a housekeeper for such work," Dorothea said.

"As did I until you came into Scotland for the express purpose of chasing her away," Michael could not help pointing out.

"Forgive me for contradicting you, Father," Marguerite said huffily, "but *you* are the one who chased her away. After the scene you enacted over the invasion of Mama's boudoir, the village girls are probably afraid to touch anything in the house without permission."

"I understand. It is somehow *my* fault that you do not know how to keep household," he said.

"*I* should like to keep household, if my precious mother-in-law would permit it," Marguerite said *sotto voce.*

Dorothea looked out the doorway.

"Marguerite! Marguerite! They are getting away, and with so much to do before the party!" she cried as she sped out of the barn in pursuit of the village girls, who were stealthily making their way out of the house.

Marguerite clapped both hands over her mouth in consternation.

"The house is at sixes and sevens, and what Lady Constance will think if she arrives to see it in such disarray, I cannot bear to think."

"Then you had better hurry after your sister to stop them," he suggested as Marguerite gave him a huff of annoyance and hurried out of the barn, carefully watching her step to avoid soiling her dainty slippers on any substance of animal origin.

Michael exchanged a look of long suffering with his head groom. Guests would begin arriving for the much-anticipated party the next day, and by then his daughters would have driven him absolutely insane with their demands and their complaints. It occurred to him that when Catriona came to him to demand that he do something about whatever crisis was rampant at the moment, she could always remedy the situation easily enough once he provided her with the funds to do so. Obviously, with the best will in the world, he had failed his daughters by spoiling them so abominably, and now he was paying the price.

"It is easier to rear a hundred horses than it is two young women," he said.

"Now that Miss Grant, or Lady Catriona, I *should* say," the groom said feelingly. "There was a female who could get the last drop of work out of a body."

It was true that when there was heavy furniture to be moved, Catriona had no qualms about running out to the barn to roust every able-bodied stable hand into the house to do her bidding.

She was nothing short of imperious. How could he have mistaken her for the usual poor relation?

"She was a terror, was she not?" he observed with what he suspected was a very silly smile on his face.

No doubt Catriona even now was leading her father on a merry dance, and, God help him, Michael envied the fellow. He envied him very much indeed.

CHAPTER 21

It was the morning of the first day of the hunt party, and Sir Michael's daughters had arisen at what for them was the ungodly hour of ten o'clock so that they could be gowned, coifed, and perfumed in time to welcome their guests properly. What their maids concealed from them was the fact that Pierre, driven mad by Mrs. Muir's meddling with his artistry in the execution of his pastries, had burned the delicate creations that were to have established Lady Redgrave and Mrs. Walbridge as the most accomplished hostesses of this provincial backwater and was sulking in the butler's pantry after having appropriated a bottle of fine old spirits from the master's wine cellar, leaving the field to his gleeful adversary, who was even now perpetrating outrages upon the culinary arts that surely were making the angels weep.

Sir Michael knew, but he was not about to shake his daughters' confidence by revealing this. He had tried to reason with the chef to no avail and, indeed, he could not bring himself to regret his failure. Mrs. Muir's cheeks were glowing with triumph, and she moved about the kitchen with an energy she had not exhibited in several decades.

"You look very pretty, the both of you," Michael reassured the excited young women as he kissed them each on the cheek. He gave Dorothea a tap on the nose. "And as soon as this ridiculous party is over, I shall go at once to London to horsewhip your husband for making you unhappy."

Dorothea gave a surprised little spurt of laughter.

"Would you, Papa? Truly?" she asked.

"Will you horsewhip my mother-in-law, too?" Marguerite asked plaintively. "She is making *me* unhappy."

"No," Michael said with no hesitation whatsoever as both girls laughed. "The dowager Lady Redgrave terrifies me."

"Papa, you are so absurd," Marguerite said.

"A coach!" cried Dorothea, running to the window and staring at the arriving coach in a way that would have caused her fashionable London friends to raise their eyebrows at such vulgar behavior. "Our first guest!"

"In fine style, too," Michael said as he moved behind her and squinted to discern the crest on the door. "The arms of the Dukes of Buccleuch."

"Lady Constance!" both girls shrieked gleefully.

"What a delightful surprise," Michael said, even though he had expected her to arrive early so she could lay siege to the best guest room and position herself as a sort of honorary hostess. The woman had hinted all during their week in Edinburgh that it was time for him to remarry and that she was available. He had told his daughters that his objection to Lady Constance, who was really a very attractive woman and an excellent companion in addition to her wealth, centered on his refusal to marry a domineering woman. But he had already fallen madly in love with Lady Catriona, and a more stubborn, imperious female he had never met.

Now if *she* had come to Scotland to lay claim to him— but there was no possibility of that, he thought glumly, even as he stepped forward to hand Lady Constance out of the duke's carriage.

"Sir Michael," the lady said graciously as she accepted his assistance and stepped gracefully to the pavement. Her auburn hair was styled with charming little curls about her heart-shaped face and crowned with a fetching hat graced with peacock feathers. Her traveling costume was of green velvet, which set off her alabaster skin perfectly.

She smelled of some expensive French scent and gave him her most beguiling smile, but he felt nothing. Not the slightest stirring of interest.

"Welcome, Lady Constance," he said. "Here are Dorothea and Marguerite to greet you."

She expertly snagged his arm when he would have bowed and made good his escape to the horse barn, a skill she had no doubt honed to perfection as the mother of four strapping sons.

"You must not run off yet. Look who I have brought with me," she said as she turned toward the door of the carriage.

"Mr. Montagu," Sir Michael said with a marked lack of enthusiasm.

"Sir Michael," that gentleman said as he alighted from the carriage with a youthful athleticism that made both of Sir Michael's daughters go starry-eyed for a moment, blast his eyes! "Lady Redgrave," he said, kissing Marguerite's hand and then reaching for Dorothea's. "Mrs. Walbridge. How kind of you to include me in your invitation." As they expressed their delight in his acceptance of their invitation, his eyes seemed to rove a bit, which was less than strictly polite while his hostesses were speaking to him, but completely understandable, Michael thought.

"Lady Catriona is not here," Michael said bluntly as Mr. Montagu turned surprised eyes toward him. Michael positively enjoyed the disappointment on the younger man's face.

"Oh. I had understood she was visiting you for an indefinite period," he said. "But she is expected for the party, surely."

"I am not in the lady's confidence," Michael said. "If

you will excuse me, there are matters in the horse barn that require my attention."

With that, he feigned deafness to his daughters' protests that he should go into the house and take tea with his guests and made good his escape. So, Lady Constance's fine young relation had come sniffing around here, looking for Lady Catriona, had he? At least Sir Michael would not be subjected to the sickening sight of the silly chub making sheep's eyes at the lady over the expanse of his own dinner table.

Lady Constance raised her eyebrows slightly at the rather lumpy pastries before her and glanced fleetingly at Mr. Montagu to see his reaction to the rather homely refreshments set before them, but she had the courtesy not to say a word.

She didn't need to, for both of Sir Michael's daughters had flushed scarlet to the roots of their hair, as well they might.

Mrs. Muir proudly had set before them the scones heavy with lard and sugar, the homely pots of homemade fruit jam, the clotted cream and a great glob of greasy butter, and the coarse brown bread that suddenly became their daily fare as children after their mother died and Sir Michael had discharged the exorbitantly expensive French chef she had insisted upon keeping at the estate. After his wife's death, Papa did not care what he ate and, in truth, even when he had a good appetite, his taste ran to the simple, homely dishes of the Scottish countryside at which Mrs. Muir excelled in preparing.

Dorothea gave a shudder of distaste and devoutly hoped Mrs. Muir would not forget herself so far as to present a great mess of haggis to her guests.

Town-bred Mr. Montagu gingerly picked up one of the scones and bit into it.

"This is quite delicious," he said, sounding surprised. "And what is this interesting . . . substance?"

"I believe that is clotted cream," Lady Constance murmured.

"One puts it on the scone," Marguerite said.

"Interesting," Mr. Montagu said as he spooned a bit onto his scone. He tasted it. "Delicious as well," he pronounced it. He turned innocently to his cousin. "Have you tasted these before, Lady Constance?"

"Yes," Lady Constance said. "Scones are a native Scottish innovation, I believe."

He took another bite.

"Quite delicious," he said. "Why do we not have such things at Drumlanrig Castle?"

Lady Constance looked faintly shocked that he would ask such a thing.

"His grace's chef is French," she said. "He has no knowledge of such things, nor would you, naturally, having been reared in London." She smiled at Dorothea and Marguerite. "This is quite a refreshing change."

"I do have a French cook," Dorothea said tearfully. "We were to have strawberry tarts, and plum cake, and meringue—" She was so overcome with emotion she could not bear to continue in that train. "And now it is all ruined. Pray excuse me. I feel most unwell."

She pressed her hands to her trembling lips, leaped to her feet, and fled the room.

Mr. Montagu rose in concern.

"Really, Mrs. Walbridge," he called after her. "Everything is quite delicious."

Dorothea gave a renewed wail of despair in answer before she disappeared from sight.

"The poor girl. I will see if I can offer her some comfort, if you will excuse me," Lady Constance said as she daintily pressed her serviette to her lips and hurried after Dorothea with a smile of maternal concern on her face.

Marguerite and Mr. Montagu faced one another ruefully. She flushed crimson, for it was not usual for her
to be alone in the company of a presentable young man.
He hesitated, seeing her discomfort, and started to rise.
Marguerite thrust out her chin. She was no longer a
debutante newly delivered from the schoolroom, but a
grown woman and a viscountess as well. If her mother-
in-law had not refused to leave her son's town house,
Marguerite, the sophisticated Society hostess, would no
doubt entertain gentleman callers every day of the week
and no one would lift an eyebrow.

"Do remain seated, Mr. Montagu," she said. "There is
no reason for you to abandon your refreshments."

"Did I say something wrong?" he asked.

"Not at all," she said. "Personally, I am quite fond of
scones and clotted cream." She dimpled. "Although I
would not dare admit as much in front of Lady Constance and my sister. I am glad you are not so difficult
to please."

In other situations, Marguerite, too, would scorn such
homely fare as this, but with the admiring eyes of this
handsome young man upon her, she could profess a
fondness for the treats of her childhood.

"How refreshing," he said with an admiring smile. "It
is not often one meets with a lady possessed of a good appetite and the honesty to admit it."

Marguerite fluttered her eyelashes at him in sheer re-
flex. She loved her husband with all her heart, but it had
been a long time since dear Henry had looked at her in
just that way. Most of the time she was made to feel like an
imbecile in her own home as her mother-in-law criticized
her appearance, her opinions, and her taste. Henry had
lately spent more time at his club to avoid mediating their
disputes, for the head servants were forever appealing to
him for instructions after being issued a number of con-
tradictory orders by their warring mistresses.

For all she knew, *he* had an actress in keeping.

"You are too kind, Mr. Montagu," she murmured as she gave another little flutter of her eyelashes. "What must you think of us?"

"I think you are absolutely charming," he said with a sincerity that made her blush as he leaned forward to press her hand. "We are practically neighbors, you know, with my cousin living so close. Surely you need not stand on ceremony with Lady Constance and me, and I hope you will tell your sister this."

At that, the door to the parlor was pushed open with so much force that it slammed against the wall.

To Marguerite's astonishment, her husband strode into the room and glared down at her as she hastily snatched her hand back from under Mr. Montagu's.

"What is the meaning of this, madam?" he demanded. He looked down his nose at Mr. Montagu. "And who are you, sir?"

"Henry!" squeaked Marguerite. Her husband looked positively dangerous, and her heart quickened with excitement. He was *jealous*. "Lord Redgrave, may I present Mr. Montagu, the cousin of the Duke of Buccleuch and a resident of Edinburgh at present. Mr. Montagu, my husband, Lord Redgrave."

"My lord," Mr. Montagu said, looking self-conscious. "If you will excuse me—"

"With pleasure," Lord Redgrave spat. He gave a smile of sour satisfaction as Mr. Montagu rose and left the room with all the haste his dignity would permit.

"Now, Marguerite," he said awfully as he turned to his defiant wife. "What is the meaning of this? You leave my house for a fortnight's visit with your father, which you exceed for a full week, and when I come here to find out what has delayed you, I find you trysting with some fellow in my father-in-law's house."

"My dear husband," she said angrily. "I am a grown woman now, and acting as hostess for my father. Mr.

Montagu is an invited guest in this house, and he has been nothing but perfectly kind to me."

"*Kind*!" he exclaimed. "The fellow was positively drooling all over you, the idiot."

"An *idiot*, is he? *You* certainly would not be guilty of paying attention to me!"

He looked so furious that a lesser woman would have cowered, but Marguerite met him glare for glare.

"You know very well that is not what I meant," he snarled. "You are only trying to put me in the wrong, and I do not like it."

"Oho! You do not like it, do you? How do you think *I* feel, being harassed by your mother day in and day out, being told to a nicety how unworthy I am to be your wife, and having all my wishes in the arrangements for my own household set aside?"

"You will leave my mother out of this," he said harshly.

"If only one could!" she cried. "But *you* have made that impossible, my lord, by refusing to make her remove to a dower house."

"Dower house! I do not have a dower house."

"Well, *build* one," she said with gritted teeth.

Lord Redgrave threw up his hands when Sir Michael came into the room.

"Redgrave! Come to see what has delayed your wife, I see," Sir Michael said, stepping up to the enraged young nobleman and offering his hand. "I had hoped you would spare her to me a little longer."

"I take leave to tell *you*, sir," Lord Redgrave said with gritted teeth, "that you have reared a singularly obstinate daughter."

"Have I, indeed?" Sir Michael said stiffly. "Then I take leave to tell *you* that your mother has reared a spineless son if he will permit his mother to rule his wife in her own house."

"You do your daughter no good, sir, by encouraging

her to persist in her unjust grievances. My mother only seeks to teach her."

"Do *not* insult my father under his own roof, Henry," Marguerite said warningly.

"He insulted me first," he said, "for when I said he had reared an obstinate daughter, I spoke nothing but truth, whereas he had the unmitigated gall to speak ill of my mother, a lady who is not present to defend herself."

"Your mother only seeks to keep me under her thumb so she can continue to rule at Redgrave House as she always has without acknowledging my right as mistress," Marguerite said. "Everyone but you can see the contempt with which she regards me."

"That is nonsense. Utter nonsense. She regards you quite as the daughter she never had."

"We have nothing to say to one another, my lord," Marguerite said. "I will thank you to leave this house."

"Leave this house? Now? After I have come all the way from London to see you?" He gave a bitter laugh. "Oh, my mother warned me how it would be if I insisted upon wedding you, but I would not listen. She said you were too young and too flighty to succeed her as Viscountess Redgrave. She said that you were sure to get into some mischief in Scotland with no one to curb your high spirits except your doting father, who has always spoiled you. I laughed aside her concerns, and what do I find when I come to surprise you?" He pointed accusingly at Mr. Montagu, who had reappeared at the doorway with Lady Constance and the new arrivals, Mr. Wieland and Mr. Sandhurst. "*Him*," he shouted in accents of loathing.

"Now, see here, Lord Redgrave," Mr. Montagu said as he advanced into the room. "I am making every allowance for your consternation in finding me alone with your lovely wife." He sketched a bow in Marguerite's direction, and she simpered at him. He really was quite handsome. "Indeed, she is such a delightful lady that I would have serious doubts about your sanity if you were not jealous. However, your lady has done nothing at all to encourage improper advances as I, I hasten to assure you, had no intention of offering them."

"What nonsense is this?" Lady Constance asked with a pretty, tinkling laugh. "I assure you, Lord Redgrave, for I assume you are he although no one has troubled to introduce us, that Mrs. Walbridge and I had only left the room for an instant. I hope you will not mind my saying so, but you are being very foolish. I suppose much might be forgiven of an impetuous young man in love with his wife."

This had the happy effect of defusing Lord Redgrave's anger.

"I fear you are right, madam," he said ruefully.

"Lady Constance," Dorothea supplied. "May I present my brother-in-law, Lord Redgrave. My lord, here are Mr. Sandhurst and Mr. Wieland, come to attend our little hunt party as well."

"A party?" Lord Redgrave said, glaring at his wife. "You did not tell me of any hunt party. And I am not to be suspicious when you delay your return to London in order to surround yourself with sporting gentlemen?"

"Do calm yourself, Henry," Sir Michael said as he clapped his hand on his son-in-law's shoulder. "I have birds enough to spare for even a sportsman of your superior marksmanship. And a stream full of trout for your entertainment. You will stay, of course."

"Good of you, Sir Michael," Lord Redgrave said at once. He smiled at his wife. "I say, my dear. I apologize for being such an ugly customer. I have missed you, you know."

Marguerite gave him a shy smile. He really was quite magnificent when he was angry, but when he smiled he was a veritable Adonis. She was suddenly reminded of why she had fallen so completely in love with him when she met him during her first season in London.

"You are forgiven. Will you join us for refreshment, my lord?" she asked as she took his hand.

He squeezed her hand but released it at once.

"I should like that, my dear, but first I must prevail upon Sir Michael to lend me pen and paper so I may write to Mother to tell her I will not return to London as soon as I had planned."

With that Marguerite gave what could only be described as a growl as her father took her insensitive beast of a husband off to his study to procure the desired writing implements.

CHAPTER 22

Dorothea gasped when her husband, Mr. Edward Walbridge, strode into the drawing room, caught her around the waist, and lifted her into his arms to kiss her nearly witless before all of her father's guests. Mr. Sandhurst, with whom she had been playing cards at the time, came at once to his feet in alarm.

Instead of melting into his arms as the odious man plainly expected, she pounded against his chest with her fists.

"Put me down, you barbarian," she said through gritted teeth as the other guests goggled at them.

"I say," Mr. Sandhurst interjected. "I must insist that you release Mrs. Walbridge at once. She does not seem to want your attentions."

Mr. Walbridge looked the young man up and down.

"And who is this pretty fellow, my dear?" he demanded. "I will have you know my wife likes my attentions very well."

"Your wife!" exclaimed Mr. Sandhurst. Both Dorothea and her husband ignored him.

"No, Edward, I don't," she said as she dealt him a clout on the shoulder. "Put me down. You are making a spectacle of me in front of all our guests."

"*Hang* your guests! You have been absent from your home for three weeks without a word of explanation. We are going back to London. Now," he said savagely. He set Dorothea on her feet with a thump that made her stagger.

Mr. Sandhurst caught her arm to steady her, and Mr. Walbridge gave him a look that made him take a hasty step backward.

"You," Mr. Walbridge shouted at a maid who was staring wide-eyed from the table where she had just placed a plate of sweet biscuits. "Tell my wife's maid to pack." The maid looked to Sir Michael for instructions and he shook his head slightly.

"How *dare* you?" Dorothea sputtered as her husband took her in a grip that was far from gentle.

"I'd like a word with you, Walbridge," Sir Michael said menacingly. "And I will thank you to unhand my daughter."

"She is my wife," Mr. Walbridge said.

"Which does not give you the right to treat her like one of your light skirts under her father's roof. It appears you have forgotten how to treat a respectable woman."

Mr. Walbridge's dark brows drew together. He looked from Dorothea to Sir Michael, both of whom were glaring at him.

"One of my—? Has the world run mad? I say, what the deuce is going on here?"

"Come with me to my study, and I will be delighted to tell you," Michael growled.

Mr. Walbridge cast one comprehensive look about the room, taking in the well-dressed and plainly affronted company. He singled out Mr. Sandhurst.

"You," he said with a snarl. "Stay away from my wife while I am gone." He gave Dorothea a narrow-eyed stare. "I will be back, and if you want to please me, Dorothea, you will be ready to return to London with me."

With that, Sir Michael clapped his son-in-law on the shoulder and practically shoved him into the study.

If he only knew how like a rebellious adolescent he looks, Michael thought with a weary sigh as he indicated a chair and Mr. Walbridge sulkily lowered himself into it.

He was young and angry, but Michael was stronger from an active life than the town-bred Walbridge and just as angry as he was. He regretted that it was beneath his dignity to indulge in a swift, satisfying bout of fisticuffs with the young hothead. Besides, Dorothea, in the illogical way of women, would not like it if Michael damaged her husband, even if she was out of temper with him at the moment.

"What is wrong with her?" Mr. Walbridge asked, suddenly looking more wistful than angry. "Why is she not glad to see me? The house is a tomb without her."

"I am surprised you noticed she was missing," Sir Michael said as he moved to the decanters on a shelf by his desk. They were starting to look dusty, and the sight made him sad. If Catriona were still in residence, they would be sparkling, with the liquor inside glowing like jewels. He poured his son-in-law a generous measure of whiskey and handed it to him, even if the young idiot did not deserve it.

"You are surprised I noticed my wife was missing?" Mr. Walbridge repeated in astonishment. "Are you *mad*?"

"I thought perhaps you had been so occupied with your mistress that you might not have realized she was gone."

"My mistress! What mistress? Who has been putting such nonsense in Dorothea's head to turn her against me? There is no mistress."

"No mistress," Sir Michael repeated skeptically.

"No, dash it all! And anyone who says otherwise is a liar. Now, are you going to order *my wife* to return to London where she belongs?"

Sir Michael gripped Mr. Walbridge by his collar and drew him to his feet. He held him in front of him so he could stare right into his astonished face.

"*My daughter* will stay right where she is until she *chooses* to return to London with you," he said menacingly. "If you think you can barge into my home and order my daughter about as if she were your servant, you are sadly mistaken."

"See here, Sir Michael! I will not put up with—"

"Ah, but you *will* put up with it," Sir Michael said. "You are under *my* roof now. You managed to convince me you were a man of integrity and loyalty when you offered for Dorothea, or I never would have permitted your marriage regardless of how rich you are. But a man who would keep a mistress and flaunt her in his wife's face is no man for my Dorothea."

"I have no mistress, I tell you!" he shouted.

"My daughter believes otherwise."

"She wrongs me."

"Perhaps so," Michael said. He prided himself on being a good judge of character, and he would have staked his life that Walbridge told the truth by the unmistakable conviction in his voice and the unflinching way he stared into Michael's eyes. Then, to his consternation, the younger man gave an anguished sob and buried his face in his hands.

"See here, man," Michael said in alarm as he put a hand on Walbridge's trembling shoulder. "You cannot fall apart now."

"You do not know what it was like to suddenly have her gone," Walbridge said as he emerged from his hands. His eyes were moist. "And to have her delay her return with no explanation."

"I think I might," Michael said, recalling those first horrible months of grief after his wife's death, when he could not even mourn her properly because he had to stay strong for the sake of his tiny, helpless daughters. Dorothea had kept watching the door to their house, certain that her mother would return to her any moment. It broke his heart.

"With respect, Sir Michael, you do not," Walbridge snapped. "I expected them to bring her corpse home to me any moment. I could think of no reason why a loving wife would not return to her husband. One of my friends suggested that she might have run off with another man, and his companions had to pull me off him. If they had not, I would have torn his lying throat out for saying such a thing. The lot of us were thrown out of the tavern." He gave another loud sob. "It never once occurred to me that Dorothea would be unfaithful to me. Never. And you *dare* accuse me of having a mistress. How can you think it of me? How can *she*?"

"You were seen," Michael said quietly.

"Whoever says so is a liar," Walbridge said. "I swear it on my mother's grave."

"See here. No need for that," Michael said. It always made him uncomfortable when people started swearing on dead relatives' graves. "I am willing to admit the possibility that there has been some misunderstanding."

Walbridge's eyes shone with hope.

"You will talk to her on my behalf?" he asked. He sounded almost humble.

"No. *You* will talk to her. Dorothea is your wife, not mine. I will call her into this room, but I insist upon being present when you speak with her. I will not permit you to bully her."

Walbridge gave a long sigh of relief.

"Thank you, Sir Michael," Walbridge said, sounding pathetically grateful.

For an alarming moment, Michael feared he was going to throw himself on his chest and weep with gratitude. He stepped back quickly to avoid this appalling prospect.

"Compose yourself, Walbridge," he said bracingly. "I will fetch Dorothea now." When Walbridge started to thank him again, he cut him off with a sharp gesture of his hand. "Enough!"

When Dorothea came into the room, her chin was set and her dark eyes were still alight with temper. She walked straight to her husband, who had stood at her entrance and held out his hand with a smile of entreaty on his lips, and slapped him hard across his face. Michael winced. He could see Dorothea's angry red handprint on Walbridge's cheek as the young man's mouth dropped open in dismay.

He looked shattered. Positively shattered.

"Dorothea," Michael said repressively to his daughter. "You are not a tavern maid. Reprehensible as you believe your husband's conduct to have been, I expect you to behave with dignity in my house."

"He will be fortunate if I do not kill him," she said, unashamed. She looked magnificent, like a young tigress laying claim to her mate. *Poor Walbridge*, Michael thought. *He had better not be guilty of the charges against him. Dorothea might well tear him apart with those dainty, pampered little hands.*

And Michael would not lift a finger to help him if he had dared to be unfaithful to his daughter. Michael was well aware that many men of his class established separate households for the women they had in keeping apart from their wives, but he had only contempt for such men. If Walbridge proved to be one of them, Michael would throttle the fellow himself. Or he would simply hand the errant husband over to Dorothea.

A man might boast of muscular strength and fists the size of hams, but no one could inflict true suffering like a woman. The quickly repressed image of Lady Catriona rose before him.

He would not think of *her* now.

He would not place himself under the cat's paw as poor Walbridge had. Dorothea looked as if she might scratch his eyes out at any moment.

"Not once," Walbridge said between clenched teeth as he grabbed his wife's shoulders and gave her a little shake. "Not *once* have I been unfaithful to you from the first moment I saw you."

"Mrs. Robinson saw you with her own eyes, right in Hyde Park," Dorothea cried. "Embracing another woman.

She recognized her. She is an actress. A rather famous one who created quite a stir by leaving the stage some time ago, presumably because she had found an important lover who no longer wanted her to display herself in public. She told Marguerite, and Marguerite did not believe her. She told her she was a shocking old busybody. But she had her husband make inquiries, and he found out that any number of his friends knew about your sordid little affair with this actress!"

Walbridge's lips went white with anger.

"Lady Redgrave is wrong. They are both wrong. I know no such woman," he declared. He threw one hand out dramatically. "Let my accuser stand before me!"

Michael shook his head. What rare entertainment his daughters and their husbands were providing for his guests. Walbridge had seemed such a sensible man when he came to Scotland three years ago to formally ask Michael for permission to pay his addresses to Dorothea. He had presented his case calmly and well. He had brought his man of business with documentation of his wealth and holdings.

Now this formerly composed and dignified young man was acting as if he were the male protagonist in the most lurid of Cheltenham tragedies.

Women. They make lunatics of us all.

Michael could not pride himself on being any better than Walbridge. For that reason, perhaps, he decided to honor the affronted husband's request.

"Very well," he said. "I will call Marguerite, Lord Redgrave, and Mrs. Robinson. All of them happen to be in the house at the moment."

The combatants turned faces of surprise to him. They obviously had forgotten he was in the room.

Michael rolled his eyes. Once his daughters had married, Michael had thought his only duty to them remaining as a father would be to dandle his grandchildren on his knee. How naïve he had been, although he hardly could have foreseen that he would be called upon to prevent his elder daughter from scratching her husband's eyes out.

Walbridge let out his breath all at once.

"Thank you, Sir Michael," he said. "We shall see who is the liar now."

Michael jabbed a forefinger into Walbridge's waistcoat with enough force to make the younger man give a surprised bleat of pain.

"I will not have either of my girls bullied by you," he said warningly. "*You* stay here. Dorothea, you will come with me."

With that he took his daughter's elbow, favored Walbridge with a parting glare, and ushered his daughter out of the room and back to the parlor, where he had no doubt his guests were sitting with wide-eyed relish on the edges of their chairs, waiting for the next installment of the drama being enacted for their delectation.

CHAPTER 23

Edward was facing the window when Sir Michael ushered Dorothea, Marguerite, Henry and Mrs. Robinson into the parlor. Dorothea looked at the back of her husband's head and was struck by something she had not noticed until now—his dark, formerly luxurious mane of hair was thinning in back. The slightest hint of what might soon be a bald spot had appeared, and she had not known it. Instead of repelling her, for a moment the sight somehow endeared him to her.

Then she felt her face grow stiff.

It was said that when men began to feel their mortality in the small, undignified signs of aging such as thinning hair and weakened eyes, they bolstered their self-esteem by gambling away their fortunes and taking mistresses. Obviously, this had been the case with Edward.

How bitter it was to have the truth confirmed in this way.

The idiot! Did he not know that she would have loved him if he had grown bald overnight? That even if he had grown stooped and squinted hideously in an effort to see through his rhuemy eyes, she still would have thought him the most handsome man in the world?

He turned, and his eyes instantly sought hers. She looked away.

"Mrs. Robinson. You say you saw me with this . . . *person*," he said as he grimaced in distaste.

"Yes, I did, Mr. Walbridge," the elder lady said clearly. "Quite brazen, you were, hugging her in public."

"I do not know what you are talking about," he said.

"Then you deny it," Dorothea said.

"I do. Most vehemently," he spat out. "Mrs. Robinson, I will not call you a liar, for I was reared as a gentleman. But I think it possible that you have been mistaken."

"There is nothing wrong with my eyes, young man," the elderly lady snapped. "I recognized her at once."

"And you were sure it was *I* you saw embracing her."

"Well," the woman said, less sure. "That is, I am almost completely sure."

Dorothea stared at the other woman.

"What do you mean?" she cried. "*Almost* completely sure?"

"Well, the man's back was to me, although I saw his profile."

"There, you see?" Edward cried out triumphantly.

"I think you are forgetting that Henry made inquiries," Marguerite interjected. "And she was known to be your mistress. You purchased a house near Green Park for her."

"Redgrave, what are you about, telling such things to your wife?" Edward cried.

Henry turned red but stood his ground.

"What are *you* about, cuddling your fancy piece in Hyde Park where anyone might see you? I am sorry for it as I can be, old man. I was sure it was a hum when Marguerite told me of it. But I asked my friends and they knew about it. You and Mrs. Smythe. Some of them had visited the house when Mrs. Smythe was holding court, and you were right there, looking every inch the proud protector."

"Dash it! We are only friends!" Walbridge shouted.

"You know no such woman, do you?" Dorothea cried. She gave a sob. She could not help it. She would have rushed from the room if her father had not caught her shoulders and held her within the circle of his arm. She turned her face into his chest and wept. He stroked her back in comfort.

"Dorothea," Walbridge said, holding his hand out to her. "See what you have done?" he added accusingly to Lord Redgrave, who hung his head.

"Well, burn it, man. I had to tell the truth," he said. "Do not make *me* out to be the villain of the piece. *You* are the one who took up with the blasted female, not me."

"And did your helpful friends tell you *when* these events transpired?" Walbridge asked through gritted teeth.

Uncomfortable, Redgrave thrust his hands in his pockets.

"A year ago, two years ago, I gather," he said. "What does it matter?"

"It was three years ago, and not an hour later," Walbridge said softly. "It stopped the day after I met Dorothea. Completely. I permitted Mrs. Smythe to keep the house near Green Park as a parting gift."

Dorothea looked up hopefully.

"Then she is not . . . you are not . . ."

"No. Not for three years. Not since I first fell in love with you," he said. Dorothea made a movement toward him, and an expression of relief spread over his face. He held out his hand to her, but before she could take it, Mrs. Robinson pointed an accusing finger at him.

"Not so fast, young man!" the elder lady cried. "It was not six months ago that I saw you with this woman. And you had the *gall* to try to convince these people that I was mistaken. What have you to say to that?"

"All right. I admit it," he said. "You did see me embracing Mrs. Smythe in the park."

Oh, treachery! Dorothea gave a shriek and would have retreated back to her father's arms if her husband had not caught both her hands in his to restrain her.

"My love, she has left her old life behind her," he said,

but Dorothea had turned her face away. "She had no protector after me. Instead, she found a man who loved her enough to marry her, and she is happy. The day Mrs. Robinson saw her embrace me was the day she told me that she had given her husband a healthy child. She was so full of joy that when she saw me by chance in the park it just came bursting out of her. Of course I embraced her. She has not had a happy life, my dear. I no longer desired her, but I did wish her well. It was not *her* fault, after all, that there is not, there will never *be*, room in my heart for anyone but you."

"Very pretty, Mr. Walbridge, but did you have to *embrace* her?" Dorothea asked.

"Yes. I did," he said. His eyes begged her to understand. "She married well, but the *ton* has never accepted her. Not completely. I could not cut her. It would be too cruel. She is a wonderful woman, Dorothea, with a great capacity for—"

"I do not wish to know how *wonderful* she is," Dorothea snapped.

Edward cupped her face in his hands.

"She is not nearly so wonderful as you," he said softly, and kissed her. Dorothea melted in his arms and her father cleared his throat.

"If that will be all, then," he said in a tone of utter disgust, "we had better return to the parlor."

"I will never doubt you again," Dorothea said as she looked up into her husband's beautiful eyes. He took her hand and kissed it before he put his hand to her waist and guided her from the room.

Dorothea's heart fluttered with happiness as she entered the parlor, prepared to explain to their guests that there had been a silly mistake and no cause for alarm, when she found that no one paid her any attention at all, for there were unmistakable signs of a new arrival.

* * *

More guests, Sir Michael thought with a sigh of dismay. How he wished all of these people would go away.

But no. He was obliged to host this interminable party, even though there seemed to be no good reason for it now. No reason at all.

He looked at his guests and considered telling them all to go away—his silly daughters, their sillier husbands, the predatory Lady Constance who was even now favoring Michael with an arch look meant to be provocative, the well-favored Mr. Montagu and his irritatingly young friends who seemed to have no purpose on earth other than to make Michael feel even more weary and decrepit than he was already, that shocking old gossip, Mrs. Robinson, and other assorted neighborhood and London gentry, none of whom he had the slightest desire to know any better than he did already.

Excellent idea! He would tell them the party was canceled and send them on their way. If they took offense and threatened never to speak to him again, all the better.

He opened his mouth to put this masterful scheme in motion when the first of the arriving guests appeared on the threshold to the parlor. The wind suddenly emptied from Sir Michael's lungs.

In a dark blue velvet traveling costume and her blond hair crowned with a fetching hat trimmed in white fur, she looked like an ice princess out of a fairy tale. She looked quickly about the room, and when her eyes lighted on him, she smiled.

God. How he had missed her.

"Lady Catriona," he said from a dry throat. He should have bowed, but he could not bear to take his eyes from her for even that short length of time.

"Sir Michael," she said in reply as her smile grew and she stepped forward. "How kind of you to invite us."

Never mind that he had not sent the audacious little baggage an invitation. He was so glad to see her that he—

Michael frowned.

"Us?" he said.

"My father, stepmother, and baby brother," she said matter-of-factly. "Mrs. Walbridge," she added as she stepped to Dorothea and the ladies kissed the air above one another's cheeks. "And Lady Redgrave," she went on, repeating the same ritual with Marguerite. Both of Sir Michael's daughters looked surprised, but they covered it quickly.

"Lady Catriona," Dorothea said as she turned smoothly to her husband. "May I present my husband—"

At that moment, Mrs. Robinson pointed a shaking forefinger to the doorway, where, presumably, said father and stepmother stood wreathed in smiles with said baby brother in the stepmother's arms. Mrs. Robinson uttered, "It is *she*! That woman of Mr. Walbridge's!" in quavering accents, and fainted into Sir Michael's reluctant arms.

He carefully supported the now-moaning woman's tottering steps to the sofa, which its occupants quickly vacated, and crouched down, patting her plump, fluttering hands in vague comfort because he could not think of what else to do with her.

"Here, Sir Michael, do get out of the way," said the voice he had ached to hear over the past week. He looked up in consternation to see Lady Catriona had somehow managed to acquire a cup of tea. "Now, Mrs. Robinson. Drink this. It will make you feel better," she said when she had made a shooing motion at Sir Michael to dislodge him from his post and taken his place next to the fallen woman.

Catriona said just under her breath, "Michael, for the Lord's sake, go say something to my father and stepmother before it gets any worse."

"Lord Grantham, Lady Grantham," Sir Michael said, seeing that everyone else seemed frozen in place. "I bid you welcome."

To his consternation, Dorothea and Marguerite, usually

the most hospitable of young ladies, glared at the earl's wife as if she were the devil incarnate.

Worse, Walbridge had grown deathly pale, and Sir Michael wondered if *he* was going to faint next. By contrast, Lady Grantham looked perfectly composed as she clutched her child to her bosom. She drew her cloak about her as if it were made of ermine, thrust her chin forward, and held her head up proudly, as if it wore a crown.

Lady Macbeth, to the life, surrounded by enemies. No doubt it had been one of her best roles, Sir Michael thought as the creepy feeling of nemesis settled into his bones and he realized who and what this woman must be, for although he had not been to a London theater in years, she might as well have had "actress" written in glowing letters across her forehead.

"How now, Edward?" the former Mrs. Smythe—for Michael knew it could be no other from Mrs. Robinson's and Mr. Walbridge's reactions—said in a warm, musical, imposing voice that, without appearing to be raised, nevertheless carried in perfect, round, resonant tones to every corner of the room. "Are *you* going to cut me as well?"

"Egad," the guilty man said weakly. "Hallo, Elvira."

With that, Dorothea's eyes rolled up in her head and she tumbled onto the floor in a flurry of lacy petticoats, unheeded by her husband, whose eyes seemed paralyzed on the spectacle of his former mistress on the arm of the earl, her husband, and their sleeping child nestling at her bosom.

"Oh, good heavens," snapped Catriona as she straightened from the sofa, where the recovered Mrs. Robinson was sipping her tea and staring at That Woman with the peculiar look of disgust and fascination that respectable women always assumed when confronted with a woman of less-than-perfect reputation. "You, there," Catriona added to Mr. Walbridge, who had torn his eyes away from the woman in question and was looking down at his wife with a heartrending look on his face. "Do you mean to leave her lying on the carpet like that?"

"No, of course not," he said hastily as he knelt down and lifted his wife's head and shoulders to turn her so she was supported in his arms. "My darling, speak to me."

His darling's eyelashes fluttered and she opened her eyes.

"Never again as long as I live," she said tearfully. "How *dare* you humiliate me this way?"

"Now, Dorothea," Catriona said bracingly as she bent over Dorothea and patted her shoulder. "I am sure he meant no such thing." She looked up at the anxious man. "Mr. Walbridge, I presume. I am Lady Catriona Grantham."

"A pleasure, my lady," he said, remembering his manners after a short hesitation.

"I presume you have already met my stepmother," she said dryly.

"Beast," whispered Dorothea.

"None of that, my dear," Catriona said to her. "I know it is very bad, but it is *I* who am to blame for bringing her here, and not Mr. Walbridge, although I had no notion of it. She really is not so bad, really, once one becomes accustomed to the idea of one's father married to a former actress." She looked up from chafing Dorothea's wrist. "Sir Michael?"

Michael had been staring at Catriona as if his eyes would never get their fill of her, or his ears tire of hearing her beloved voice.

"At your service, Lady Catriona," he said, jolted out of his reverie. He bent down beside her. "Dorothea, my dear. Come along." He put an arm under her shoulders and started to raise her.

"Oh, Papa," Dorothea cried. Her pretty face crumpled.

"Dorothea, my darling," said her husband brokenly as he took her arm. "Let me help you to your room."

Her eyes narrowed and she gave him a look of utter loathing.

"Do not touch me," she said as Sir Michael raised her to her feet and, with a steadying arm around her waist, guided her toward the door. Marguerite went to Dorothea's other side and was whispering soothing words to her as she turned a look of absolute hatred on her brother-in-law.

"Sir Michael," said Catriona.

He turned to look at her.

"Ah, Lady Catriona," he said dryly. "Forgive me. I forgot all about you for a moment." This was such a big lie that he wondered his tongue did not turn black. "I fear we have not yet acquired a new housekeeper. If you would be so good, will you choose bedchambers for your father and stepmother? And the blue room for yourself, of course."

"Do you mean to tell me you are going to let *her* stay?" Marguerite demanded.

"We will leave at once," Lord Grantham said as he drew himself up in his dignity. "I will not have my wife insulted."

"Papa," said Catriona. Her voice was pregnant with meaning, but for the life of him, Sir Michael could not decipher it. "You agreed." She caught Lady Grantham's eye. "And so did you."

The earl let out a long sigh.

"As you wish, girl. That is, Sir Michael, if we are welcome."

"Any relation of Lady Catriona's is always welcome here," Sir Michael said to the earl, but he was looking at Catriona. "As is she."

"Thank you, Sir Michael," Catriona said.

"Papa," said Dorothea.

"Then *we* are leaving," Mr. Walbridge said. "I mean no offense, Lady Grantham," he said to his former mistress. "It would be best, you see, if I were to take my wife home at once."

"I would not leave this house with you if it were hell it-self," Dorothea spat out. She took Marguerite's arm to lean against her for support, and the two of them left the room with their noses high in the air.

Mr. Walbridge stood looking forlornly at the door-way through which his wife had disappeared.

"She does not mean it, you know," Lady Grantham said kindly. Everyone turned to look at her like so many spectators following the combatants at a lively sporting event.

"It is over. My life is ruined," Mr. Walbridge said.

"Nonsense," Lady Grantham said. "She will forgive you if the two of you are half as much in love as you told me you were three years ago when you ended our asso-ciation."

"Forgive me, my dear," the earl said, touching her arm. "But I rather think this is neither the time nor the place to have this discussion."

Sir Michael had to admire the earl for the dignity with which he bore up under the rather trying social position in which his wife's former relationship had placed him.

Lady Grantham gave him a look of infinite regret.

"My darling, you see that my past constantly rears its ugly head to haunt me," she said in throbbing, tragic ac-cents. "I told you I would cause you embarrassment if you married me."

One could have heard a pin drop in the room.

"Oh, do not be so dramatic," Catriona snapped in dis-gust. "Really, Elvira. Come along now, and let us get you settled into your rooms. Mr. Timms!"

"Lady Catriona," the butler said as he slipped into the room from where he obviously had been eavesdropping outside the door.

"Is the green suite available?"

"Yes, my lady," he said, unembarrassed at being caught out.

"Excellent. It has a separate dressing room where Nurse and Christopher can stay."

"Lady Catriona," Mr. Montagu said as he took a step toward her with his hand out. "When you disappeared, I never thought I would see you again."

"Which time was that?" she asked brightly. When he looked affronted, she patted him on the shoulder. "Do not be offended, Mr. Montagu," she said kindly, "but I will offer you a word of advice. Do not deliver any dramatic speeches to me when my stepmother is in the same room. You are bound to be sadly upstaged, you know."

"Good to see you, Montagu," the earl said genially. He gave him a wink. "See that you make her happy."

Mr. Montagu's face grew as bright as the sun.

Oh, dear, Catriona thought, irritated with them both. Her father might as well have waved a wedding contract under the man's nose.

"If you please, Father," Catriona said as she took the earl's arm and fairly pulled him from the room.

CHAPTER 24

"Why are you avoiding me?" Catriona asked as she stepped into the garden path from the shadows and confronted Sir Michael.

He dropped the cheroot he had been smoking onto the ground and stepped on it. One did not smoke in the presence of a lady, not even in one's own garden.

"I am avoiding all my guests," he said bitterly.

She grinned at him.

"I have missed you," she said. "You are the only honest man I know."

He remained silent, just looking at her. He could have said he missed her, too, but this beautifully dressed noblewoman was a stranger. He had seen the way the neighboring gentry hung on her every pronouncement, for all the world as if they hadn't known her for the past two years merely as the late Mrs. Tilden's companion. This woman was poised and self-assured. The woman he missed was the kind, bossy one who caused such havoc in his house that he had become very, very sure he could not live without her.

Michael had been driven from his own house because he could not endure another moment of watching half of the guests in his parlor fawn upon Lady Catriona, the Earl of Grantham, and the countess, and the other half forming a disapproving, supportive circle of defense around Dorothea, who spent most of the evening scowling in the general direction of the Granthams. Mr. Walbridge had wisely insisted that he had an urgent engagement in London and left before dinner, leaving the field of combat to Lady Grantham and Dorothea, who insisted that she would not be driven from her own father's house by That Woman. Lady Grantham was giving a dazzling performance as the noble Roman matron enduring with dignity and fortitude the slights of lesser creatures envious of her position.

Mr. Walbridge had exacted his revenge, however. With him, he took Pierre, his chef, and Mrs. Muir had fairly danced for joy at having her kitchen to herself again while Dorothea and Marguerite had indulged in a hearty bout of hysterics.

Michael detested big, emotional, dramatic scenes. Now his whole life was one big, emotional, dramatic scene.

"Perhaps you should go in," Michael said curtly to Lady Catriona. He had no hesitation in laying the whole irritating affair at her door. "The night is damp, and it would be a pity for you to ruin your gown."

She was dressed all in peach brocade, and there was a small, jeweled comb in her hair that had captured the light of the chandelier at dinner and shone like a tiara. It was rather much for a dinner party, Michael grumped to himself. The precious hunt ball, after all, was not until tomorrow night.

At dinner, Mr. Montagu could not take his eyes off her. With her beautiful face, bright blue eyes, and gorgeous golden hair, she had shone like the sun in the ravishing peach brocade gown and a delicate necklace of diamonds with matching earrings that rendered absolute nonsense his daughters' shrill accusations that she had taken advantage of her position in Mrs. Tilden's house so she could help herself to the lady's outmoded jewelry.

"I have others," she said airily.

Others. And every one of them worth a queen's ransom. No doubt she had burned the clothes he had

purchased for her in Edinburgh. Or given them to her
father's many housemaids to use as rags for dusting.
He had been so pleased to be able to purchase fashionable gowns for her, garments far superior to any
she had worn in her life, or so he had thought.

What a besotted fool he had been!

According to Lady Constance, who had been seated on
Michael's right at dinner, the Duke of Buccleuch had
promised to make his young cousin, Mr. Montagu, a gift
of one of his estates if Lady Catriona would consent to be
his wife. It only needed this, she implied, for Mr. Montagu
to be a worthy son-in-law in the earl's eyes. The young couple, she had confided, although all the tittering guests
knew this by now, had met two years ago and fallen instantly in love, but her father would not consent to their
marriage. He had sent her to Scotland to forget him.

Now the young lovers were reunited, Lady Constance
had said with a romantic sigh. How well they looked together, Lady Catriona with her golden hair and Mr. Montagu with his dark. Such beautiful young people! Lady
Constance seemed to have forgotten all about her dislike
of Michael's former housekeeper, whom she once had
condemned as a sly, sneaking thing, bent on stealing the
silver if she could not bring Sir Michael 'round her thumb,
mark her words! And Lady Constance had more than
once pronounced Catriona's hair to be a rather brassy, vulgar color in Sir Michael's hearing before she had learned
Catriona was the daughter of an earl.

After the seemingly interminable dinner, there had
been dancing, just an informal affair for the young people at one end of the parlor with the young ladies taking
turns at the instrument. Sir Michael could not bear to
watch Catriona smiling, advancing and retreating in
counterpoint to the attentive Mr. Montagu's steps on the
highly polished floor a moment longer.

He needed air. He needed calm.

He needed his bloody cheroot, blast it! He looked at

it, now crushed under his heel like the shreds of his old complacent life.

"You are troubled," Catriona said softly.

She was standing so near to him that he could smell her perfume. She used to smell of simple floral scents such as lily of the valley or orange blossom, no doubt purchased from the apothecary in Dumfries, but this perfume smelled of something darker and more exotic originally purchased, no doubt, in Paris or the Far East and conveyed to London to be resold to rich society ladies at exorbitant expense at one of the fashionable London shops. Michael's late wife, whose face he suddenly could no longer picture clearly in his mind, had delighted in such expensive fragrances. He thought sadly of the exquisite crystal perfume bottles that had graced Lady Stewart's vanity table, now all dry and dusty.

Just like him.

Catriona touched Michael's hand, and he closed his eyes to blot out the sight of her lovely, concerned face.

"Of course, I am troubled!" he said through clenched teeth. "Stay away from me, Catriona, or I shall do something we shall both regret."

"Look at me," she said.

He opened his eyes, knowing it was a mistake.

"I should not regret it," she said softly.

"Go away," he said. "I beg this of you, Catriona. Go back to the house, go back to London, I care not which, but go."

"Michael," she said in gentle reproach, "that is most uncivil." She moved so close that he could see the tops of her creamy breasts peeking above her décolletage. "You do not really want me to go away."

"I am only flesh and blood, my dear girl," he said earnestly as he tried not to look at those pearly orbs. "It is not safe for you to be alone with me."

"Is it not?" she asked eagerly. She leaned even closer and walked her graceful fingers up the lapel of his coat.

"And what dreadful, wicked things might you do to me if I stay?"

He had to laugh at that. He could not help it. But his laughter died when Catriona angled her face to align with his. He could feel her sweet breath on his lips.

Suddenly he could bear it no longer. He seized her in his arms and kissed her, forcing her soft lips open with his tongue and plundering her mouth. At the same time, he explored the bare skin of her upper back with his shaking fingers. When he managed to make himself stop kissing her, he cupped her face in his hands. She had such perfect skin. Her lips were swollen, and there was a big, radiant smile of triumph on her face.

"At last," she said breathlessly. "I have been wanting you to kiss me like that since the moment I arrived."

"No," he said, recoiling from her. "No, I must not."

"Ah, but you already have," she said teasingly. "Since the damage is done, you may as well kiss me again." She raised her face invitingly.

"No, Catriona," he said, retreating. "This must stop."

"Oh, do not be such an old stick," she remonstrated playfully, pursuing.

He caught her shoulders in his hands and held her back from him.

"That is exactly what I am," he said ruefully. "An old stick. Old enough to be your father."

"We have been all through this," she said, rolling her eyes. "You are *not* old enough to be my father. Not unless you were a very depraved little boy. And, even if you were, what is *that* to the point?"

"No. You deserve so much better than me." He swallowed and tasted his own bitterness. "Mr. Montagu, for instance—"

Her complacent smile disappeared, and she angrily struck his hands away.

"Mr. Montagu is an admirable gentleman with many

good qualities, but we will leave him out of this discussion, if you please," she said.

"And what is wrong with Mr. Montagu?" Michael persisted, loathing himself for the flash of pleasure her words brought.

"Nothing at all, save he is not you."

"What you feel for me, dear girl, is infatuation. I could never take advantage of your misguided affection for me to deprive you of the match to which your birth and your father's wealth entitles you. You could be the bride of the most important man in the kingdom, a duke or an earl, at the very least. Or, with your father's wealth and permission, you can afford to make a love match with a handsome young man. I am neither, my poor girl. You will thank me one day for not taking advantage of you."

"Oh! Oh!" she said as she gave him a surprisingly forceful shove that caused him to stagger back while she followed, giving him a little jab in the chest to keep him off balance. Her eyes were blazing with anger, and he had to scramble to remain upright. He began backing away from her with his hands raised in a defensive position against this furious young woman. "Let us summarize this, shall we?"

"My dear Lady Catriona—"

"When I merely was Cousin Sophie's companion, you could not take advantage of me because it would have been vastly improper for you to dally with the employee of your late wife's relation."

"And so it would have been—"

She gave his shoulder another push backward.

"And when poor Cousin Sophie died, you could not take advantage of me because I was then your own defenseless dependent with no male relation to defend me from your lascivious advances."

"Or so I thought at the time," he said indignantly, "but—"

She smacked his upraised hands.

"And now that I am revealed to be a woman of position and fortune with a father to see after my interests, *now* you cannot take advantage of me because by some freak of nature you are some ten years older than I and my father is an earl."

"Certainly not! Everyone would accuse me of—"

"Sir Michael," she said, suddenly coming to a halt. He warily put his arms down. For a moment she looked so fierce he thought she might rake his face with her fingernails. At that silly thought, he reflected that perhaps for the past few days he had spent entirely too much time in the company of ladies of romantic predisposition whose minds fed upon the melodramatic utterances of the heroines of the Minerva Press novels. "Just when, and under which circumstances, *could* you be prevailed upon to take advantage of me?"

"Never!" he declared. "As I am a gentleman! Under no circumstances will I take advantage of you."

"You make it sound rather lurid, I must say. I was not suggesting that you set me up as your mistress, as Mr. Walbridge did with my stepmother. We could marry, you know," she said, looking up at him from under her lashes, "although I rather had hoped *you* would introduce the subject instead of forcing me to do so."

"That we could not," he declared. "Your father would never permit it. As a father, *I* would not have permitted it if either Dorothea or Marguerite had fixed upon so unsuitable a match."

"Have you *asked* him?" she said impatiently.

"Of course not! I would not be so presumptuous, and he would be deficient in his duty to you if he would permit any such union. He would think me a fool."

"My father married an actress. He can hardly object if I want to marry a perfectly respectable titled gentleman."

"A mere baronet," he scoffed. "And a Scottish title at that."

"The best man I know," she whispered. "I want you and no other."

"You do not mean it," he said kindly. He was filled with self-loathing as he gave her a paternal pat on the shoulder. "You merely *think* you do. These passions are strong in the young, but sadly short lived. You would regret our marriage before the wedding cake grew stale, I promise you. And then you would despise me for taking advantage of your innocence. I am the father of two daughters, so I know something about the way young ladies form attachments. Dorothea fell in love with her riding master at the age of fifteen. Marguerite quite fancied her music instructor. Once these persons were removed from their orbit, they quickly turned their thoughts to other, more eligible prospective husbands."

"Yes, and we can see how well *that* turned out," Catriona said dryly.

"Catriona," Michael said reproachfully. "You know what I mean."

"I do, and I will thank you to remember that *I* am hardly fifteen," Catriona said as she grabbed his hand and shoved it away. "Do not patronize me, Sir Michael! Next you will say you look upon *me* as quite one of your own daughters, and after that kiss, we both know that would be the most outrageous lie."

"Mr. Montagu—"

"Yes, Mr. Montagu, the duke's precious cousin, who has hinted that his grace would make us a present of a very pretty estate near Drumlanrig if we marry," she said, tossing her head back so the little jeweled clip in her hair twinkled madly in the light of the absurd little torches Dorothea and Marguerite in one of their frivolous fancies had insisted upon setting along the paths of the garden. "If it would make you so happy to see us together, I shall take very great care to be with him every moment."

With that she started to flounce away.

"See here, Catriona!" he called after her. "That is not at all what I—"

"No?" she said archly as she looked over one creamy shoulder at him. "That is a great pity, then. You will soon see what you have thrown away, you foolish man, for I intend to make you suffer for it."

"You already are making me suffer," he said softly. If she heard, she gave no sign of it as she stalked away in her expensive evening slippers.

When she was gone, he gave a heavy sigh, sat down on a cold, hard bench, and stared into the trees as the moon rose.

It is for the best, he told himself.

CHAPTER 25

The insufferable prig, Catriona thought as she gathered her skirts and ran the last few steps to the house. She burst through the French doors of the parlor overlooking the gardens and all but fell into Mr. Montagu's arms, as he had been looking out the glass doors at the time and had opened the door when he saw her on the other side.

"My dear Lady Catriona," that startled young gentleman said. "Are you all right?"

"Perfectly," she said as she forced a smile to her lips. "I have not missed all the dancing, have I?"

"No, you have not," he said, offering his arm. "I would be delighted if you would honor me—"

But she had already started dragging him to the floor. When the music started, she called out to Dorothea, who had been sitting at the instrument with the air of a martyr.

"No more of your stately minuets, Mrs. Walbridge, if you please. Let us have a waltz."

Some of the elder ladies tittered and fanned themselves at so daring a suggestion, even though the once-scandalous dance had been accepted in the most respectable ballrooms of the most staid houses in England for some time.

Mr. Montagu circled her waist with one hand and took her offered hand with the other, but although he held her no closer to his tall, manly person than was strictly proper, Catriona felt her face flush with embarrassment. She cast down her eyes.

"What is this, Lady Catriona?" her partner asked archly. "Shy with *me*?" She could hear the smile in his voice, and she realized he thought she was being flirtatious with this show of maidenly shrinking.

"It has been a long time, Walter," she said, leaning back to give herself a bit more distance from him. At that, the irritating man drew her closer. How could she have fancied herself in love with such an obtuse creature, even if she had been young and stupid at the time? She was about to tell him in no uncertain terms that she was not about to let him maul her before the other guests as if she were some Haymarket strumpet when she saw Sir Michael quietly enter the parlor through the French doors and nod to the earl and countess, who were seated nearby.

Michael felt his temperature rise when Catriona let her fingers trail along the collar of Mr. Montagu's coat and smiled up into his besotted face.

"Sir Michael," the earl called out, slurring only slightly from the quantity of wine he had enjoyed at dinner. "Do come and sit with us old married folk and admire the exertions of the more youthful of our company."

Michael turned and saw the countess was making a place beside her on the sofa. Her smile trembled a bit at the edges, and he realized she wondered if *he* was about to snub her, too, in sympathy with his daughter.

There was no question. Michael had to join them now, for the poor lady had done nothing to deserve a slight from him. He forced himself to smile at the countess and take the seat she offered with a polite expression of thanks.

"Handsome girl, if I do say so myself," the earl said, indicating Catriona who, to Michael's annoyance, laughed when Mr. Montagu drew her closer and patted him flirtatiously on the shoulder.

"She has a great look of my lord," the countess interjected with a glowing look at her husband.

Sir Michael accepted this politely, even though the earl was a corpulent gentleman with a red nose and brown, thinning hair and his daughter was a slim, golden goddess.

"My lady is blinded by partiality," the earl said, as if he could hear Michael's thoughts. "No, Catriona is the image of her mother, and a more difficult, headstrong female I had never met, unlike you, my dear countess." He patted his wife's hand affectionately. "A good-looking woman, but there was no pleasing her, nor arguing with her. But she gave me a beautiful daughter, so I am not repining."

"She is that," Sir Michael agreed.

The earl gave him a playful jab on the shoulder from around his wife's back that nearly toppled him from his side of the sofa.

"I must thank you, Sir Michael, for watching out for my girl while she has been in Scotland. It would not do for her to fall in love with any of the local lads, would it? I had the devil of a time with her over Montagu years ago, I do not mind saying, and it led to our estrangement, which is now happily at an end. Once she has set her mind on something, there is no changing it."

"This does not surprise me," Michael said dryly.

The earl laughed heartily.

"Quite a handful, is she not?" he said proudly. "Well, she will win her Mr. Montagu in the end, after all. He asked me for permission to pay his addresses to her in the interval after dinner tonight, and I have granted it." He took his countess's hand and gazed deeply into her eyes. "I am truly in love for the first time in my life. I would have Catriona know the same happiness."

"My dear, it is vastly improper of you to tell others of this before Mr. Montagu has declared his intentions to

Catriona and been accepted," his wife chided. She looked pleased, nonetheless.

"Ah, but it is just Sir Michael," the earl said gaily, "another old father like me, determined to ensure his child's happiness. I was wrong to insist that Catriona marry an older man in the first place. Now I am just as determined to see her shackled to Montagu." At that moment, Mr. Montagu bent his lips to Catriona's ear and said something that made her burst out laughing and give him a flirtatious rap on the shoulder. The earl actually got a little teary eyed. "Ah, but it is good to see my girl so happy. I have missed her so much."

I will miss her every day for the rest of my life, Michael thought glumly.

"I say, tomorrow at the ball would be a perfect time to announce the betrothal," the earl said. He gave Sir Michael another shove behind his wife's back. "The sly little minx insists they are only friends, but they have been smelling of April and May since we arrived."

"She has not accepted him yet," his wife reminded him with a coy smile. Quite obviously there was no doubt in either the earl's or the countess's mind that Mr. Montagu's suit would be successful.

"Speaking of matches, old man, what say you to Lady Constance?" the earl said. "Fine woman. Has her eye on you, and no mistake."

"I am flattered, but I hardly know the lady," Michael said stiffly as he gave a short nod in acknowledgment to that lady's pantomime of patting the sofa next to her in a signal that he should join her.

"Her husband left her quite well to pass, I understand," the earl said.

"So I am told," Michael said repressively. Lady Constance was still smiling flirtatiously at him and patting the sofa. He smiled and turned his head, hoping she would think him too thick to understand her meaning. The last thing he wanted now was to sit beside Lady Constance and endure her usual hints that his house must be very quiet and lonely now that his daughters were grown. And wasn't it a pity that he was possessed of this absolutely *immense* ballroom, and no hostess to organize parties and fill it with guests?

The lady was on the catch for a husband, and it was *not* going to be him!

"Why do you not take my wife for a turn about the room, Sir Michael?" the earl suddenly suggested.

Both Michael and the countess looked at him in surprise.

"My dear, I am perfectly content to sit beside you," she said affectionately. "And if I let you out of my sight, we will have Lady Constance over here making up to you."

Michael had to hide a smile and offer silent applause to the countess for managing to get that sly bit of business in. She managed to transform Lady Constance with one masterful sentence into a pathetic husband-hunting shrew. He had felt sorry for the countess's embarrassment, for if a man wished to marry an actress it was no bread and butter of his, but it was apparent that Lady Grantham could take care of herself.

"I know how you love to dance, my dear, and it would give me great pleasure to watch you," the earl said. "I am too advanced in my cups not to make a sad spectacle of myself, but you are always grace personified."

She beamed at him.

"You are always so kind to me," she said, and smiled up into Sir Michael's face. "Shall we, then, Sir Michael, since my husband grants his permission?"

"I would be delighted," the reluctant Sir Michael said, extending his hand to her since he obviously had no choice.

"Do not hold her too closely, mind," the earl warned jokingly as they walked away. "Or I shall have to have my friends call upon you."

"Oh, my lord!" exclaimed the countess. "You are such a tease!"

Dorothea, seeing her father take the floor with That Woman, gave him a look that could curdle milk and ended the waltz in a dramatic clash of chords. With that, she stood, and Marguerite, also giving her father a dark look, took her sister's place and began playing a country dance. Dorothea immediately left the room, and Michael was torn between finishing the dance with the countess and running after Dorothea to comfort her.

How could he not have known his daughter would see his dancing with her husband's former mistress as a betrayal? He found his head pivoting on his neck as he went through the insipid opening movement of the country dance to watch the doorway as if he expected Dorothea to reappear. He knew that making his apologies to the countess and following his daughter would make everything worse.

He was about to do it, though, when his eyes met those of Lady Constance, who had been watching the little drama. She shook her head at Sir Michael in censure at his insensitivity and went after Dorothea, no doubt to give her a mother's comfort.

The countess's color was heightened, and the smile was fixed on her face, but she continued with the dance after one anxious look at him to see if he meant to abandon her.

"This is most awkward for you, and I regret that," Lady Grantham said as a movement of the dance brought them together. "I told my lord that we should leave your house and end this awkwardness, but he said he refuses to behave as if he were ashamed of being married to me. Besides, Catriona threatened to go off again if we left the house." She gave him a misty smile. "She is so in love with Mr. Montagu, you see. She could not wait to come back to Scotland. It is all so romantic."

She gave a nod of her head toward Catriona, who was

twirling merrily in Mr. Montagu's arms. The fellow was eating her up with his eyes. It was disgusting! Michael turned away from the sight of the woman he loved encouraging another man to make a cake of himself.

He knew very well that she was just making up to Mr. Montagu to make him jealous. The woman had not the least guile in her, and her attempt at deception was heavy handed at best. But he could hardly say so without sounding like a conceited coxcomb, so he remained silent.

"I do so want dear Catriona's happiness," the countess said. "She has been excessively kind to me, all things considered. She positively dotes on her baby brother. I predict that she will be an excellent mother."

An excellent mother, Michael thought in horror. Naturally Catriona would want children of her own. Why did this not occur to him until the countess brought it up? She was young. She was healthy. Michael shuddered. He adored both of his daughters, but the thought of having infants at his age made him weak.

"And we shall hold you quite in the light of an honorary grandfather to Catriona's children," the countess said gaily, for all the world as if she expected Sir Michael to be gratified by this sentiment, "for your role in bringing this courtship to its happy conclusion."

Well, that certainly put him in his place, did it not?

Michael forced himself to smile.

"Yes. An honorary grandfather. To Lady Catriona's children. A delightful thought, countess," he said as he felt a chill touch his heart.

When the music stopped, he bowed to the countess and escorted her to her husband, who gave a prodigious yawn.

"Time for us old fellows to retire, is it not, Sir Michael?" the earl said with a wink at Sir Michael. "Come, my lady. Just watching these energetic young people makes me long for my bed."

Michael did not miss the wicked look he gave his wife, or the rosy blush that suffused her face. He looked like an aged satyr about to chase a particularly buxom nymph around the rim of an ancient Greek vase.

Michael had no intention of making such a fool of himself by chasing a vibrant young woman. The music had stopped, and Michael looked toward the floor to see that Catriona had started to turn from Mr. Montagu, and that young gentleman had caught her hand and was speaking earnestly to her. Catriona smilingly shook her head at him and approached her father and stepmother.

"You need not seek your bed just because your old father is doing so, my dear," he said when Catriona had announced her intention of retiring and Mr. Montagu, following her, begged her to have another dance with him. "Stay and dance, my girl!"

"I can hardly do so if you, my stepmother, and Sir Michael are all determined to retire," she said, looking straight into Michael's eyes. "It would be excessively improper."

"There! You see? Lady Constance has returned to the room," the earl said as he watched that lady take a chair by the door. "She will be a more than adequate chaperone to see you and Mr. Montagu do not get into mischief." He gave Mr. Montagu a friendly buffet on the shoulder that nearly sent him stumbling.

"Mr. Montagu," the countess said with a significant look toward that gentleman, "no doubt has something very particular he wants to say to you."

Catriona stifled a yawn.

"So he has said. Mr. Montagu just wants me to dance with him again, but I can hardly do so without occasioning the sort of remark that Papa will not like," Catriona said. "The hunt itself is tomorrow. I intend to be well rested for it. So Mr. Montagu will have to content himself with another partner."

"Ah, yes," the earl said with a comical roll of his eyes

toward Sir Michael. "The hunt. We are all looking forward to it." He smiled at his countess. "Although we old men would derive far more pleasure from staying behind with the ladies, eh, Sir Michael?"

"Yes, Sir Michael," Catriona said sweetly. "You must rest your gouty knee, mustn't you? I wish you all a pleasant night."

Gouty knee, indeed.

"But Lady Catriona—" Mr. Montagu said, looking crestfallen.

If only you knew her as well as I do, my lad, you would not gaze after her like a moonstruck calf, Michael thought as Catriona deliberately ignored her lovesick swain and flounced from the room.

"There, there, lad," the earl said. "Tomorrow will be soon enough to pop the question."

"As you say, my lord," Mr. Montagu said with a bow to the earl and his lady. "Since Catriona does not mean to stay, I will retire as well."

He bowed to the earl and countess and left the room. The earl turned to Michael.

"I had not known you were a fellow sufferer," the earl said sympathetically.

"I beg your pardon?" Michael said stiffly, thinking of Mr. Montagu. Had he somehow revealed his feelings toward Catriona? "I am afraid I do not understand you, my lord."

"The gout," the earl said as he offered his arm to the countess.

"Lady Catriona is pleased to make a joke," Sir Michael said, nettled. "I do not have the gout."

"That is excellent news," the countess said in a tone that revealed she did not believe a word of it. "But just the same, my serving woman has an excellent recipe for mustard plaster that never fails to give my lord relief. I should be delighted to write it out for you."

"Your ladyship is too kind," Sir Michael said, gritting his teeth in annoyance.

"We cannot have you laid out on your bed of suffering tomorrow," the earl said heartily, "when we will require your good offices to dance to my daughter's joy at the ball."

CHAPTER 26

Sir Michael was in the stable at dawn, seeing to the assignment of his horses for the hunt. He was well aware that some of the most avid horsemen in the county would participate and that this was a good time to show them what his excellent Hanoverians could do on the hunting field.

They were not as light or as swift as some breeds, but Lord, could they jump!

"There is a beauty," Lady Catriona said as she walked into the barn and stroked one gloved hand along the muzzle of a pretty little mare Sir Michael's head groom was just leading out of her stall.

Michael turned and looked at her.

"That is just what I was thinking," he said softly.

Today Catriona was wearing a beautifully tailored habit in a rich brown shade that should have looked drab and ordinary but lent a creaminess to her skin that made him think of chocolate and other delicious and strictly forbidden delights.

She smiled.

"Gallantry, Sir Michael, and at such an hour."

He tried to look stern, when the truth was his eyes had been starved for the sight of her.

"You should not be here," he said curtly. "The other ladies are no doubt still abed, sipping their morning chocolate."

"I came early to stake my claim," she said, unsmiling,

as she moved forward swiftly and laid her hand upon his arm.

"Lady Catriona," he said reproachfully. It was unfair of her to accost him this morning, when he was feeling so vulnerable after an evening of watching her smile up into Mr. Montagu's face as they danced. "I have told you—"

"To her," she said brightly as she pivoted and took the reins of the mare from the head groom, who smiled and touched his hat to her. "Was it not clever of me to steal a march on the other ladies and come to choose my mount early?" She murmured into the horse's ear. "What is your name, pretty one?"

Since it was apparent she did not expect the horse to answer her, Michael went to the horse's other side and ran a practiced hand through her shining mane.

"Her name is Éclair, I am sorry to say," Michael said wryly. "She was born a month before Marguerite's marriage, so she had the naming of her."

"It suits her," Catriona said as she brought her lips close to the horse's nose, as if she might kiss her. Michael had to look away from her soft, pursed lips. The woman was deliberately torturing him. "You will walk out into the yard with us, I hope, Sir Michael," she added, still cooing at the horse. "It is such a fine morning."

He could have refused with the excuse that he had too much work to do with helping his people ready the horses, but he did not. The morning light turned Catriona's hair to spun gold and the wind blew little tendrils of it about her pretty face. She was every inch the earl's daughter, and as unattainable as the sun by such as he.

"We should not be alone like this," he told her when the head groom was out of earshot.

"Nonsense," she said with a toss of her head. "I daresay anyone seeing us will assume you are giving me some fatherly advice on retaining my seat."

"My dear Catriona, I utterly refuse to discuss your seat with you."

"Most proper," she said. Her face was straight, but her eyes were dancing. "And how is your gout, Sir Michael, dear?"

"I have no gout, you little baggage." Against his will, his lips twitched. Then he looked up to see Mr. Montagu approaching them at a run. "Here is your most ardent admirer," he could not help himself from saying, even though he sounded like a jealous old fool.

Catriona compressed her lips in annoyance.

"Mount me," she said.

"I beg your pardon?" Sir Michael said, taken aback.

"Quickly, before he reaches us," she said impatiently.

"Oh. I see." Sir Michael sheepishly joined his hands so she could put her booted foot in them and spring to the saddle. She rode away as Mr. Montagu breathlessly reached Michael's side and gazed forlornly after her. She turned in the saddle and touched her hat to them in a humorous little gesture, as if she were a gentleman, saluting the ladies.

Mr. Montagu laughed aloud.

"It appears the lady does not wish to speak with you," Michael could not help saying with a note of triumph in his voice.

"Catriona does delight in her little jokes," Mr. Montagu said cheerfully enough, just as if it were necessary for *him* to explain anything about Catriona to Michael. He clapped Michael on the shoulder, a familiarity he did not appreciate. "Come, Sir Michael, you must help me choose a mount that will make me appear to advantage in Lady Catriona's sight, for today I have something most particular to ask her."

"Come along, then," Michael said ungraciously as he managed to tear his eyes away from Catriona, who had raised her whip in a saucy salute to a few more guests venturing out of the house. "I am sure we can find something that will suit you."

To his discomfort, Mr. Montagu did not remove his hand from his shoulder.

"If the answer to a certain question is favorable, Sir Michael, I mean to repay you for your kind offices here by purchasing a number of horses from you," Mr. Montagu said.

With Catriona's money, he meant.

Michael masked his annoyance with a light tone.

"As the countrymen say, it is unwise to count one's chickens before they are hatched," he said.

Mr. Montagu gave a hearty laugh and clapped Sir Michael on the back.

"I think we can count *that* little chicken safely hatched, sir!" he said, gazing at Catriona's progress with what Sir Michael thought was entirely too proprietary an air. "But wish me luck, by all means, old man."

Old man. Insolent puppy!

Michael knew the words would stick in his throat, so he said instead, "Here is a horse I think you will like. Chesterton." He stopped before the horse's stall and fed the handsome stallion a bit of apple from his pocket. He would have preferred to mount Montagu on the most broken-down nag in his stables, except that he had no such horse. As a matter of pride, he offered Chesterton, one of his best and, in fact, the horse he normally rode himself. He would not be so mean spirited as to give the man who dared assume Catriona was his for the asking an inferior horse.

"Not bad," Mr. Montagu said as he annoyed Michael even further by failing to look impressed by a horse that he knew was one of the best in the country. Just as if he were a connoisseur of horseflesh, which he obviously was not, Mr. Montagu looked the horse over carefully and even had the gall to look at his hooves and run his hands up its powerful legs. "This one will do," he said, and took the reins without so much as a word of thanks or a backward look, as if Michael were one of the grooms. He led the horse outside and mounted him in one clean motion. Then he was off across the yard in pursuit of Catriona and the fortune the earl would settle upon her.

"Stupid imbecile," Michael muttered to no one in particular. "Tiring *my* horse out before the hunt begins."

"The young can be so thoughtless," Lady Constance said from behind him. He turned to see that while he had been gazing off after Mr. Montagu, Lady Constance apparently had approached unnoticed. She was drawing on her expensive leather riding gloves and was dressed from head to toe in black with a jaunty red flower in the buttonhole of her severely tailored habit. The ensemble made her auburn hair and dark eyes look even more dramatic, as she and her dressmaker no doubt had intended. "Come now, Sir Michael. Do not tell me you have forgotten what it is to be caught in the throes of young love."

"Please, my dear Lady Constance," he said with an exaggerated grimace of distaste to pass the matter off as a joke. "Do not be warbling of young love at such an hour. It isn't decent."

"Oh, do not be such an old grump, Sir Michael," she said, laughing. "Can you not see they were made for one another?"

"No, I cannot," he said, feeling testy.

Lady Constance took his arm and laughed up into his face.

"I agree with you that such strong emotions are rather fatiguing at our age," she said.

"*You* would hardly know about that, dear lady," said Michael, who might be in a foul temper and living quite out of the world in rural Scotland, but knew what was expected of him as a gentleman when a lady made such a self-deprecating remark.

"Always so gallant, Sir Michael. You know very well that we are of an age," she said with a coquettish giggle as she patted her elegant hat with a complacent hand, "although I endeavor not to look it." She took a stronger grip on his arm. "Sometimes I envy them their youth and passion, Catriona and Walter. But I believe that the affection and mutual respect of a more mature attachment can be just as fulfilling. Our lives do not end simply because our children are grown."

Help, he thought in alarm as Lady Constance batted her long, darkened eyelashes at him expectantly.

Others might have thought him a monk, but Michael knew a great deal of women, having reared two of them, and he knew this was his cue to kiss her.

Kiss her, he knew, and he would have the devil's own time avoiding parson's mousetrap, for she would have his daughters, the busybody neighbors, and probably the duke himself ranged against him with, for good measure, the ethereal ghost of Mrs. Tilden floating approvingly above. He could just see all of them getting together to discuss the problem that was Sir Michael's single state and deciding that this must not continue and putting Lady Constance forward as the instrument of his deliverance from bachelorhood.

But fail to kiss her, and he would be guilty of an ungallantry that would be an intolerable affront to a woman who had done nothing to deserve such an insult. Lady Constance was an attractive, intelligent, and desirable woman who had no fault save that she was not Catriona. There had been a time when he would have been perfectly willing, nay, eager, to kiss Lady Constance. But that time was long past.

"Speaking of children," he said, "I must thank you for speaking to Dorothea last night. I could hardly desert the earl and his lady to do so. The matter was excessively awkward."

The subject, heaven be thanked, successfully diverted her attention from the kiss that did not happen.

"Poor Dorothea," she said with a sigh. "It was my pleasure to stand in the place of her dear mother at such a trying time, Sir Michael." She looked down in pretty modesty. "Girls need a mother long after they have put their hair up and taken to wearing long skirts. It was only natural that Dorothea look to me for comfort when she was troubled."

Oh, bother. She was off onto *that* again, when he thought he had distracted her from the idea of marrying him.

"As for Lady Catriona," she said in a less sentimental tone, "it was the outside of enough for her to bring That Woman into your house."

"Well, she could hardly know that her stepmother and Dorothea's husband—"

Lady Constance waved away his excuse with an impatient wave of her hand.

"Possibly not, but she *did* know Lady Grantham had been an actress."

"No doubt," Michael said, nettled, "but it is hardly the place of any of us to pass judgment on the lady, or on the earl's choice of a wife, for that matter. Everyone had been urging Lady Catriona to reconcile with her father, and she has done so."

"It is one thing to reconcile with the man, but quite another to foist her vulgar stepmother on her betters," she said with a sniff.

"Some might argue that the countess has no better in rank among this company," he said. He felt an unworthy sense of satisfaction when she stiffened like a poker.

"Well, if one wants to be strictly literal, that may be true," she said coldly. "But women know the intricacies of these matters and Lady Catriona, you may be sure, knew perfectly well she might give offense by bringing That Woman here. And parading her child before your daughters, neither of whom have conceived. I call it plain bad manners."

"I beg your pardon?" he asked, frowning.

Lady Constance regarded him with a look of annoyance.

"Well, Dorothea has been married quite long enough to have a child," she said. "Of course she is concerned that she may be barren."

"She said nothing of it to me."

"Of course not," she said. "One does not blurt out such confidences to a *man*."

"But I am her father. Who else should she tell?"

She cast her eyes down modestly.

"As to that, a young girl would naturally confide in a lady she sees quite in the light of a surrogate mother."

"My daughter has told *you* that she fears she is barren?" Sir Michael said with raised eyebrows. "I do not believe it."

"Dorothea has too much pride to say so in so many words," she admitted, "but to one who knows her so well, she did not need to do so."

"She has all the time in the world for the travails of childbirth," Michael said bleakly.

Lady Constance lay one gloved hand on his arm.

"Forgive me," she said. "You are thinking of poor Lady Stewart, of course. But your wife was not strong, and having children was too much for her. Your girls, thank heaven, have your own constitution and will stand to the business splendidly, mark my words." She gave him a patronizing smile. "A woman knows these things."

"You relieve my mind," he said, unwilling to give her further opportunity to enlighten him on the subject of his own daughters. "Shall we look to the horses?"

But Lady Constance was not through with him yet. She maintained a grip on his arm and held him in place when he would have turned toward the horses' stalls.

"Your daughters have too much affection and respect for you to question your ways, Sir Michael," she said, "but when you marry, they will be greatly relieved to see you in good hands."

"Another subliminal truth they told you without the

medium of words, no doubt," he could not help saying with some impatience in his voice. "Could it be that you are volunteering to spoon chicken broth into my drooling mouth in my old age, Lady Constance?"

"You are hardly ready for that, my dear Sir Michael," she said kindly. "I predict that with good care, you have many good years ahead of you."

"I am glad to know this, dear lady," he said dryly. "Now, if we may turn to the horses . . ."

"Of course. I do not want the other ladies to steal a march on me. There are some young ladies in our company who think they are quite top of the trees when it comes to riding, but I can still hold my own."

"I am sure you can, madam," he said. "Cerise is a perfect little lady," he added, indicating a mare in her stall. At his gesture, the groom opened the door to the stall and led the horse out.

"What a pretty creature," Lady Constance exclaimed. "What delicate little feet she has! I am sure we shall get along famously."

They walked out to the yard, and Sir Michael threw her up into the saddle, delighted to see her ride away at last. He shook his head in weariness. And the hunt had not yet begun.

As a good host, he rode to the back of the pack as his guests went racing forward. He was always anxious in the crush of the horses when ladies participated, but fortunately his daughters had elected to stay behind today. Lady Grantham had decided to stay with her son. So the only ladies riding were Lady Constance and Lady Catriona, but the two of them were quite the handful.

Lady Constance was not precisely the bruising rider she had implied herself to be, and he was constantly having to drop back with her. It became apparent she was making no attempt whatsoever to keep up.

He had a glimpse of Lady Catriona at the head of the riders with Mr. Montagu, and he was heartily sick of hearing Lady Constance call his attention to what a dashing picture they made.

At one point, though, he could see there was a little flurry of confusion among the riders ahead and he abandoned Lady Constance to investigate, praying all the while that no one had been hurt. He came upon the scene to see his worst fears realized.

"My ankle," said Lady Catriona with a grimace when she turned over from her landing place on the ground. The faster riders had not been able to stop in time to aid her, but the earl had dismounted and dropped to his knees at her side.

"Lady Catriona," Michael exclaimed as he dismounted quickly and dropped to other side. "My poor girl. Lie still, now, and let me see if you are injured."

"I say, what are you doing?" objected the earl when Michael carefully explored Catriona's ankle with his hands.

"Feeling for broken bones, of course," Sir Michael said. His tongue felt thick in his mouth. Her ankles were so slender and well formed. "I think it is only a sprain."

"That will be enough of that," her father snapped.

"Papa, Sir Michael is only trying to help," Catriona said.

"Such a pity," Lady Constance said in satisfaction when she rode up and assessed the situation. "And the ball is tonight. Such a shame you will have to miss it."

Michael gave her a look that shut her up immediately.

"I will not miss it," Catriona said. "If you would be so kind, Sir Michael." She held her arms up to him and he drew her to her feet and stood supporting her with an arm around her waist so she could keep the weight off her injury.

At that moment Mr. Montagu came riding up with anxiety writ huge upon his handsome face. He stopped the horse so quickly that it reared a little and gave a little scream.

Michael winced. If the young hothead ruined Chesterton's mouth, he would thrash him within an inch of his life.

"Catriona, my darling," the young man cried out in throbbing accents. "When I saw you fall, my heart nearly stopped. I could not stop in time to aid you—"

"Because you did not have your horse under proper control," Michael said rudely. The idiot was too intent upon showing off for Catriona, no doubt. He wouldn't be surprised if the accident was Mr. Montagu's fault for charging through the riders at reckless speed.

"Catriona, I will take you to the house," Mr. Montagu said, making as if to dismount.

"No need," she said. "Sir Michael has me in hand." She looked at her anxious father. "You, too, Papa. I insist that you continue. Poor Sir Michael, as host, is obliged to see to my comfort, but there is absolutely no need for the rest of you to cut your pleasure short because I was silly enough to take a tumble from his horse. Oh, Sir Michael! Do take a look at her. I will never forgive myself if she has taken harm through my stupidity."

"That horse should be destroyed," cried Mr. Montagu.

"Do not be silly," Catriona said. "Éclair is a perfect lady. If anyone should be destroyed, it is I for being such a clumsy rider."

Mr. Montagu was incoherent with horror at such a thought, and would have gone on passionately and at great length about it if the earl had not testily commanded him to stop being such an old woman. The apologetic look Mr. Montagu then gave Lady Constance had that lady's lip curling with displeasure.

"Do get me out of here," Catriona whispered to Michael, "before my ankle swells to twice the size of my head."

"Of course," he said as he swung her into his arms.

She laughed.

"What? Are you going to carry me all the way to the house?"

"No," he said as he carried her over to his own mount and lifted her to sit sidesaddle on it. The other riders had gone on, even Lady Constance, who cast a dark glance backward and was sped on her way by a triumphant look from Catriona, but Michael still had his hands at Catriona's waist, looking up into her eyes. He could not make himself move away from her.

"Sir Michael," she whispered.

"Yes?" he forced his lips to answer.

"I hope it will not be necessary for you to cut it off," she said anxiously.

That broke the spell. Sir Michael rolled his eyes at her, much as he would at one of his daughters if she had uttered such an inanity.

"Do not *you* turn into a little drama queen," he scoffed. "Cut off your foot for such a trifling injury?"

"I meant my boot," she said, sounding testy. She flexed her foot in its boot of exquisite butter-soft leather and flinched a bit. "The pair is quite new, and one is hardly any good without the other."

"Then we should return before it swells up any bigger," he said as he led the horse forward and took Éclair by the reins.

Naturally, all the inhabitants of the house poured out the front door to greet them when Sir Michael walked up to door with Catriona in his strong arms. He looked so solemn and concerned, she could not resist teasing him.

"I rather like this," she said, tightening the arm she had around his neck and bringing her face close to his. "If it were not for the pain in my ankle, it would be perfect."

"Here they all are to greet us," he said impatiently

when he began running the gantlet of Catriona's curious well-wishers. "Brace yourself, my dear."

"Catriona! Oh, I hope you are not too badly hurt!" called her stepmother, who, as usual, had her son in her arms despite the fact that a nurse had made the journey into Scotland with her. Catriona made a mental note to speak to her about the unfairness of using poor Christopher as a device to establish her superiority over the other ladies present. Elvira was far from being the youngest or highest born of the ladies, but *she* had managed to give her husband an heir, a feat that neither Dorothea nor Marguerite, who had been so horrid to her, had managed to duplicate. She was not about to let anyone forget it.

"Just a silly sprain," Catriona called out cheerfully.

"I suppose I should come see to it," the countess said dubiously as she looked about for the nurse to take her son.

"We both know you haven't the least talent for nursing, darling," Catriona said as her stepmother attempted to pace Sir Michael's long strides and ended up panting alongside, rather like a mongrel that had been chasing carriages in the road. "Sir Michael will take care of me."

"But would that be proper?" Dorothea cried out, scandalized, although she could not hide her pleasure at seeing That Odious Woman rebuffed.

"Possibly not," Catriona said, "but he is probably the only one who knows what to do."

"I have been caring for the sprains of my horses for years," he said dryly. "This will be no different."

Catriona gave him a surprisingly hard rap on the back of the head for comparing her to a horse. She could feel his smile against her temple, and she felt her heart swell.

"There, you see? Sir Michael will merely pretend I am one of his mares, and all will be perfectly proper," she said airily, but her sentence ended on a little cry of pain because her ankle was jarred as he moved up the steps.

"My apologies," he said at once. "We will have that boot off you soon."

"But not by cutting," she said hastily.

"No, not by cutting," he said. "We will save the boot at all costs."

He set her on the bed and knelt before her, brushing her heavy skirts up to the knee with businesslike swiftness as he took her foot in his hands. He looked up into her eyes.

"This will hurt," he warned her.

"Do your worst," she said with a little laugh that turned into a gasp of pain as he started to slowly move the boot down her calf.

"Steady on," he said soothingly. "You do know this is not at all like caring for my horses."

"I had hoped not," she said on a little gurgle of laughter that ended in a sob.

"Another moment," he said. "There!" He held the boot aloft. "And none the worse for wear."

He put down the boot and touched her eyelash and the teardrop glimmering there.

"You did well," he said. "Now, let us look at what we have." His warm hands enclosed her ankle, and she closed her eyes at his touch. "Not too much swelling," he commented with satisfaction.

"I'll wager that when your daughters were small, you would kiss them if they were brave and did not make too much of a fuss when they were injured."

"So I would," he said, "but *you* are not my daughter."

"There. I must say that is progress of a sort," she said cheerfully, and he gave her a rueful smile. Then he sobered and drew closer to her.

He is going to do it, she thought in anticipation. She closed her eyes as his lips drew closer.

But he drew back at the last moment, leaving Catriona seething with disappointment.

"Why?" she whispered.

"Ah, there you are," he said to Mrs. Muir as he indicated she should enter the room. He reached for the hot water and cloths she brought. "Thank you, Mrs. Muir."

"Do you want me to stay, sir?" she asked hopefully.

"That will not be necessary, thank you," he said pointedly.

The old lady dropped him a dejected little curtsey and left the room.

"I am afraid we are scandalizing the household," he said ruefully.

"Do you mind?" she asked. "Should I apologize for placing you in a compromising position?"

He gave a snort of derision.

"Hardly. There now," he said as he competently wrapped the ankle. "Rest it well, and I think you will be ready to dance until dawn with your precious Mr. Montagu."

"You are jealous," she said, smiling.

"It is not my place to be jealous," he said. "In some ways the match is suitable. I should offer you my congratulations."

"What a hypocrite you are," she said. "You know I do not love Mr. Montagu."

"He loves himself enough for both of you," he said.

"Precisely," she said on a crow of laughter. She touched the side of his strong face with her hand. "Oh, Michael," she said with a sigh. "Why can you not see the truth?"

"Why cannot you?" he said with a rueful smile, but he did not pull away.

To her exasperation, the maid she had hired in haste in London came excitedly into the room with a big, rectangular box in her hands.

"From Edinburgh, my lady," the girl said in tones of congratulation. "For you."

Catriona could have screamed at the interruption.

"For me? I was not expecting a parcel from Edinburgh," she said with a frown. "There must be some mistake."

Sir Michael had straightened and stood up. The look on his face was remote.

"No," he said. "There is no mistake."

She gave him a questioning look and would have dismissed the young maid, but the girl gave an involuntary little cry of disappointment at being denied a glimpse of what was inside the tantalizing box and Catriona relented.

"Is it from you, then?" she asked Sir Michael. Her heart had begun beating fast as she touched with reverent fingers what she knew at once as a dressmaker's box.

"Yes. I had forgotten all about it, actually," he said with a deprecating gesture of his hand. "You probably do not want it now."

It could be only one thing. She carefully opened the box and parted the nest of filmy white tissue paper surrounding the treasure inside.

"Oh," Catriona said with a cry of pure feminine rapture as she carefully lifted the exquisite pink silk gown from its protective shroud of tissue paper. "It is so beautiful. I shall wear it tonight."

"But, my lady," the little maid objected. "Have you forgotten about the white gown with the crystal beads from Paris?"

"I can have a half dozen Paris gowns at the snap of my fingers," she said, looking straight into Sir Michael's eyes, "and none of them will mean as much as this. Go away, Molly."

"My lady?" the maid said.

Catriona carefully placed the gown on the bed.

"Go away," she said. "I shall ring for you when I need you."

The girl looked from Catriona to Sir Michael, bobbed a curtsey, and fled.

Catriona advanced on Sir Michael, limping.

"This is the kindest thing anyone ever did for me," she said.

"You said it yourself," he said, backing away from her. "You could have a half dozen Paris gowns at the snap of your fingers."

"But you did not know that." She put her arms around his neck and raised on tiptoe. Then she gave a little gasp of pain and staggered, which left him no choice but to catch her in his arms. She smiled up at him. "This is a shockingly expensive gown by Edinburgh standards. By *your* standards. Mrs. Walbridge, Lady Redgrave, and, heaven help you, Lady Constance will be furious when they learn about it."

"Lady Catriona, I do not want you to read anything into this gift but what it is, an act of kindness toward a young dependent."

She raised one eyebrow.

"*That* is not the kind of gown that a respectable gentleman buys for an impecunious dependent. I shall definitely wear it tonight."

He picked her up in his arms and carried her to a chair. He had to forcibly detach her arms from his neck to get free of her so he could stand up and step back.

"You only want to annoy my daughters and Lady Constance," he said.

"That, too," she said, smiling up at him. "You do love me. You do."

"You are mistaken," he said stiffly. "You are a stubborn girl. A match between us would be most unsuitable. Mr. Montagu is the man for you. Your father approves, the *duke* approves. If you were my daughter, *I* would approve."

"I am *not* your daughter," Catriona said through clenched teeth.

"No, my dear. That you are not," he said with a sigh.

"Someday you will thank me for refusing to take advantage of—"

"Do not *dare* tell me that," she said, stamping her foot and giving a howl of pain.

"Catriona, for the Lord's sake," he said, hurrying to her side in concern and putting a hand on her shoulder.

"Oh, go away!" she cried out as she burst out in frustrated tears. "Just go away!"

CHAPTER 27

Michael chided himself for his feeling of disappointment when Lady Catriona appeared in the drawing room before dinner in the white crystal beaded gown from Paris. She looked like an ice princess. She even wore a little tiara in her golden curls and a necklet of blue sapphires at her throat.

"Exquisite," breathed Marguerite at his side. "Oh, I would give my *eyes* for such a gown."

The countess gave a self-satisfied smile and said to her lord loudly enough for Sir Michael to hear, for the earl was a trifle hard of hearing, "You see, I was right. She wanted to wear some little pink gown run up by some dressmaker in Edinburgh, but I told her that tonight she must look her very best." She gave an inclination of her head to Mr. Montagu, who had turned from staring like a mooncalf at Catriona, for the countess's theater-trained voice had carried quite clearly to him as well.

"Go ahead, boy," the earl said encouragingly to Mr. Montagu, who eagerly approached Lady Catriona. That lady smiled regally and placed her white-kid-gloved hand on his and permitted him to escort her to a chair. Sir Michael frowned. There was a smile on her lips, but he could tell she was favoring her right leg, for she was leaning slightly on Mr. Montagu, the besotted young idiot. The ankle must still be paining her.

The countess gave a fond sigh.

"Have you ever seen so charming a young couple?"

she asked of the earl. "It appears our little girl is quite grown up," she added, for all the world as if she had dandled Catriona on her knee. "She will make a beautiful bride."

"Has she accepted him, then?" Sir Michael could not help asking.

The countess turned to him in surprise.

"With the hunt, and then the ball to dress for immediately after, he has not had a chance to speak to her, for Catriona was resting in her bedchamber when the men returned and her maid said she was not to be disturbed," she said. She indicated the dark head bent solicitiously over the blond one with a fatuous smile. "But, really, Sir Michael, is there any doubt that she will have him? He is perfect for her. What more can she want?"

A sensible man, he almost said, but that would have been churlish.

"What more, indeed?" he murmured. "If you will excuse me."

He approached Dorothea, who was sitting with her brother-in-law, Lord Redgrave, and staring holes into the back of the countess's head. With a nod of his head, he indicated that Lord Redgrave was to retire and took the seat on the sofa next to his daughter. He laid his hand on hers.

"And how are you, my dear?" he asked.

She looked straight ahead.

"As well as might be expected considering my husband has run off to London and left me here, where my own father is kowtowing to That Woman merely because she is married to an earl."

"The countess means you no harm," he said. "She has no designs on Edward, and he has no designs on her. He insists that he broke off the connection when he met you, and I believe him."

She looked away from him, but he put his hand under

her chin and turned her face so that he could look into her red-rimmed eyes.

"I think you believe him, too," he added gently.

Dorothea gave a tired sigh.

"There have been too many angry words between us. The case is hopeless. He hardly will want me now." She cast a look of absolute hatred toward the countess and the earl. "And *she* has given *him* a son."

"What of it?" he said with a shrug. "Your mother did not give me a son, and I can tell you I got along quite well without one. I do not want some little pip-squeak strutting about the place, telling me what I should do, or sending me off regularly to town to extricate him from some mischief he has got himself into or settle the debts he has run up." He touched her cheek. "I am content with my girls, I promise you."

"I have not even given Edward a girl."

"Well, and you are not likely to do so until you put this unpleasantness behind you. He is sorry. Forgive him."

"You make it sound so simple," she said with a sigh.

"It is."

"Oh, Papa," she said. "I am so unhappy."

"I know, darling," he said, patting her shoulder. "We will get through the business, I promise you." He gave her a straight look. "My offer to go to London and give him a horsewhipping still stands."

She choked on a gurgle of laughter.

"Oh, Papa. I have missed you," she said. She gave a coy glance toward Lady Constance, who was talking to Marguerite. "I hate to think of you rattling around in this great house. Are you not lonely?"

"No, you don't, my girl," Sir Michael said in a mock-stern voice. "I know a female is feeling better when she starts matchmaking. Let your poor old father have some rest from such plots, I beg of you. And rest I shall not have with Lady Constance to order my days."

"Pity," Dorothea said. "You do not think you could come to love her, then?"

"No," he said, rising. "If you will excuse me, I must do my duty as host." He gave her a humorous roll of the eyes. "The things I do to please the females in my life."

He walked across the room and offered his arm to Lady Constance, which caused that lady to cast a look of triumph at the countess, whom Sir Michael with equal correctness could have escorted in to dinner. He regretted that she no doubt took this for partiality toward herself, but he actually chose Lady Constance for this honor in deference to Dorothea's feelings rather than his own desire for her company. He knew the countess, far from feeling slighted, would prefer to go in to dinner with the earl.

That would leave Catriona and Mr. Montagu to go in to dinner together, but that could not be helped.

"My dear Catriona," Mr. Montagu, seated at Catriona's left hand, said in an urgent undervoice when the rest of the diners were distracted with other conversation, "I must and will speak!"

"I beg you will not," she said hastily as she glanced toward the head of the table where Sir Michael's dark head was bent close to Lady Constance's. The sight offended her grievously. Lady Constance might think herself the last word in elegance and sophistication, but Catriona knew mutton dressed as lamb when she saw it.

"But, Catriona, you must allow me to express my devotion—"

"In the middle of *dinner*? Are you mad?" she whispered back, just as urgently.

"But we have not been alone for the space of—"

"Ah! Roasted capon. My favorite," Catriona said, indicating a platter on the table. "If you would be so kind, Mr. Montagu."

"What? Oh, yes. Of course," he said as he helped Catriona to a slice of capon's breast.

"And some peas as well, I beg of you," she said brightly. "I must say, I am famished."

"Yes. As I was saying—"

"I do hope there will be lemon cakes at the ball tonight. I am very fond of lemon cakes."

"As am I," he said impatiently. "Lady Catriona, from the first moment I saw you—"

"Of course, strawberry tarts are not to be scorned," Catriona said, "but sadly, they are out of season. Do take some of the capon for yourself, Mr. Montagu. It is quite delicious."

In that manner, Catriona kept Mr. Montagu distracted from the subject of their marriage, for a female knew—even one who had been living quite out of the world—when a gentleman was determined to propose to her.

Oh, how her ankle ached. When would this interminable dinner be over?

The earl, observing his daughter and her swain, called his wife's attention to the striking couple.

"Oh, I say, this looks promising. They look very serious with their heads together," he said. "We shall have our announcement yet, will we not, my dear?"

The countess gave a sentimental sigh.

"We must have the wedding in London in St. Paul's," she said. "I am quite determined."

"Whatever you say," her husband agreed. "Heaven knows my girl has waited long enough for her young man." He patted his wife on the hand. "I predict that within a year after the ceremony, our Christopher will have a little nephew to play with in his nursery."

Sir Michael, who could not help overhearing part of this conversation because the earl and countess were seated quite close to him, frowned mightily.

So, she had accepted him. She must have done if her parents were planning her wedding.

He regarded Catriona, whose devoted swain was gallantly offering her bits of every dish on the table.

Deliberately, he turned his eyes away from her and did not look that way again. And when Lady Constance next claimed his attention, he concentrated painfully upon her every word.

After dinner, the ladies had gone to the parlor for tea and cakes, but the gentlemen did not linger long over their port because Sir Michael had to get into place with his daughters for the receiving line so they could welcome the guests who had not been honored with invitations to the dinner.

Indeed, he had not known he had so many neighbors. "Many of them are our friends from London," Dorothea said when he voiced this to her.

Still, as the house filled with perfect strangers, he could not be sorry. Dorothea was quite in her element as hostess, and it was well worth the botheration of this infernal party to take that sad, hopeless look from her eyes. Marguerite, too, seemed to be in delightful spirits. He cast a glowering look at her husband who was, quite rightly, looking at Marguerite with a proud smile on his face. At least the fellow seemed to be behaving himself. Perhaps he would be more considerate of Marguerite's feelings and allow her to play the hostess in her own home from now on.

He had not done so badly by his daughters, after all, although he might yet make the trip to London to horsewhip Walbridge if he did not settle matters with Dorothea soon.

"Have you seen Lady Catriona?" Mr. Montagu asked anxiously when the receiving line had disbanded and the party had moved into the main ballroom.

"Not since dinner," Michael replied.

"I cannot find her anywhere," the young man cried. He looked on the verge of tearing his hair out.

"See here, man," Michael said disapprovingly. Had the man no pride at all? He hoped *he* had not behaved like a lovesick ninny when he was courting his wife all those years ago, but he probably had. "Surely you can do without her company for the space of half an hour. No doubt she wished to have her maid refurbish her hair or rest her ankle for a little while. No female of my acquaintance would intentionally miss a ball unless she were at death's door, so I think I can safely assure you that Lady Catriona will arrive soon."

At that, she appeared in the doorway to the ballroom, and all eyes turned to her.

"She changed her gown," the countess said in surprise.

"I say, Elvira. Do you not think it is cut rather low?" the earl asked with a frown.

Sir Michael's heart gave an odd little lurch.

Lady Catriona had changed from what any dolt would recognize instantly as a shockingly expensive crystal beaded gown from Paris into the pink silk gown he had purchased for her. And the earl was perfectly correct, the gown was definitely cut rather low.

It was like a gift she gave to him, a secret gift between the two of them. Which was why he was so nettled when Mr. Montagu gave a sigh of rapture.

"She is exquisite," he sighed. He seized Michael's hand and pumped it up and down. "Congratulate me, Sir Michael, for I am the most fortunate of men."

"Indecent," said Lady Constance, although there was envy in her dark eyes.

"Quite shocking," said Dorothea with equal envy, "and so I told her in Edinburgh when she wanted us to purchase it for her. So unsuitable! I am embarrassed for her."

Mr. Montagu had gone straight up to Catriona and taken her arm. She shook her head at him, which delighted Sir Michael no end until he realized she was saying no to a dance, and leaned lightly against Mr. Montagu as he solicitiously guided her to a chair and sat down beside her, clearly intent upon living in her pocket for the whole of the evening.

"Is there no sight so sweet or so bitter to a father," the earl said from beside him.

"I beg your pardon?" Michael asked distractedly.

"My daughter and Mr. Montagu. I daresay you feel quite as I do, seeing Catriona about to be swept off by her bridegroom."

"It is settled, then," Michael said heavily.

"It is. We will make the announcement later, when all the guests have arrived. I was pleased to see you had your butler bring out ample champagne. You think of everything, Sir Michael."

"My pleasure," Michael said automatically as he watched Catriona, although he suspected it was the officious Lady Constance who had ordered the champagne brought from the cellar. He would not stay here staring at Catriona like a lovesick fool. "If you will excuse me, the musicians are about to start. I must open the ball." He held out his hand to Lady Constance, who had been standing nearby. "Lady Constance, if you will honor me?"

"With great pleasure, Michael," she said softly.

"Look at her, making sheep's eyes at Sir Michael," Catriona said pettishly to Mr. Montagu. "Or mutton's eyes, I should say."

He laughed.

"Do not be unkind, sweet. She has quite a *tendre* for the old fellow. I think they look charming together."

"They do *not* look charming. They look ridiculous."

"Ah, do not grudge them a little happiness," Mr. Montagu said expansively. He took her hand and kissed it. "I am certain they do not grudge us ours."

"Mr. Montagu, I have told you—"

"I know, I know," he said with a fatuous smile on his face. "You still wish to punish me a little because I did not fight for you two years ago. I understand. But do not let that stand in the way of our happiness."

"I am not being coy, Mr. Montagu," she said sternly.

"Of course not," he agreed with a readiness that made her want to box his ears. "There! The rest of the dancers are joining them now. Come along. We will be careful with your ankle."

With that, he escorted her out to the floor and took her into his arms. It was a waltz, and she gritted her teeth when he had the effrontery to pull her much too close to him.

"I believe that is close enough," she said with a brittle smile for the benefit of any who might be watching.

"As you say, my dear Catriona," he said with a mischievous smile. "Lord, I love that gown. You look like a strawberry tart that I could gobble down in one bite."

Catriona rolled her eyes.

Had his conversation always been this inane?

Michael watched from the side of the room after he had deftly surrendered Lady Constance to another partner and left the floor. The sight of that fellow's hand at the waist of Catriona's pink silk gown made him want to punch something. Hard.

"I think it is time, do not you, old fellow?" the earl said from his side. He puffed himself up a bit and strode confidently to the orchestra's platform. The musicians, seeing his signal for silence, screeched to a confused halt that had the dancers looking at them in surprise.

"I have an announcement," the earl called out. He held his hands out for Catriona and Mr. Montagu. The young man grinned and confidently went to join the earl, but Catriona hung back. Her eyes were huge with dismay. Then she hastily went to her father.

"Papa, what are you doing?" she said into his ear.

"Making Montagu, here, the happiest of men," he said with a friendly poke at that beaming young man's shoulder. He raised his voice. "Ladies and gentlemen, I am pleased to announce the betrothal of my daughter, Lady Catriona, to Mr. Montagu."

There was a pleased little flurry of voices that quite drowned out Catriona's gasp of dismay.

"Papa!" she cried out.

A beaming Mr. Montagu reached over and took her hand with his. She slapped it away.

"Catriona?" he said, frowning.

"There has been some mistake," she whispered to her father, ignoring Mr. Montagu. "I did not consent to this. You cannot make me marry him."

"But I thought you wanted—" The earl turned to Mr. Montagu for enlightenment. "Did you not have the wit to ask her, boy?"

"I was leading up to it," he admitted with a sickly smile on his face. "Catriona, do not make me look a fool in front of all these people, I beg of you."

"Smile, girl," the earl said as he gave a look at Mr. Montagu that should have cut him to ribbons. "Just smile and accept their congratulations. We can call it off later, if need be."

"Call it off? But—" objected Mr. Montagu.

"Silence, you," the earl said. "You told me she had agreed."

"But she would have done, if I could have got a word alone with her," Mr. Montagu said between clenched teeth. "The girl will not pay attention for two minutes together before her mind is gadding on about capon's breasts and lemon cakes—"

"For the Lord's sake, smile, girl," the earl ordered.

Catriona turned and smiled to the guests waiting to express their good wishes, although she wanted badly to burst into tears. She allowed her stepmother and Lady Constance to kiss her cheeks. She hugged a tearful Dorothea. But when she saw a solemn Sir Michael standing before her, she could not stop her lips from trembling.

"I wish you most happy," he said.

With that, she burst into tears and shuffled awkwardly from the room, favoring her right ankle with Mr. Montagu right behind her.

"My Catriona," the earl said uneasily, "is overcome by happiness. You know these giddy girls."

"So romantic," sniffed the countess happily.

Sir Michael's eyes narrowed.

He couldn't say anything about *these* giddy girls, but he knew *this* giddy girl quite well, and those had not been tears of happiness welling in her eyes. He hardened his jaw and went after them as the most expensive champagne in his cellars was wasted in a toast to the beautiful young couple's health and happiness.

CHAPTER 28

"Walter, I am as sorry as I can be," Catriona said after trying, and failing, to shut the door to her bedchamber to prevent Mr. Montagu from entering. "I have no wish to hurt you."

"How could you do this?" he demanded. "How could you dash my hopes and make me look a fool before everyone? You know how I feel about you."

"No, I do not, Walter," she said quite clearly. "I know how you feel about being my father's son-in-law and about the dowry that would come to you on our marriage. I know how you feel about the estate the duke will bestow upon you if you manage to marry an heiress. But I do not know how you feel about *me*."

"I love you. You must know that."

"No, I do not," she insisted. "You know nothing about me. You never did. I was a stupid girl two years ago. I have grown up since then. And I realize that what I felt for you was the infatuation of a silly, romantic fool. My father was perfectly right about that."

"But we have his blessing. He said we could marry."

"*I* did not give my consent! You would not be marrying my father. You would be marrying *me*."

"But you wore this dress to entice me," he said as he ran his hand lightly from the sides of her breasts to her waist.

She slapped his hands away.

"I did not wear it to entice *you*, you silly creature!" she snapped. "I do not love you. I love another."

Walter grabbed her shoulders and pulled her into his arms where he held her so tightly that she gave a squeak of consternation.

"Careful, Walter," she cried out sharply. "Mind my ankle."

"Who is this man? I swear I will drive all thoughts of him from you," he declared passionately. Then he bent and kissed her so hard that the inside of her lip was cut on her teeth.

"Stop that," she said, pushing him away in her distaste. Just then, her ankle nearly gave way and she had to grasp his shoulder to remain upright.

"You *will* love me! You *must*," he said as he tried to kiss her again.

The door opened with enough force to make it bounce against the wall and a furious Sir Michael Stewart strode into the room, grabbed Mr. Montagu by his meticulously arranged neckcloth, and shook him like a rat.

"I believe," he said furiously, "that the lady said no."

"Sir Michael, please stop!" Catriona cried.

He stopped shaking Mr. Montagu.

"Do you want him after all, then?" he asked in surprise.

"Good heavens, no!" she said in disgust. "But look at him! He is turning purple because you are choking him with that blasted neckcloth. You do not want his dead corpse to explain to the duke, his cousin, do you?"

Sir Michael dropped the man at once and he fell, groaning, to the floor.

"Get out of here," he said as he gave Mr. Montagu a jab with the toe of his kid evening slipper.

"*Him*, Catriona?" Mr. Montagu said in reproach. "You prefer *him* to me? He is old enough to be your father."

"I am *not*, you young idiot," Sir Michael snapped. "Now get out of the lady's room before I draw your claret."

Mr. Montagu lurched to his feet, brushed off his coat with a sneer of disgust on his face, and drew himself up to his full height.

"With *pleasure*," he said, and stalked from the room, taking care to close the door with a bang as he passed through it.

When Mr. Montagu was gone, Sir Michael gathered Catriona into his arms and just held her against his chest for a moment.

"They say drowning men see the whole of their lives pass before their eyes as they are dying," he said with his lips against her temple. "I never believed them until your father made that announcement. It was like that for me."

"Me, too," she murmured against his chest. His heart was beating as fast as her own.

"I am a selfish old man," he said as he placed reverent kisses against her closed eyelids. "I have tried to do the right thing, but it will not do. Will you marry me, Catriona?"

"I will! Oh, I will, Michael."

She threw her arms around him and kissed him, but it put a strain on her ankle, which caused her to stagger and pull him down on the bed with her as she fell.

"I am very glad I purchased this gown," he said languidly when they emerged from their embrace. He caressed her back with his warm hands. "But it is rather wasted in a ballroom."

She slapped his shoulder and they both laughed. Then he sat up bolt upright.

"What is it?" she asked.

"I have gone about this all wrong," he said. "I have asked you to marry me *before* I spoke to your father."

"Is that all?" she said, drawing him back into her arms.

"What if he will not consent?"

"He will consent. He and Elvira will be delighted to have me off their hands."

"I will not move to London," he warned.

"Nor will I," she said, sitting up and trying, in vain, to smooth the now-crumpled silk of her gown. "I plan to stay and become a leader of Dumfries society to put Lady Constance's nose out of joint."

"My sweet girl," he said as he kissed her again. "I will go to seek out your father at once."

"We will go together," she said. "I do not want any confusion this time about which gentleman I want to marry."

"As you wish," he said as he held out his hand for her.

Instead of taking it, she moved close by his side and put one arm around his neck.

"I find my pesky old ankle is paining me again," she said, smiling up at him as she placed his hand around her waist. "Do you mind?"

"Not at all," he said as they went arm in arm to ensure their happiness.

BOOK YOUR PLACE ON OUR WEBSITE AND MAKE THE READING CONNECTION!

We've created a customized website just for our very special readers, where you can get the inside scoop on everything that's going on with Zebra, Pinnacle and Kensington books.

When you come online, you'll have the exciting opportunity to:

- View covers of upcoming books
- Read sample chapters
- Learn about our future publishing schedule (listed by publication month *and author*)
- Find out when your favorite authors will be visiting a city near you
- Search for and order backlist books from our online catalog
- Check out author bios and background information
- Send e-mail to your favorite authors
- Meet the Kensington staff online
- Join us in weekly chats with authors, readers and other guests
- Get writing guidelines
- AND MUCH MORE!

**Visit our website at
http://www.kensingtonbooks.com**

More Regency Romance
From Zebra